IN THE BLOOD

IN THE BLOOD

Fay Sampson

This first world edition published 2009
in Great Britain and in the USA by
SEVERN HOUSE PUBLISHERS LTD of
9–15 High Street, Sutton, Surrey, England, SM1 1DF.
Trade paperback edition published
in Great Britain and the USA 2009 by
SEVERN HOUSE PUBLISHERS LTD

British Library Cataloguing in Publication Data

Sampson, Fay
  In the Blood
  1. Women genealogists - Fiction 2. Murder - Investigation -
  Fiction 3. Great Britain - History - Stuarts, 1603-1714 -
  Fiction 4. Detective and mystery stories
  I. Title
  823.9'14[F]

ISBN-13: 978-0-7278-6776-6   (cased)
ISBN-13: 978-1-84751-141-6   (trade paper)

Typeset by Palimpsest Book Production Ltd.,
Grangemouth, Stirlingshire, Scotland.
Printed and bound in Great Britain by
MPG Books Ltd., Bodmin, Cornwall.

ONE

Nick read aloud the notice in the church porch. 'PLEASE CLOSE THIS DOOR TO KEEP OUT OUR SISTERS THE SWALLOWS. I like it! Just imagine them dropping their offerings on the congregation's heads during the sermon.'

Suzie was silent. This was always a special moment for her, discovering a new parish where her ancestors had once lived. She would be entering for the first time a church where generations of them had been baptized, married and buried. Another link in the chain that connected her and her own teenage children to their past.

All she had at the moment was one record from the parish register. She looked back at the sunny churchyard.

Southcombe Marriages Register
1676 Joshua Loosemore and Loyalty Turner 14th June

Had it been a fine summer's day like this for their wedding?

Nick stood aside with a flourish of his arm, indicating to her to enter first. He was happy to drive her here, but this was her quest, not his.

The inner door was heavy oak, resisting her push. Yet the hinges were smooth, and it opened without a creak. The light was subdued after the bright churchyard.

She walked down three steps to stand in the south aisle. Descending to a lower level was appropriate; this was like an archaeological excavation. She was hoping to delve three centuries down into her history.

Cool air washed over her arms. For the first time that day, she wondered whether her sleeveless cotton dress was enough.

Her eyes were adjusting to the dimness. Light filtered through stained glass. She noted they were the strong blues and reds of Victorian work, not the more subtle greens and misty gold of medieval glass. She looked around her for something older.

A cry of dismay, almost of anguish, broke from her.

'What's up?' The door thudded shut, darkening the church further. Nick stood on the step above her.

'The blasted Victorians again. Look at the floor!'

The ancient stones, which she had planned to search for the names of villagers carved on memorial slabs, had been overlaid with tiles of red and cream.

'It's like a nineteenth-century hallway! And where are the old pews?'

Instead of medieval bench ends, eccentrically carved, these pews offered only a uniform, stylized rose motif overlaid with a sticky-looking varnish. She would find no mermaid or Green Man, no sailing ship or tinners' rabbits. Suzie hurried to the central aisle and turned to the altar. Her foreboding was confirmed: the carved tracery of the old rood screen, which had once separated the nave from the chancel, had been stripped away. There was little left of the church interior her ancestors would have known. What evidence they might have left her had gone.

'How could they think this was better than what they destroyed?' she cried in frustration.

'Oh, come on now. It's got its own charm. Look at those wall tiles. They're rather special, aren't they?'

Suzie threw a glance where Nick pointed. It was true. Instead of the usual whitewash, with monumental plaques to eighteenth- and nineteenth-century gentry decorated with florid cherubs, these walls were banded with green and cream tiles, each painted with a different flower depicted with careful detail. She recognized woodbine and honeysuckle, primrose and coltsfoot. They had, she grudgingly admitted, the artistic originality she had hoped to find on the pews. They were not typical of Victorian restorations.

'That's not what I came for,' she said, still unwilling to be coaxed out of her disappointment.

'There's more on the ceiling,' said her husband, craning back his head. 'Imagine painting that. The artist must have stood up there on some nineteenth-century wooden scaffolding, or lain on his back to do it. Like Michelangelo in the Sistine Chapel.'

'Hardly.' A fairer part of her mind knew she should be showing interest, admiring this unexpected artistry. But frustration would not let her share his enthusiasm.

'Gives you a crick in the neck, just thinking of it.'

The vault of the ceiling, now that she reluctantly followed his eyes, was painted with variations of the smaller images on the wall tiles. They twined into every corner, in a riot of cream, white and yellow blossoms and green foliage. This had been a labour of love for whoever had painted it.

'There were probably medieval paintings on these walls once,' she said through stiff lips. 'Doom, a skeleton at the mouth of hell, resurrection.'

'It's a bit unfair to blame the Victorians for scrubbing those out, isn't it? More likely it was Cromwell's Roundheads knocking the place about a bit.'

'Not *Oliver* Cromwell. Thomas,' she corrected him. 'Henry VIII's vice-regent, a century earlier. He was the one who had all the popish stuff swept away at the Reformation.'

'Whatever.'

'That's not the point. I came here hoping to find my seventeenth-century ancestors. And what have the Victorians left me? Nothing.'

'It's called reality, love. It's like that archaeology programme you're so keen on. One week they uncover a fabulous Roman mosaic; the next, they're lucky to find half a broken flint. Sometimes the evidence is there; sometimes it's not. Who were you looking for this time, anyway?'

'The ancestors of Joshua Loosemore and Loyalty Turner. I can trace my family back to when they married in the 1670s. But then the trail goes cold. From the date of their wedding, they should have been born around 1650. But that was the time of the republic, after the Civil War. There's a gap in the parish registers, as there often is at that time. Southcombe's church records don't start again until the Restoration of the monarchy in 1660.'

'So?'

'So I need some other evidence – a clue, at least. I thought there might have been Loosemores and Turners buried in this church. The poorer people outside wouldn't have had gravestones, but Joshua's family might have been affluent enough to rate a burial inside the church. They'd have had to pay extra, of course. Six shillings and fourpence, I think it cost.'

Nick tapped his foot on the red and cream floor tiles. 'And you think, under here . . .? We're never going to know now, are we? I don't imagine the vicar would be enchanted if you suggested digging this up.'

'It's the rector, actually.'

They both turned. The light from the newly opened door shone through the young man's hair, so that it curled up from his head like tongues of pale flame.

'Sorry.' He grinned at them. 'Shouldn't be pedantic, should I? But I do like people to get my title right.'

Suzie waited for Nick to ask him what was the difference between a vicar and a rector. He did not. She recognized the usual male reluctance to admit ignorance. He might ask her later, in private. She rehearsed the dictionary definition in her head. *A rector is the incumbent of a parish whose tithes are not impropriate.* Nick would probably not tell her that he still did not understand what that meant.

She was being churlish. Nick was lovely. He was endlessly tolerant of her enthusiasm for family history, willing to share these weekend explorations with her.

'We were admiring your wall tiles and ceiling,' he said tactfully to the rector. 'They're rather unusual, aren't they?'

A dazzling smile lit up the young man's face. 'I should say so. You won't find another church like this in the county. Come and have a closer look at the tiles. Do you see? Every flower is different, and all accurately observed. Look at that stitchwort. She must have been quite a botanist, as well as a remarkable artist.'

'She?'

'Didn't I say? Celia Montague, eldest daughter of Southcombe Manor. Brought up a brood of brothers and sisters after her mother died in childbirth. Never married. Did all this around the 1860s, when her father paid for restoring the church. I often wonder what he said about her shinning up a ladder to paint that ceiling. Must have been quite a woman, for those times. Sad story, though. Father remarries. Stepmother takes over the housekeeping keys of the manor. Celia retires, hurt, to live with brother. Dies two years later, probably of a broken heart.'

The two men had moved away, clambering through the pews of the north aisle to study the wall tiles more closely.

Suzie stood her ground. She should have been interested. It was a good story, an unexpected artwork with a human drama behind it. Yet she still felt cheated; she had come wanting to find seventeenth-century yeomen, not the nineteenth-century squirearchy, however unusual.

She turned her back on the men and returned to the south aisle, walking forward towards the Lady Chapel. She was scanning the walls in the fading hope that something from the older church might remain.

There? That arched alcove high up in the wall, at the front end of the nave. That must have been the doorway which gave access to the rood screen, before it was destroyed. There would have been a walkway along the top of it, to reach the great central crucifix, flanked by the figures of the Virgin Mary and St John. Not now. You could look straight up to the altar without interruption. Mystery was dead.

Only the mystery of her forebears thickened.

Just before that blank doorway, which would now have opened on to empty air, a board on the wall caught her eye. Wood, not a marble plaque. A list of names, picked out in black and red with touches of gold. It would, almost certainly, be a list of Southcombe's rectors, predecessors of the young man with the blond curls who was chatting to Nick. They would probably date back to the Normans, or at least the Plantagenets. She dismissed it from her mind, as she had dismissed the Victorian artist. Rectors had little to do with her family history. She had no reason to believe that any of her ancestors had ever been clergymen, here or elsewhere.

Her faint remaining hope was that there might still be grave slabs uncovered by tiles in the floor of the chancel or the Lady Chapel, and that she might find a name she recognized. It was unlikely. The Loosemores and Turners might have aspired to be buried inside the church, but places in the chancel would be reserved for the gentry, not her family.

She cast a brief sideways glance at the board as she passed . . . and stopped. It was not a list of rectors. It was something she had never seen before in a parish church: a list of churchwardens, going back – she peered up at the first name – to 1594.

Her heart beat faster. This was remarkable. Here, recorded for posterity, were the ordinary parishioners who had served this church down the centuries since Elizabeth I. Well, perhaps not the *most* ordinary – these would not be labourers and cottagers. Churchwardens were men, and sometimes women, who were householders of some means and standing in the community. But they were not just the rich and powerful, whose marble plaques hung heavy on most church walls, nor the university-educated clergy, moving in from some other parish or county. Here were parishioners whose roots were in these few square miles of countryside, who worked its fields, gave birth to its children, drew their surnames from its farms and trades.

Her eye raced down the list of names, more excited now because against some of them was the name of a house or a farm. Too fast. She was in danger of missing the very information she was so desperately hoping for.

She began again, more slowly, forcing herself to give close attention to every word. Unfamiliar names scrolled past. Even these might prove significant; she had yet to unravel the surnames of some of the wives on her tree.

Her eye snagged in the 1600s. A lump of denial rose in her throat. She was fooling herself, hoping too much.

No, it was real. *1659–60 Thos: Loosemore of Wayland.*

It was him; it must be. Joshua Loosemore's father. The same surname, seventeen years before Joshua's marriage. So Thomas Loosemore must have been a youngish married man then, but a householder thought fit to take his turn serving the village.

Thomas Loosemore. The sudden significance whisked her back into the present. She almost crowed with delight. Thomas was the Christian name she and Nick had chosen for their son seventeen years ago, and after it they had added Suzie's maiden name: Loosemore. Their Tom was Thomas Loosemore Fewings. Excitement was rising. It had not been a wasted day. This was a gift she could give Tom, a piece of his past.

The men were coming back towards the door.

'Did you know we were here?' Nick was asking. 'You came so quickly after we arrived. Do you check up on all the visitors to your church? Make sure we're keeping the swallows out?'

The rector laughed, a little embarrassed. 'Oh, I wouldn't exactly call it "checking up". I mean, you don't exactly look as if you were likely to steal the candlesticks. And we don't keep the valuable stuff on display any more. But, well, it's God's house, and if he has visitors, somebody ought to be here to make them welcome.'

'This board,' Suzie said, cutting in too fast, her voice high with excitement. 'All the churchwardens from the year dot. I've never seen anything like it. It's wonderful.'

The young man's eyes lit up. 'We've got a list of the rectors, too, down the other end by the door. Did you see it? It's a funny feeling to think I'll be on it myself, one day.'

'But just about every church has that. This is special.'

He rallied from her dismissal of his place in history. 'Oh, good. I'm glad you like it. Your husband tells me you found us a bit of a disappointment. We usually pride ourselves on being rather a star attraction, as far as Victorian restorations go. Definitely different. But *chacun à son gout*. Would you like a copy of our parish history – one pound fifty? It's for parish funds.'

She took the black and white leaflet he pressed on her. Nick extracted his coin purse from his pocket and fished in it for change. The rector indicated a wall safe and the coins clattered into its depths.

'Thank you,' she said, forcing a smile for the eager young man.

He can't understand, she thought. *He's a priest. He can't see how remarkable that board is, with its record of the laity.*

'Don't forget to shut the door when you leave,' he said. 'If we get birds trapped inside, they leave such a mess, and it's the devil of a job to get them out again. Oh!' He ran his fingers through his curls in rueful dismay. 'Sorry. Not the most appropriate metaphor. I don't think St Francis would approve.'

'I know what you mean,' Nick assured him. 'We had a jackdaw down the chimney once. We read your notice in the porch. We'll shut the door.'

When he had gone, Suzie scrabbled in her shoulder bag for a piece of paper. 'After all that, I nearly forgot to copy it down.'

'What? I thought you decided you'd drawn a blank here.'

'The board!' She almost stamped her foot. 'He's there. Joshua's father. I've found him. His name is Thomas. Thomas Loosemore of Wayland, churchwarden of this village the year after Oliver Cromwell died; the last year of the republic. *Thomas Loosemore*. Don't you see? Just wait till I tell Tom.'

Nick's affectionate smile teased her. 'A churchwarden in the seventeenth century? You really believe Tom will think that has anything to do with him?'

TWO

'That was rather churlish of you, to walk away from the poor guy when he was dying to tell us about his church.' Nick softened his censure with a sidelong grin at her. The car was winding through summer lanes heavy with cow parsley. Above the high hedgebanks the fields were busy with machinery turning hay.

All Suzie could recall of the rector was a bush of blond curls, backlit by the sun from the doorway.

'I was just so disappointed. I didn't go to Southcombe for the Victorians. My people had left the parish by then. I needed more evidence about the early ones and I didn't think I was going to find any.'

'He didn't just talk about the Victorians. He was telling me about what his church is doing now. Did you know they get fifty people on a Sunday? That's pretty good for an out-of-the-way village that size. The guy must be doing something right. And they've got this link with a congregation of Christian Arabs in Palestine, near the Israeli border. They sent someone out to see just how tough it gets, and she came back with olive wood carvings and embroidery they'd made, to sell for them. Did you know that things are so bad there that everyone who can is leaving? He says that Christians in the occupied territory have dropped from twenty per cent to just one per cent.'

'That's terrible,' she said. 'In the land where Christianity started. How could they bear to leave it? All that history, those memories?'

'You're doing it again!' Nick thumped the steering wheel. 'You can't spend all your time living in the past. What about now? What about the barrier cutting off six out of their seven wells? What about their olive orchards being cut down and leaving them with no income? What about the checkpoints they can't get past in time to see to their animals or keep a hospital appointment?'

'That's not fair!' His words had cut her surprisingly deep.

'I don't just live in the past. I spend half my week working for old people, remember. Family history's only a hobby. I'm entitled to that, aren't I?'

'Hobby?' The teasing grin was back. 'Sometimes it sounds like an obsession.'

She tried to shape an answering smile. 'Well, yes, it is addictive. Everyone says that. You see, it's like a detective story. Only, as soon as you solve one case, two more open up. Every new person you discover has got a father and a mother. What can I find out about *them* and the lives they led? And as well as the fun of problem solving, there's the thrill of using your imagination to put together a human story from a few dry scraps of information. They may be dead now, but these were real people too, you know. And they're part of who I am.'

'Possibly. It's a wise child that knows its father.'

'Cynic.'

'No; realist. You shouldn't always believe what's on the birth certificate.'

It was not worth even a friendly argument. She settled back to watch the scenery dipping down from the high inland farms to a distant glimpse of the sea.

Nick was telling the truth, of course. It was quite common for brides to go pregnant to the altar. There was no way of knowing now whether the groom was the father of the child or just a husband of convenience. He might have been paid by the squire to take on a sturdy young woman who had proved herself fertile by one of his sons. Even without that doubt, linking a marriage to an earlier baptism was speculative. Was the William Tozer who married in Nether Pickwell in 1821 the same as the William Tozer christened there twenty-five years before, or had someone else of the same name moved into the parish? How certain was any bloodline?

She watched a hamlet of thatched cottages whisk by.

Did it matter? If these names she was researching were not her forebears, then they were people like them. This was her ancestry, her roots. Knowing it changed the way she saw herself. Like the time she had walked into another church-yard, looking for the grave of her great-grandparents. She had hunted in vain for a humble headstone of a farm labourer hidden away in the long grass and ivy under the hedge.

She had almost missed the real grave, right beside the path that led up to the church door, fenced off significantly with a railing. A large upright slab of polished red granite, such as only someone of standing in the village would have. Her first reaction had been disappointment, which she recognized wryly as inverted snobbery. Did it mean she was not, after all, of peasant stock, as she had imagined? She had found the Kelly's Directory for 1891 and discovered that Arthur Loosemore was the village shopkeeper. Every new discovery changed her perception of the past, and of herself.

And today, Thomas Loosemore of Wayland. She hugged the name to herself, warm as the summer's day around her. This had not been a futile journey after all. Far from it. She would have something to tell Tom.

She looked sideways at Nick and felt a rush of renewed affection. He was, to be fair, remarkably sympathetic to her hobby. Now that Tom and Millie were in their teens, she and Nick had taken to setting off most Saturdays for a pub lunch at some village on Suzie's family tree, followed by an exploration of the church and its surrounding countryside. He seemed incurious about his own past in Lancashire, but he enjoyed these expeditions to uncover hers almost as much as she did. As an architect, his own designs were futuristic, but he loved to work with wood and stone. He would examine with professional interest and respect the way his ancient predecessors had used them. So he liked discovering out-of-the-way villages they would never otherwise have come across, adding to their list of good food pubs and finding gems of historic churches. Like today. Nick had been genuinely delighted by the unexpected floral artwork of Southcombe's church and he had listened with real interest to the rector talking of his congregation's present-day work.

She studied his profile. The well-cut nose and chin, the curve of his black hair, contrasting with his astonishing deep blue eyes, were remarkably like Tom's. Nick kept himself in good shape. She was so lucky. She put her hand out and squeezed his knee by way of apology. He shot her another quick grin, before a tractor lurching round the bend recalled his attention to the road.

Suzie watched while the two vehicles negotiated each other. Her pleasure in studying Nick's face was followed by a small stab of regret. She might have given her maiden name of Loosemore to Tom, but it was Nick's gift of genes to their son that predominated. You had only to look at the two of them to see that.

Besides, Nick was probably right about Tom. Why should she expect a seventeen-year-old boy to care that one of his distant ancestors had been a godly churchwarden, just because they shared the same name?

As they swung into Mahonia Drive, Suzie felt, not for the first time, her heart dip in disappointment at the sight of her home. It was ungrateful of her. It was a nice house – of course it was – worth quite a bit in today's market, according to Nick. A double-fronted, detached semi-bungalow from the 1960s, set in a big garden. Nick and his fellow architect turned a respectable profit.

Suzie could understand why he was successful, after outings like today's. The same loving care that took him patiently round the county with her on her family research, was extended to discussing with clients the design of their dream house. Word got around. Nick Fewings was the architect who would shape your home around the way you liked to live, would make it ecologically sustainable, with sympathetic use of natural materials.

Yet she thought of her own modern kitchen, with its maple-fronted integral appliances, the polished green granite tops, the spacious conservatory looking out over curving lawns and the beds of flowers carefully chosen for their gradations of colour and height, a solar-powered water feature bubbling over pebbles, the maturing fruit trees and ornamental shrubs. Their garden would not look out of place on the cover of a horti-cultural magazine. Mostly Nick's work, too, of course. She was better at cutting things back than growing them, let alone planning how it should look in the future.

She ought to be grateful for this home. But sitting in the car, looking at the brick and stone-clad facade, she knew that, left to herself, it was not what she would have chosen. At least, not now that her past was opening up to her. The trees might be growing tall, but this house had been built during her lifetime. It had no history to speak of. She could not drift through its rooms imagining the women who had kept house there before her, the clothes they wore, the wars and political upheavals which had shaken their security, the infectious illnesses, almost unknown today, which had taken their children. In her gleaming kitchen there were no ghosts of the daily maid-of-all-work who had come to cook and clean, sweating over sink and stove, carrying coals to the fireplaces. In this house, there was only one fireplace, with a log-effect gas fire. Surprisingly realistic, but Nick agreed he would have preferred the real thing.

These days, when she pictured the home of her dreams, it was not one of Nick's innovative creations. She could not decide whether it would be a Tudor farmhouse, a Georgian town house, or an Edwardian villa. But what would once have been her place in such a house? She was increasingly unsure whether she was one with the mistress or the maid.

'Tom!'

Suzie came to with a start and realized that Nick had parked the car in front of the garage. He was standing on the drive calling for his son.

No answer.

'Lazy sod. I told him to water the front garden while we were out. He's supposed to do something to warrant the amount of allowance I give him.'

She followed him into the house.

'Tom?'

The only sound was the faint chatter of the television in the conservatory. Nick went ahead. Thirteen-year-old Millie lay with her thin pale legs draped over the flowered cushions of the wicker sofa. She was eating crisps and watching a film which appeared to be about Robin Hood.

'Where's Tom?'

'Out.'

'I don't suppose he said where he was going?'

'Nope.'

Nick turned to Suzie. 'Is he coming back for supper?'

Suzie shrugged. Then, not wanting to sound quite as laconic as Millie, said, 'I've no idea. He didn't tell me he wasn't.'

'Did he say what he was planning today?'

'Tom doesn't usually discuss his movements with me. Does he with you? I assumed he'd be with Dave this afternoon.'

Dave, Tom said of his best friend, was a nerd, but a

likeable nerd. Tom had other friends for clubbing with on Saturday evenings.

'I thought at least we'd agreed about watering the garden. And I like to know where he is. He's our son. We're supposed to be responsible for his movements.'

'He's seventeen.'

Nick sighed. 'All the more reason to worry about what he gets up to.'

'Tom's fine. He's a nice boy. He's never been in any trouble.'

She was disappointed too, but for a different reason. Despite Nick's scepticism, she was longing to tell Tom of her discovery of his namesake.

The note in her shoulder bag with this new information pecked at her mind like a chick ready to hatch. She must do something to release it. She edged away from the conservatory.

'Have you done your homework?' she heard Nick ask Millie.

'Boring.'

Their voices faded as she slid into the study and seated herself at the desk. The computer sprang into flickering life. She spread out the piece of paper and frowned as she deciphered what she had scribbled from the board in the church.

She clicked on her folder for 'Family History' and the sub-folder 'Loosemore'. There was a thrill of anticipation as she opened a new page.

Generation 10: THOMAS LOOSEMORE.

It always gave her a thrill to type in the heading for a new entry. Ten generations back from her own now. That was good going. She had only been at it for less than a year.

She began to type. *On the wall of the church of St Ruman in the village of Southcombe there is a board . . .*

There were hands squeezing her shoulders. Nick was standing behind her. 'So this is what you're up to. I should have known by now, shouldn't I? I did wonder whether a cup of tea might be in order.'

'Sorry. I just wanted to get it down before I forgot anything. This one's for Tom.'

'You're wasting your time, you know. He won't thank you for it.'

She spun the desk chair to smile up at him. 'You're probably right. Did I tell you about this poster I saw at the Family

History Society? *THERE ARE PEOPLE WHO CAN TELL YOU ALL ABOUT THEIR ANCESTORS THREE HUNDRED YEARS AGO, WHO DON'T KNOW WHERE THEIR CHILDREN WERE LAST NIGHT.'*

'Too true.'

The smile vanished. Outrage swept over her. She sprang to her feet. 'Nick! That was a *joke!'*

A twist of hurt replaced the laughter in his face. 'I was only agreeing with you.'

'Well, don't!' It was several moments before she could control her indignation enough to kiss him. 'Sorry, love . . . Did you say you'd put the kettle on?'

The evening meal was nearly over when Tom came home. Suzie felt the familiar lift of her heart as he breezed through the door. He was so like Nick physically: tall, lean. Her hands ached to plunge through the thick dark waves of his hair. Yet there was an added charisma to Tom, which she felt in the core of her body as her son's laughing blue eyes caught hers. Where Nick was quiet, considerate of others, Tom was mercurial, a glinting, sparkling bauble of a boy, designed to catch attention and ensnare hearts. She felt for the girls in his life, that kaleidoscope of names which seemed to change every week.

'We saved some ragout for you,' she offered. 'I can warm it up again.'

She saw the amused, sidelong glance he gave the congealing food.

'Thanks. I'll do myself a pizza.' He headed for the freezer.

Why did it always hurt so much when a child refused a meal you had so lovingly cooked? What was it about food? That sacramental quality, which made the shared family meal so important.

Nick's voice pursued Tom. The forced harshness of it told Suzie how reluctant he was to play the role of the heavy parent, yet he felt that his loyalty to Suzie demanded it of him. 'Where have you been? You were going to water the front garden; we agreed. And supper's always at half past six.'

Tom appeared briefly in the kitchen doorway, the cardboard package in his hand. His eyebrows lifted, his eyes danced. There were never teenage rows with Tom. He seemed incapable of taking offence. If anyone lost his temper, it would be Nick, goaded out of his normal calm by Tom's refusal to take anything seriously.

'I'll do it. No sweat. And it's only quarter to seven. Hey, what's fifteen minutes between friends? Eh, Mum?' The laugh he threw her enrolled her as his co-conspirator.

'It's food wasted. And your mother's time and effort.'

'Starving babies in Africa?' He could raise one eyebrow to an astonishing height.

'Just waste.' Nick was struggling to keep his voice low and reasonable now. 'Not living lightly on the planet. Like consuming that junk food when there's a perfectly good meal on the table.'

'So why does Mum put pizzas in the freezer? She knows I like them.'

'Nobody asked *me* if I'd prefer a pizza to ragout,' Millie objected. 'And the answer is, yes, Mum, I would.'

Suzie was tossed between them, a weapon in their arsenals.

The microwave pinged as Tom pressed the settings. She scrabbled for a way out of the argument which hung in the air, though Tom was evading it.

'I came across a new ancestor today in Southcombe, Tom. You'll never guess what he was called. Thomas Loosemore. I've never found that before in the family history. When we christened you, I'd no idea that it had been a Loosemore family name.'

He turned his merry eyes to hers. 'Mum, Thomas has got to be one of the three most popular names in history: Thomas the Tank Engine, Tom Hanks, Thomas Paine, old Uncle Tom Cobbley and all. You could have chosen something more original.'

'But Thomas *Loosemore*? We gave you both names. Anyway, you should be grateful that Tom's so normal. I found a boy in the register around 1700 christened Maher-shalal-hash-baz.'

'Cool. Hey, that'd be a great chat-up line with the girls. "Bet you can't guess what my name is." They'd never believe it. Baz . . . Yes, I like the sound of that. Or Hash, even. That's better still. Can't I get my name changed by deed poll?'

'Better than Millie,' said Millie. 'Honestly, Mum!'

As a ploy to divert attention from her feeling of rejection over the food, it had not been a great success.

THREE

Later that evening Suzie was seduced into slipping back to the study. She told herself she really did need to get the information down while the memory of the day was still fresh. She found the computer file she had started.

10. LOOSEMORE. The tenth generation, counting back from her own.

Was that a mistake? If she was Generation 1, what did that make Tom and Millie? Generation 0? Perhaps she should have started with them. But there could be no fixed point. Families grew. One day, Tom and Millie would have children of their own, her grandchildren. She would become an ancestor. She liked that thought. For now, the children were not the least bit interested in her hobby. Perhaps when they had families of their own it would make a difference. By then, she would have thick sheaves of their family history to give them.

She laid out her scribbled note from Southcombe church on the desk beside her and set to work.

As yet, we do not know where Thomas Loosemore was born or who his parents were. Since he was churchwarden of Southcombe in 1659–60, he must have been born well before the Civil War of 1642–49.

It was not everyone who could trace their ancestors back to the Civil War, she reflected proudly. Of course, it helped, living in the same county, with all the records to hand and the chance to visit the actual villages and towns, like today.

Suzie turned her attention back to the seventeenth century.

We assume that Thomas is the father of Joshua Loosemore, who married Loyalty Turner in Southcombe in 1676. We do not yet know the name of his own wife.

He lived, and probably farmed, at Wayland.

Her hands stilled on the keys. It had not occurred to her until now. They must have been close to Wayland this afternoon, if it still existed. They could have gone to look at it.

Was it a hamlet or a farm? Surely the talkative rector would have known. If only she had asked him while she had the chance. Instead, she had barely spoken to him.

She concentrated on the screen again.

Following the execution of Charles I in 1649, Oliver Cromwell ruled as Lord Protector. Many parish registers for this Commonwealth period have been lost, including Southcombe's. The gaps occur most frequently in parishes where a Royalist or High Church parson was ejected from the living and replaced by a Puritan incumbent . . .

She re-read the words she had typed. A thought struck her. She could go to the library and look up that book. What was it called? Walker's *Sufferings of the Clergy*. Yes, that was it. She had been told it recorded all the horror stories of these evictions. If Southcombe was among them, it should be there.

On Tuesday she walked up the steps to the central library. This was her afternoon for self-indulgence, her weekly treat to herself. To the right as she entered was, appropriately, the Register Office, recording modern-day births, marriages and deaths. A couple in their thirties, with a little boy, sat waiting in the lobby. What turning-point in their lives had they come to register: a brother or sister for the child, a belated wedding, a bereavement? It was hard to tell from their passive faces.

She went on upstairs to the Local Studies Library, to pursue similar turning points in the lives of her ancestors. She signed in. In the column for 'Subject of Research' she wrote 'FH', for Family History. So, she noted, had most other people.

There was a man with a map spread out across the tables. A couple of girls, probably students, were exchanging whispered giggles across two of the microfiche readers. Other researchers bent over books and notepads, or scanned the shelves. There was an air of quiet enjoyment. It was not just Suzie; even those who used this library for their work seemed to find pleasure in what they were discovering.

She seated herself in front of the catalogue computer, clicked 'Title', and typed in 'Sufferings of the Clergy'. There it was: 'Walker, John. *The Sufferings of the Clergy during the Grand Rebellion.*'

She knew the book by reputation only. It was a rant against the ejections of High Church, Royalist clergy from their livings after the Civil War, when the Parliamentarians had made the country a Puritan republic. She had never used it before. She made a note of its classification number.

It was almost a surprise to find it there on the shelf, where the catalogue said it should be. A brown ridged leather spine, with gilt lettering. She pulled it out, savouring the feel of the binding in her hand, the weight of its pages. In spite of what Nick had said, this history held its own reality. She checked the title page. This was a later, edited edition. Walker's book had originally been published in 1714. So it was not a contemporary account of Cromwell's Commonwealth, even then. It would be highly coloured and partisan; she had been warned about that. But it was still evidence. It all helped to put flesh on the bones of ancestors who would otherwise simply be names on a family tree.

It was, of course, too much to hope that it would mention her own family members, the Loosemores and Turners. Why should it? But what was going on in their parish was part of their experience. These were the stormy events through which they had lived out their humbler lives. It was *her* history. Even unreliable evidence was better than nothing. No smoke without a fire.

She took the book to one of the empty tables. It seemed to be arranged alphabetically. She leafed through its pages to find the parish of Southcombe.

A hollow disappointment. There was nothing there. She had felt so sure that the gap in the registers for the 1650s must point to an ejected parson. But perhaps not. In those fractured times, continuity might have been broken for less dramatic reasons.

She was right about the alphabetical sequence, wasn't she? She had found the Ss. *Soreton, Squire, Ward.* No mention of Southcombe.

Idiot! She was reading the surnames of the clergy, not the names of their parishes. More haste, less speed. She thumbed back to the main body of entries.

This looked more like it. Page 139, *Southill, Southmore.* She turned back one more page, willing it to produce a result.

It was there: *Southcombe.* CHAMBERS, ARTHUR. An account of his origins, his degree at Oxford, his induction to Southcombe. Then the meat.

'He was miserably harassed, and forced to hide under the

roof of his house. When discovered and apprehended, he was first ill-treated by the mob to make him disclose the whereabouts of his money. Then a militiaman, one Thomas Loosemore . . .'

She stopped, breath held in disbelief. This was more than she had dared to hope for. Now her eye raced on.

'. . . one of his own parishioners, seized him by the hairs of his head and dragged him down the stair of the parsonage house. The venerable rector, being advanced in years, suffered a broken skull of which he died ten days later.'

She stared at those final words. Could this be the same Thomas Loosemore, churchwarden a few years later, the pillar of village society, who had laid violent hands on his royalist rector, thrown the old man downstairs and . . . killed him?

She sat back, stunned. This was not what she had expected.

Time lengthened out while she absorbed this information. It significantly altered the image of the man she had formed in her mind.

At last, she took the book to the photocopier, inserted her coins and folded the printout into her bag. She walked out of the library, without even remembering to return the book to its shelf.

She stepped off the bus. The noise of traffic from the main road faded as she walked down the leafy side road. Usually she could not wait to get home and write up her research. Today, as she approached the house, she felt a growing reluctance, a sense that her pleasure had been tainted.

It was ridiculous. She should have been delighted. She had never uncovered anything like this before. Not only a personal mention of her ancestor, but a story colourful enough to evoke the envy of her fellow members of the Family History Society. She should be on a high.

So why did she feel this constriction in her throat? What did it matter now that Thomas Loosemore of Southcombe had killed someone? It was far in the past. Hadn't she mocked those researchers whose sole ambition was to prove they were related to someone like Lord Nelson or Charles Dickens, and who shied away from any hint of something unsavoury in their past? Wasn't the point of family history to follow open-mindedly where the evidence led and just enjoy whatever you

found? Real family historians weren't shocked if a supposed
pilgrim ancestor turned out to be a transported felon. The ones
Suzie knew were more likely to punch the air and cheer. The
more colourful the story the better.

She reminded herself how she had gurgled with laughter to
find, in the local barber's gossipy diary, a dodgy turnpike-gate
keeper on one branch of her tree. She had savoured the entry.

*1799. Folly-Lane Gate was taken by James Taverner. It
returned the last year £48.0.0. This Taverner kept the same
Gate some years since, when 'tis thought there was more travelling than at present, and returned but £28.0.0 in the year.
Here, I shall leave the Reader to make his Remarks.*

There was no doubt who the barber thought had pocketed
the missing tolls. That sort of scandalous discovery only added
to the general gaiety.

So why was she wishing she could fold the marbled covers
of Walker's book shut and return to the time when she had
never opened them?

The house was cool, peaceful. Millie's skinny figure was
hunched over the kitchen table. She was apparently doing her
homework.

'How's things?'

'It's French. Boring.'

'Can I help?'

'I didn't say it was difficult. Just boring.'

Suzie deposited her shopping in the kitchen. For once, she
didn't hurry to the computer to add today's findings to her
family history. She began instead to think about the evening
meal. Randomly, she found herself assembling onions, fish,
wine, herbs, kitchen knife.

She stared down at the sharp blade. It was ridiculous to
feel upset. Those were bloody, brutal times, when the country,
even families, had been ripped apart by civil war. She and her
family were living in the twenty-first century, in a peaceful
suburban estate. There was still bloody strife, civil war, God
knew. The television screens were full of it. But not here, not
to them. Violence was not *their* reality.

Usually when she had made her weekly trip to the Local
Studies Library or the Record Office, she was eager to pour
out the results to Nick. If he was bored to tears by now, he
managed not to let it show, bless him.

This Tuesday, however, she found she did not want to share her findings.

'How was it today?' he asked later, as she passed him his plate of fish. 'Turn up anything interesting? Granny in the workhouse? Cholera epidemic? Sister on the game?'

The words that would have told him of her discovery were strangely reluctant to pass her lips. She felt oddly ashamed of what she knew. It made no difference that she recognized she was being silly. Hadn't she relished finding there were smugglers on her mother's side of the family, even though she knew that these gentlemen of the night had sometimes killed Revenue Officers?

That was different. There had been nothing as personal as this. None of her ancestors had actually been named as responsible.

'*Thomas Loosemore, one of his own parishioners, seized him by the hairs of his head . . .*'

She had flicked through more of the pages of Walker's book afterwards. She had found no other instance where a layman abusing a clergyman had been so named. Thomas Loosemore's guilt for his rector's death was unavoidable.

She looked up suddenly and found that Tom was listening for her reply too, his dark head tilted, his blue eyes on hers, alive and questioning.

'Nothing much,' she said, after too long a pause. 'I photo-copied some stuff. I still need to sort it out.'

'You mean, it's Tuesday and we can talk about something other than family history?' said Millie. 'Put out the flags.'

'Don't rile her.' Tom's eyes smiled at Suzie across the table. 'She's doing a great job. How many generations have you got back now, Mum?'

She seized gratefully on the diversion. 'Thirteen, on one line. That's the 1500s. It's hard to go further back than that, because the registers only began in 1538, and even then some parishes have lost their early books. Unless, of course, you're the landed gentry, with pedigrees going back to the Norman Conquest.'

'Some hopes! That's not us, is it?'

'In this game, you never know what you may turn up.'

Then, looking across into Tom's warm blue eyes, it came to her. This was what was so upsetting her. Tom. Her baby.

The son they had christened Thomas Loosemore. She had
been so unreasonably pleased to find his namesake. It had made
her eager to find out more about him, to offer Tom detail,
colour, a living man behind the name. It would be her gift to
him. Someone to catch his imagination. Someone of whom
he could be proud.

But instead, she found she had given him *this* name. The
name of a violent young man, guilty of manslaughter. It made
her feel like a wicked fairy godmother with a poisoned
christening gift.

She toyed with the fish on her plate, extracting a bone.
Rubbish! She was making far too much of it. It had happened
three and half centuries ago. She did the arithmetic in her head.
Ten generations back from her, so eleven from Tom. That made
Thomas Loosemore two, four, eight – she counted the generations on her fingers as she went on doubling – one out of a
thousand and twenty-four ancestors on the same level of Tom's
family tree. Less than a tenth of one per cent of his heredity.

Suzie and Nick took their coffee into the conservatory. Nick
switched on the television to catch the weather forecast at the
end of the local news.

'Sunshine and showers? Looks like we may not need to
water the garden this weekend.'

'Tom will be pleased.'

A viewer's photograph of a sunset beach was replaced by
the two presenters at their desk. Their smiles were less genial
than usual, their faces concerned.

'And don't forget, if you think you have any information
about where Julie Samuel may be, let the police know. Here's
the number again.'

'See you tomorrow. Enjoy your evening.'

On to the national headlines.

'She goes to our school.' Millie was leaning against the
doorway behind them. She was trying to sound casual, but
there was a rise of excitement in her voice. 'What's up? She
gone missing?'

'You know as much as we do. It sounds like it.'

'Is she in your class?' Suzie asked.

'Nope. Year Eleven. Tom knows her, though. She's one of
his. Or was a couple of weeks ago.'

'What do you mean, "one of his"?' asked her father.

Millie and Suzie exchanged glances. Suzie had not needed to ask.

'You know. On his scorecard.'

And now Suzie was less sure. What exactly did that mean? Year Eleven. She did some swift mental arithmetic. It was what, in her own school days, had been called the fifth form. GCSE year. So, a girl of fifteen or sixteen. Tom was in the sixth form. The arithmetic was troubling, if Millie meant what Suzie thought she did. Still, it was the summer term. Surely this Julie Samuel would be sixteen by now?

Guilt smote her. The girl was missing. She might even be dead. It was every parent's nightmare. And all she, Suzie, had been worrying about was whether Tom had been having under-age sex.

But I should worry, shouldn't I? He's my son.

Every parent's nightmare . . . Millie.

'Excuse me. Got to get on the phone,' Millie said. 'It'll be all over school in the morning. Do you think they'll have a camera crew outside the gates? Better do my hair properly tomorrow, hadn't I? I might be on the telly.'

'Millie!'

'*Sorry!* But it's the first time anything interesting's happened in the three years I've been there.'

'A girl's missing, maybe in danger,' Nick said. 'Can't you think of anyone but yourself?'

Millie flounced away.

'She doesn't mean it,' Suzie said. 'It's not cool to show you're afraid.'

'Afraid? You mean . . .?' Nick's eyes registered sudden alarm.

What *had* she meant, Suzie wondered?

'We don't know yet what's happened to this girl. She may just have run off, on her own or with someone else. But she could have been . . .' Her voice trailed off. It was too difficult to say the word 'murdered'.

'You think Millie might be in danger?'

She was more uncomfortable now, afraid of seeming melo-dramatic. 'Probably not. But until we know, any girl could be, couldn't they?'

'Maybe I should take her to school tomorrow in the car. Could you meet her in the afternoon?'

'Yes, but she won't like it, in front of her mates.'

'Better safe than sorry. You'll probably find their parents are doing the same.'

'Should we tell Tom, after what Millie said about the two of them?'

A silence. There was a murmur of voices from upstairs. A brief cry from Tom.

'I suspect Millie just has.'

FOUR

I t was not easy to watch Tom's distress. When he came home from school next day he did not leap upstairs and switch on his computer, as he usually did. He came down to the kitchen in a pair of old jeans and went out of the back door without speaking. Suzie saw him stride under the apple tree to the far end of the garden. After a while, she followed him far enough to see what he was doing. She hesitated. Should she go and say something to him? Something sympathetic and motherly, inviting his confidence? She bit her lip and turned back to the house.

'What's he doing out there?' asked Nick, setting down his briefcase an hour later.

'Turning over the compost heap.'

'What! It must be flying pigs time. I never even asked him. I just said I'd need to do it this weekend.'

'I think he needs something physical.'

'Why?'

'Isn't that what we all do when we don't want to think about something?'

'Such as? Oh, you mean this Julie Samuel thing. They haven't found her, have they?'

'I shouldn't think so. Millie would have said something.'

They watched the lift and swing of his shoulders beyond the lines of runner beans. There was something almost angry in the movement. Tom was tall, becoming well built, Suzie realized, almost as if she were watching a stranger. The gangly leanness of a teenager, whose limbs seemed to grow faster than he learned to control them, was filling out into manhood. She had not been sufficiently aware of it.

She had to call him in for supper. She could have shouted from the doorway, but she walked across the lawn. A trellis fence made a partial screen for the vegetable garden.

She stood awkwardly, watching. Slabs of dark compost flew from one pile to the next bay. Tom's face was red with exertion; sweat darkened his tee shirt. She could not tell if he knew she was there.

'Supper's ready.'

'Oh, yeah. Coming.'

He rested the spade at last and leaned on it. He was panting slightly.

'Is anything wrong?' It was like putting out a foot cautiously to test a sheet of ice.

'No. Why? Should there be?' He was not looking at her. A lock of black hair fell over his lowered face.

'This.' She gestured at the compost. 'You don't usually go gardening after school.'

'Felt like it. Dad said it needed doing.'

He was already moving abruptly to restore the spade to the tool shed. He walked ahead of her to the kitchen.

Nick and Millie were already sitting at the table.

'Hello. How's things?' Nick was trying too hard to pitch his voice at a reassuring cheerfulness.

'Fine.'

Tom scrubbed his hands at the kitchen sink and sat down. Another day, Suzie might have told him to change his dirty clothes.

She served the meal in a brittle silence no one wanted to break.

'No way, Mum.' Millie stuck out her sharp chin as she gathered up her school bag. 'You are not coming to meet me from school again. It was so embarrassing yesterday.'

'It's just until they find Julie Samuel. When a teenage girl goes missing, we're bound to be anxious.'

'Mum, she's sixteen. She could have cleared off of her own free will. Gone anywhere. Doesn't mean she's been murdered.'

'Without taking anything but the clothes she was wearing?'

'OK, but say something *has* happened to her, don't they say that most victims are killed by someone they know? You've been watching too many crime programmes about unknown bogeymen on the prowl.'

'Well . . . all right then. But stick with your friends and come straight home.'

'Yeah, yeah.'

Millie did not refuse Nick's offer of a lift to school in the car.

*   *   *

When the doorbell rang late that afternoon Suzie knew immediately it was to do with the sense of unease that was haunting her.

Millie got there before her. She turned, wide-eyed. 'Mum, it's the police.'

Suzie came down the hall, arranging her face to express the polite surprise she did not feel.

There were two of them, a square-set, middle-aged man and a younger woman with a black ponytail, contrasting with her crisp, white shirt.

'Yes?'

'Mrs Fewings?' said the young woman.

'Yes,' said Suzie again.

Identity cards were flashed. Sergeant Lucy Morris and Constable Elton Wall.

'Is your son Tom in?'

'Why?' Her mouth was dry, her voice thin.

'We'd like to ask him a few questions. Just routine enquiries.'

'Is it . . . about Julie Samuel?'

The policewoman's dark eyes were disturbingly direct. They held Suzie's. She was afraid they would read her mind.

'Yes. We need to talk to all her friends. Somebody must know something that will help us find her.'

'Tom . . . she wasn't his girlfriend . . . well . . .'

'I think it would be best if we let Tom tell us about that. May we come in?'

'Oh yes, of course. I'm sorry.'

She led the way to the sitting room and stood aside for them to enter. She did not go to the foot of the stairs and call up to Tom, as she would have done if his friend Dave had come to call. Instead, she went to the study, where Nick was entering figures on the computer.

'It's the police. They want to talk to Tom.'

He swivelled round. There was concern in his eyes, but no real anxiety.

'Of course. We ought to have expected that. They'll want to check up on all her friends. Have you told Tom?'

'I'll go and get him.'

Tom was lying on his bed. It struck Suzie that there was something odd in his being in his room alone. Most weekday nights, Dave was round here, or Tom was at Dave's.

'There are two police officers downstairs. They want to talk to you about Julie Samuel.'

Tom swung his feet off the bed. His face was expressionless. He followed her downstairs.

Nick was already in the sitting room, chatting to the offcers.

'Ah, here you are, Tom,' he said heartily. 'Come and sit down.' He patted the sofa beside him.

'Would you like some tea or coffee?' Suzie said. Her voice was still embarrassingly faint.

'Thanks. Black coffee, no sugar,' said the police sergeant.

'Could I trouble you for tea? Two sugars?' said Constable Wall.

The hiss of the kettle prevented her from hearing what was being said in the other room. She loaded a tray with mugs, coffee for Nick and herself, tea for Tom. The voices stopped as she entered the room. There was an awkward pause while she handed out the drinks. The policeman, she saw, had been taking notes.

'So, Tom,' said Sergeant Morris over her coffee mug, 'you think you and Julie were going out for a couple of weeks.'

'Couldn't have been more than that.'

'It was only a fortnight ago. With all the talk about her disappearance, I'd have thought it would have sharpened your memory.'

Tom flushed. 'All right, then. Two weeks.'

'And why did you stop seeing her?'

He shrugged. 'I never like to get too serious. I wouldn't want the girl to get the wrong idea.'

'Had you done anything which might have given her the wrong idea? Tom, I know this may be difficult for you. If you feel you could talk more freely without your parents . . .'

'Is that legal? He's only seventeen,' Nick interjected.

'That makes him an adult in our book.' The sergeant's look at Nick and Suzie sharpened with authority, making her suddenly look older. 'We could have asked to see him alone from the start. Sorry to be so formal. Tom's not under caution. This is just routine enquiries. Still, he's entitled to have a solicitor present if he feels it necessary, but there's no need for you to be here.'

Suzie felt fear rising, as if at an unspoken threat.

'They can stay,' Tom said quietly. Then his voice sharpened. 'I've got nothing to hide. I didn't have sex with her, if that's what you're getting at.' His face looked mutinous, the dark brows close together.

'That's not the impression her friends gave. I gather she looked on you as a rather hot conquest.'

Tom's eyebrows shot up. 'The little . . .!' He shut his mouth tight.

'Do you want to reconsider your statement?'

'No.'

Constable Wall wrote busily.

'So when was the last time you saw her? Alone, I mean.'

'Must have been Saturday night, nearly two weeks ago. I took her to the over-sixteens club on the quay. She'd just had her birthday, so she could get in.'

'And afterwards?'

'What do you mean?'

'Did you take her home? Go on anywhere else?'

'I told her it was over while we were dancing the last number. I like to do it with a bit of style. Sort of grand finale. Not just leave them waiting for the phone to ring. She went home in a taxi with some of her friends.'

'Was she upset?'

'A bit stunned, I guess. They usually are. I don't go in for rows. But she didn't go tearful on me, not then. Just sort of tossed her head and flounced away.'

Suzie was uneasy at the harshness in Tom's voice. His characteristic smile was missing.

'You see yourself as some sort of Don Juan?' asked Sergeant Morris.

'Come again?'

'Never mind. And that was the last time you spoke to her?'

'She phoned. That's when we had the waterworks.'

'When?'

'Next day. Sunday.' Tom looked down at the hands clenched on his lap. 'I wasn't mean to her. I always tell the girl I think she's been great when I wind things up. But I made it clear we were finished.'

'And who have you been dating since?'

Tom studied his fingernails. 'No one.'

'No one?' That was Constable Wall. 'You ditched Julie, but you hadn't got anyone else lined up?'

Tom's head shot up. 'No. Look, I've got mates my own age. Schoolwork to do. I don't spend all my time pulling chicks.'

'But you do . . . "pull" them. Does that mean you . . .?' She shot an apologetic glance at Suzie and Nick.

'Just an expression.'

The officers exchanged glances.

'Thank you, Tom,' said Sergeant Morris. 'You've been a big help. If you'd just like to check your statement we'll get you to sign it.'

The formalities were nearly over. Suzie felt embarrassed now that she and Nick had elected to stay.

The ponytailed policewoman watched Tom sign his name. 'If there's anything else you remember in the meantime . . . Anything Julie said which might give us a lead to what she was thinking. Anything significant you've forgotten in that phone call . . .'

'It was as much a surprise to me as everybody else when she went missing, if that's what you mean.'

'Of course. But any little detail. You never know what will help.'

'If I remember anything, I'll let you know.'

The officers were starting to rise.

Tom burst out, 'What do you think's happened to her? Does it look like she's run away? Or . . .? She wouldn't have, would she? Not because I broke it off?'

'We've got a full-scale search going on, son,' said Constable Wall. 'One way or the other, we're going to find her.'

The house was oddly quiet when they had gone. Tom went back upstairs. There was no thump of his friend's feet on the stairs, no teenage laughter from Tom's bedroom.

Suzie and Nick did not speak to each other about what had happened.

FIVE

Suzie closed down her computer in the cramped office behind the charity shop. She stacked the red-and-white leaflets ready for distribution to the local churches and libraries. One o'clock.

As she closed the office door and walked through the shop, Margery laughed from behind the counter. 'Finished for the weekend? OK for some.'

Suzie smiled at the shop's manager. 'Go on, you know you love it.'

'You'll take the blue one?' Margery turned her ready warmth on a customer holding out an embroidered dress of Indian cotton. 'I've been eyeing that myself. It's a terrific bargain, isn't it?'

Suzie watched her fondly. Margery was a widow with no children. Managing the charity shop was her life, the volunteer staff and the customers her family. What must it be like to have no children to enliven your life with their unfolding futures, no one to worry about?

With that thought, the afternoon seemed less bright than it had done. She *was* worried. For Tom, brooding alone when he came home from school. For Millie, who was now refusing to be taken either to or from school, though there was still no word of what had happened to Julie Samuel and people were beginning to fear the worst.

Suzie made her way past a down-at-heel young man who seemed to spend part of every day browsing the second-hand bookshelves. She stepped out into the sunshine.

It offered what she did not want today: space to be alone with her thoughts.

She stood at the bus stop and was surprised to find herself shiver, though the day was fine. It must be the shock of yesterday, she thought, having the police in her home questioning Tom. But of course they had to. They would be checking up on all Julie's friends, looking for any clue about what might have happened to her. They could hardly leave out a boy who had dated her recently. Still, she wished Tom had not been quite so closely involved.

She cast a glance past the cathedral towards the library. Friday wasn't her normal day for research, but it would be comforting to go and lose herself among records of the past and forget the present. She could buy a sandwich to eat in the cathedral close and then head for the library, instead of going home to spend the afternoon thinking about her children.

A sour taste rose in her mouth. The Local Studies Library was where she had made that unexpectedly unpleasant find in *The Sufferings of the Clergy*. It was proving oddly difficult to shake off the depression it had caused her.

She must put away the thought. That Thomas was far in the past. What mattered was the distress her own Tom was suffering. For all his protestations about not getting serious, he must have cared for Julie, mustn't he? Why else was he so visibly upset?

Anyway, she did not want to go to the library today. Her happy discovery in Southcombe church had been spoiled. Her mind wandered back to that Saturday, to her first vision of Thomas Loosemore, the rural churchwarden, pillar of the community. Not a violent militiaman, dragging an old clergyman downstairs by his hair. She no longer wanted to connect that Civil War Thomas Loosemore with the living Tom.

It was unfair. She had been so delighted to find his name in red and gold lettering on the churchwardens' board. *Thos: Loosemore of Wayland*. She could still see it now.

Her heart leaped. Churchwarden. Was it possible? In some parishes, churchwardens' accounts, centuries old, had survived. Had Southcombe's? Was there a chance that the transactions of his year of office might even now be sitting in the Record Office in the twenty-first century, evidence that he had been, after all, what she had thought he was: a man Tom could respect?

The day looked suddenly brighter again. She jumped on the bus and then hurried up the road to her house. Dropping her bag, she went straight to the study. The computer seemed to take an age to boot. What did she care when the virus protection was last updated? The desktop cleared eventually; the wallpaper was Nick's photograph of a stone cross on the moor, from yet another parish where she had found her family. She clicked on the Internet and selected from her list of Favourites the county's Genuki page of genealogical resources. Parishes beginning with S: *Southcombe*. It was a small village. As she had expected, there were only half a dozen entries for the sources available. Parish registers from 1596 in the Record Office, an illustrated booklet on the parish church in the Local Studies Library. That must be the one the rector had sold them. Nothing about churchwardens' accounts.

Would they be listed here, if they did exist?

She remembered seeing the accounts for Childon, where another churchwarden ancestor had been responsible for hanging a new set of bells. Back to parishes beginning with C. No mention there of Childon's churchwardens' accounts. Yet they were certainly in the Record Office, on microfiche. She had transcribed some of them.

There was only one way to find out. The Record Office was on the outskirts of town, on an industrial estate. It was on her side of the city. It was, just, within walking distance. Up over the brow of the hill to where the leafy suburban gardens ended, and then down the other side past the Park and Ride. She could do it. She recognized in herself the same need for physical action that had driven Tom to the compost heap.

As she walked, fast, she was thinking of those spadefuls of compost flying through the air, the sweat on Tom's face. And she discovered what she had not realized then, watching him: that physical activity was no way to blank out the thoughts you did not want to face. The rhythmic effort of her body walking fast uphill left her mind with nothing else to do but go where she did not want it to.

Tom and Julie. Julie's friends implying that she had boasted that they had had sex together. Tom's angry denial.

She was panting now, but the top of the hill was in sight.

Surely the police could not believe he had anything to do with Julie's disappearance? Not her handsome, laughing, loving Tom. And he *was* loving, to her. Like Nick. She felt his hands on her shoulders from behind, his voice laughing in her ear. They had always been close. It was Millie who had become a teenage stranger.

She flinched as she remembered the anguish in Tom's last

question. *She wouldn't have, would she?* Poor Tom. Did he
really fear the girl would have committed suicide over the
ending of a mere fortnight's friendship? It didn't make sense.
Not if she had initially seen Tom as her conquest, rather than
herself as his.

What exactly had Tom said to her in that last phone call,
when Julie had been weeping? If that *was* their last
conversation.

The thought from the Family History Society poster sneaked
up on her: how well do we know our own children?

Where were these crazy thoughts going? She was Tom's
mother, for heaven's sake. She loved him. She trusted him.

She had reached the ridge: a broad ring road, busy with
lorries. She picked her moment to cross to the central reservation and then made it to the other side. The view changed
dramatically. No longer mellow brick houses in mature
gardens. The vast shining roofs of warehouses clad the
slopes below her like an alien civilization. Further off, a
patchwork of fields rolled out towards the wooded ridges
of the distant hills. An old landscape: villages and farms
going back to Saxon times, even older Iron Age hill forts
on the skyline. A clash of cultures. She was more at home
in the past.

It felt odd to be a pedestrian on this industrial estate. The
warehouses were not scaled to the individual. She found the
Record Office in a quiet cul-de-sac.

She had hoped for a feeling of sanctuary inside, but these
purpose-built premises were more impersonal than the old
Local Studies Library in town. She had to leave her belongings in the locker room. Only a clear plastic envelope was
allowed in the search room. No familiar handbag, no shopping bag heavy with files for reference. She must concentrate,
think what she would need inside. Paper, a pencil – no pens
allowed with original documents, of course – a couple of
sheets of her notes about Thomas Loosemore to remind her
of the dates. She closed the locker door on the rest and her
pound coin dropped into its slot. She was ready. She slipped
the key into her pocket.

Inside the spacious search room warmth began to return.
There were the familiar staff, smiles of recognition as she
checked in. She was a regular visitor here.

She found the red files of parish indexes. S. Southcombe.
She ran her finger down the entries.

There. *Churchwardens' Accounts. 1586–1748*. That included
the whole of the seventeenth century.

Or possibly not. She reminded herself that, too often, the
trauma of the Civil War had left a gaping wound in the records
for the mid-century, especially where a priest had been evicted
from his living. Accounts, as well as registers, might have
been lost.

She jotted down the reference number and took it to the
enquiry desk.

'Which table are you sitting at?'

In her haste, she had forgotten to claim a place at a table.
The search room was less than half full. She located the nearest
free one to the desk and came back with the information.

'I know,' grinned the archivist. 'I never remember my table
number when I'm ordering a bar meal. Maybe we should just
hand out wooden spoons with a number painted on them, like
they do in some pubs.'

Suzie sat down and waited. The woman came bustling from
the store room.

'Here we are. Looks like it's time we got this lot on microfiche. It's not often we have to hand out the original account
books these days.'

Suzie's hands thrilled to the touch of the leather-bound
volumes. They were long and narrow, designed for columns
of figures. She took a deep breath and opened the first one.
The late 1500s. She thumbed her way through to the beginning of the next century. Still too early. If Thomas's accounts
were here, they must be in the next volume.

She approached the 1650s with held breath. Yes, the
sequence went on through Cromwell's Commonwealth from
year to year, unbroken. A few more pages. 1657, 58 . . . It was
here. At the foot of this page.

*'And we doo appoint Thomas Loosemore to be Churchwarding
for the next yeere following.'*

She turned over one more leaf. The writing changed. The
blood beat hard in her throat. She was looking at Thomas
Loosemore's own handwriting.

It was a well-formed hand, evidence of a man who was
confidently literate. It was surprisingly easy to read. She had

been afraid the accounts might be written in an antique script she would struggle to interpret.

'For riding to ye court at Pearport & taking ye Oath and an Article Book £0..3..0d.'

Southcombe to the Bristol Channel. She tried to picture the map and did quick sums in her head. About twenty miles? The county's roads were notoriously bad, making wheeled traffic a rarity. So Thomas Loosemore was no country yokel, knowing nothing beyond his own small village. He had travelled. He had ridden to the archdeacon's court in the bustling port and market town. There, he had taken his oath as church-warden and received the book of Articles listing the duties he must perform. She read on.

'Paid to Ambrose Downey for one dayes work about the Church Gate. £0..1..4d.

Paid to Sarah Thorne for washing the linning and keeping clean the Church £0..2..0d.

Paid to Roger Harris for Carrying of Timber £0..1..6d.'

It was comforting, this long list of the church's house-keeping, which Thomas Loosemore had overseen for his year of office. There was no hint here of violence, of cruelty. The Civil War was not long over. It had rent communities apart. But life went on. The wooden shingles on the church roof needed replacing; the linen for the communion service had to be laundered; bread and wine must be paid for.

Who was the minister now, who officiated at these communion services, now that Arthur Chambers was dead? What did Thomas Loosemore feel as he approached to take the bread and wine from his hands? Did he remember those other hands which had fed him the sacrament a decade before? The hands he had stilled for ever?

If this was the same Thomas Loosemore.

Suzie snatched at the sudden hope. She had jumped to conclusions. In the absence of surviving registers for this period, she had assumed too eagerly that the churchwarden Thomas Loosemore must be her missing ancestor, father of Joshua Loosemore. And why had she accepted as inevitable that the Thomas Loosemore who had killed his rector was the same man?

She could be wrong. Hadn't Tom himself pointed out that his name was one of the commonest? Wasn't that the point of the saying 'every Tom, Dick and Harry'? There could have been two of them in the same parish. Cousins, perhaps.

But which – if there were two – was the father of Joshua? If she had to choose between the violent militiaman and the faithful churchwarden, what evidence was there to show which one was Tom's more likely ancestor?

She had the record of Joshua's marriage in 1676. That put his likely birth in the early 1650s. Was it likely that the militia would have enlisted his father, then a young married man? Yes, it was perfectly possible. Might Joshua's father have been appointed churchwarden a decade later, probably in his late thirties? He would have needed to be a householder, paying the church rate. Again, yes, it was entirely credible. So, were these different men? Not necessarily. Both, she had to admit, were plausible stages in the same Thomas's career.

Yet it was reassuring to read the passage of this less eventful year in the village's history, Easter to Easter, 1659–60.

'Paid for three sea-faring men yt had a Pass £0..1..0d.
ffor the Gypsies & carrying ym to ye next Parish £0..10..0d.'

The arrival and departure of these strangers must have been the most colourful passages of Thomas's year of office.

How had he handled the eviction of those clearly un-welcome gypsies?

She comforted herself with the thought that the villagers of Southcombe must have looked up to Thomas Loosemore. They had entrusted him with the care and the running of their church and parish.

She noticed with a start that the surface of the table where she was working had turned white. It was sprinkled with a residue of fine particles. She had a horror that the book in her hands had been crumbling to dust as she turned the pages. The evidence of her past was disintegrating.

She touched the white particles with a tentative fingertip. They did not feel like crumbs of paper. Something sharper.

Sand? Of course. Thomas Loosemore had sprinkled the wet ink of his accounts with sand to blot it. These grains her fingers were touching linked her to his own hand. She tried to imagine it. Knotted and calloused from work. Thomas Loosemore of Wayland was almost certainly a farmer. Was the soil of Southcombe embedded under his fingernails? These were the hands that had held the reins of his horse as he rode

his proud journey home from the archdeacon's court as the
new churchwarden. Were they also the same hands which had
dragged Arthur Chambers to his fatal fall?

The front door burst open. There was whistling in the hall.
Swift steps bounded up the stairs, followed by heavier ones.

Suzie, coming through from the garden, caught a glimpse
of Tom's trainers vanishing over the top step and into his
bedroom. They were followed by another slower pair of legs
in neat grey trousers, which almost certainly belonged to his
best friend Dave.

She smiled with relief. It was a week since Dave had been
here. A week in which Tom had been withdrawn and silent,
in which none of his friends had come to the house.

There was the sound of rummaging upstairs, the rush of
the cistern in the bathroom. Then Tom came leaping downstairs, three at a time. Behind him, more cautiously, came a
boy less tall than Tom, and plumper. His stooped shoulders
made him look shorter than he was. Ginger hair fell forward
over a serious, fair face dusted, rather attractively, with freckles.

'Hello, Mrs Fewings.'

'Hello, Dave.' She smiled at him. Dave was always beauti-
fully polite.

Tom grinned and ruffled her hair. 'Hi. What sort of day
have you had?'

'I thought that was my line. Fine. How was yours?'

'So-so. Citizenship wasn't bad. I got to be the leader of a
terrorist outfit. I had to convince Western governments why
they shouldn't cut off aid to my country just because I'd won
the election.'

'Did you succeed?'

'Not with all of them. It didn't help that I wasn't going to
go down on my knees and say sorry for everything we'd done
in the past.'

'Including killing innocent civilians?'

'Who's innocent? They were all in it together. They were
the ones who stole our country from us. What about state
terrorism?'

Why is he suddenly so cheerful? Suzie longed to ask. *Has
there been some news about Julie? Have they found her alive?*

She was afraid to open that conversation, in case the answer was no. Even if it was only for a few hours, that haunted look had gone from his eyes. He was his old self, laughing, teasing, sharing his thoughts with her.

He circled round her into the kitchen. 'I'm starving.'

'So what's new?'

'How about you, Dave?'

'Yes, if that's all right, Mrs Fewings.' Dave was nothing like as athletic as Tom, but he always had a good appetite.

Cereal rattled into the bowls. Milk sloshed. She watched contentedly as Tom wolfed his down. Dave ate more slowly.

It was all right. He was Tom again. The black cloud had lifted. However much he might have blamed himself at first for Julie's disappearance, he had got over it. And with the lifting of his mood, her own spirits rose. It had been an innocent friendship, over and done with two weeks before Julie vanished. It was just unfortunate timing that he was the last boy she had been seen with. It was foolish of Suzie ever to have worried that the police might suspect her Tom of having any connection with it.

SIX

They found Julie's body in the rank weeds of the ditch below the canal towpath.

Suzie did not usually buy the local paper. But she could not pass the headlines shouting at her as she left work. JULIE FOUND DEAD.

She bought a copy and hastily unfolded it. The huge black letters on the front page took up more space than the story beneath them. There was a photograph of a fair-haired laughing girl. It was the same picture which had been used over and over again in the intervening days, in newspapers, on television, appealing for information. It was grotesque that she was still smiling like that today.

I must not think of what her body looked like a week later.

Or whether she had been sexually assaulted, the thought came unbidden a moment later.

Cold crept over her. How was Tom going to feel when he learned this terrible news? Remembering his reaction to her disappearance, she felt sure the break between him and Julie had not been as final as he had said.

She made herself turn the pages and read on. Hundreds of people must have strolled or cycled past that spot these last few days, enjoying the country walk within easy distance of the city's quay. Suzie pictured the glossy ribbon of the canal, the broader, livelier river glimpsed across the playing fields, the distant fishing village down the estuary. Not until a too-curious terrier went scavenging into the docks and hedge parsley had the undergrowth in the ditch given up its secret.

She refolded the paper, returning to the photograph of the fair-haired girl on the front page. Looking down at it, her heart constricted with sudden guilt.

Millie. All her concern had been for Tom. They had grown careless about their daughter. Nick running her to school and Suzie fetching her on foot had only lasted a day or so after Julie's disappearance. Their parental fear had faded into embarrassment under Millie's withering scorn. They had allowed things to go back to normal.

But things could not be normal now.

That afternoon, she set out for the school, feeling self-conscious but determined. She was not the only one. There were more cars than usual at the kerbside, a cluster of other parents outside the railings.

Millie and her friends came surging down the school drive, talking animatedly. When she saw Suzie, Millie stopped short. Suzie braced herself for a violent reaction. She saw her daughter's face struggling between indignation and the urgent need to communicate her news with someone. She watched her break into a run.

'Her head was bashed in,' cried Millie, when she was scarcely through the gate. Her grey eyes shone with unusual brightness, both scared and excited. 'That's what they're saying at school.'

'They must be guessing,' Suzie told her. 'The police aren't revealing any details of how she died yet.'

'You know about it, then?'

'I read the paper.'

Millie looked disappointed. They started to walk homeward.

Millie kicked at a Coke can. 'That's how they do it, isn't it? The police don't make that stuff public, so then the murderer gives himself away by showing he knows all the gory details, when he couldn't have unless he did it.'

'I suppose it *was* murder.'

'Get real, Mum. What else would she be doing there in a load of nettles? It's not like she collapsed in the middle of the towpath, is it?'

'It might have been an accident. And the other person panicked and hid her there, so nobody would connect him with it.'

Why was she making excuses for an unknown person who had committed such a terrible crime? She was the mother of a teenage girl, for heaven's sake. Shouldn't she be baying for his blood? He was still on the loose; he was still a threat to Millie.

How did she picture him? A pervert, a psychopath, an abusive relative, even? What was it Millie had said? Most murderers are known to their victims.

'He'd have to be some sort of shit to just chuck her in the ditch. Her family have been going through hell. Her kid brother's been off school all week.'

I'm a mother. That's how I should be thinking, isn't it? About her family. It's awful of me even to think that it might have been her father.

Or a boyfriend? Amorous horseplay that got out of hand?

Her hand was unsteady as she unlocked the house and followed Millie indoors.

'You all right, Mum? You're looking a bit queer. Here, sit down. Shall I make us a cup of tea?

She brought the mug and set it in front of Suzie. She waved her own, splashing tea across the table.

'It's sort of better now, in a way, isn't it? I mean, it's awful, but at least we *know.*'

Suzie nodded, without looking at Millie. 'Yes. We know.'

But she did not know enough.

She grieved for Tom. She dreaded the sound of his return. She and Millie could, of course, have waited at the school gates and walked home with him too. Plenty of other seventeen-year-old boys were collected by their mothers, Ford Fiestas jockeying with 4x4s outside the school gates. But not on foot, like a small boy starting primary school. Tom would never have forgiven her.

She pictured him, on any normal day, strolling across the park with his mates, calling in at the newsagent's for sweets or ice-creams. There was no need for him to change his routine because a killer might be on the loose. He was a boy, at risk in the city at night when young men emerged drunk from the pubs and clubs, but surely not in the afternoon, from a man who had abducted a teenage girl.

If it had been a stranger.

He'll know the news by now. He won't be strolling home carefree like that today. The posters were screaming it outside the newsagent's. I saw the headlines. Millie knew before she left school. They'll all have been talking about it, Tom and his friends. She could imagine the sort of prurient questions they might be asking him. 'What was she like?' 'Did you . . . you know . . .?'

Had Tom risen in street cred in their eyes because he was

the last boy to date a murdered girl? Or would they back away from him? Would some of the horror brush off on Tom, so that the others were no longer quite comfortable in his presence, as people will cross the street to avoid meeting a bereaved friend?

How was Tom responding? Was he toughing it out, his voice too loud, his jokes too macho? Or did he find it difficult to speak to his mates about it? Would they respect his genuine grief?

How much, she wondered, *do I really know him? What sort of person is Tom with his friends? Would it surprise, even shock me if I knew?*

She reined in her thoughts abruptly, before they could go any further down that road.

At least it was reassuring to know he had Dave, a solid, if unimaginative buddy.

She heard Tom's key in the lock and went to meet him in the hall.

'Hello, Mum.' His face showed nothing, and that in itself was alarming. Tom's face was usually like the summer sea when a brisk breeze is blowing – shifting, dancing, sparkling with laughter. Its vitality could make her heart turn over with love.

Today his face was calm, his blue eyes darker than usual, unfathomable. His mouth was steady, just a little turned down. Nothing harrowed, horror-struck. She did not need to be told that he knew. He had already absorbed the shock, come to terms with it. It had changed him, but she did not know how.

'You heard?'

'Yeah. Rotten.'

He seemed to be waiting. She realized that she was blocking the foot of the stairs.

'How do you feel about it?'

'Same as everyone else. What do you expect?'

What *did* she expect?

'I just thought . . . since you and she . . . Would you like some tea?'

'No, thanks.'

She could not ignore his pointed stare any longer. She moved aside. He went upstairs, quite slowly, steadily. His bedroom door closed quietly behind him.

'It's weird, isn't it?' said Millie when Suzie returned to the kitchen. 'Tom being the last boy to date her. Everybody's talking about it. Sort of *looking* at him. It's not as if he knows anything about it, but they're sort of like, "Look! That's him, Tom Fewings." They keep pumping me to see if I can tell them anything about him and Julie. Like, did they have a row or something? It gets up my nose.'

'Do you? Know anything, I mean. Did he ever talk to you about her?'

'Don't *you* start. No. I mean, honestly, Mum. Do you think he shares his love secrets with me? Some chance.'

Millie slid off the table, her skirt riding up to her hips as she did so. She picked up her school-bag and made for the stairs, like Tom.

This is all I have, thought Suzie. *These few minutes when they come home from school and fire off whatever is at the top of their minds that day. Then they retreat – homework, computers, out with friends, television. There's no more time to talk. I'm a stranger to so much of their lives.*

Why am I feeling sorry for myself, today, of all days? Surely all that matters is that a sixteen-year-old girl is lying on a slab in a police mortuary? What must her parents be feeling? I cannot bear to think of that.

SEVEN

Nick was hoeing the weeds between rows of Brussels sprouts. His movements were calm, rhythmic. There was none of that furious activity with which Tom had turned over the compost heap. It reassured Suzie as she walked down the garden towards him to pick broad beans. The sight of him working brought back her father, her grandfather, generations of men who had tended vegetable plots for their families. Centuries ago it had been a necessity for survival. Labourers, husbandmen, growing the food they needed. For Nick, gardening was relaxation after a day at his architects' practice. It was not a matter of life and death. If a crop failed, there was always the supermarket. Nevertheless, she liked to see him working the soil like this. It gave her pleasure to cook his vegetables fresh from the garden.

She stood and watched him for a while. He threw her a glance and went on working. The compost had darkened the natural clay soil. As the blade of the hoe turned over the dry surface, the tilth beneath looked rich, fertile.

'What do you think will happen now?' she said.

'About what?' The hoe swung backwards and forwards. Felled groundsel and dandelions scattered the soil.

'Tom. Do you think they'll want to question him again? Now that they've found her.'

Nick clasped his hands on the handle of the hoe and looked at her keenly over them. 'Why? The poor girl's been murdered – at least, that's what everyone's assuming. "Treating her death as suspicious" is a bit of a euphemism, under the circumstances. Terrible, but what's that got to do with Tom?'

'They questioned him before, when she went missing.'

'They questioned all her friends. You'd have to expect that. Naturally, they'd hope for clues about what she might have done, where she could have gone. Well, now they know. Tom was just one of those friends. They don't need him to help them find her now.'

'Still, I'm worried for him. I think he may be worrying too.'

'Why? Look, what is this? You're not suggesting the police could think he had anything to do with her death, are you?'

'Of course not!' The words came out too loud, too fast. 'It's just that it would be dreadful for him if they did suspect him, wouldn't it?'

'Don't be ridiculous. Why would they? Tom's a normal, healthy seventeen-year-old, not some sexual pervert. By all accounts, he's got half the girls at his school swooning over him. Why on earth would a red-blooded heart throb like him need to get his kicks from doing something as foul as that? Even the local plods can see that wouldn't make sense.'

For a moment a treacherous thought crossed her mind. *We don't know it was murder. What if it was some awful accident?* She censored it immediately. Nick's confidence was reassuring.

'You're sure? They won't want to interview him again?'

'Of course I'm sure.' Nick's voice was vehement. 'I'm surprised that you're not. You don't think the police *should* suspect him, do you?'

She managed a small smile. 'No, of course not. Thanks, anyway. That's a relief. I couldn't help worrying.'

'Why? Has he said anything to you?'

'No.'

'How he's taking it? He seemed a bit quiet at teatime.'

'He doesn't want to talk about it.'

'No, well, come to think of it, I suppose if one of my ex-girlfriends had been murdered, I'd be pretty much knocked sideways. It doesn't bear thinking about.' He poked at another weed. 'How's Millie?'

'Millie?'

'Your daughter. Our thirteen-year-old, sexually developing girl child. In view of what's happened, shouldn't we be worrying about her?'

'I hate to say it, but I think there's a side of her that's almost enjoying it: the newspaper headlines, the ghoulish speculation. I don't suppose she's old enough to imagine that it could have been her. Not properly. She may say she does, but that's just her being a drama queen. It's not real.'

'Just as well. We don't want her having nightmares. Thank God there's something of childhood left, even if it makes her a callous brat. It's a sort of innocence. But we'll need to be more careful of her now, without scaring her. Can you meet her from school tomorrow?'

She stared at him, the focus of her fear shifting from Tom. 'You think . . .'

'This time, it *is* real. Until they find him, anything could happen. I'm surprised Tom was the one you were worrying about.'

She turned her eyes away. 'Yes, I'll meet her . . . Your runner beans are doing well. They look nearly ready for picking.'

There was a pause before Nick gave a short laugh. His answering voice took on a lighter tone as well. 'It's the same every year. I can never convince myself that one row's enough for four people. By next week you'll have enough to feed the street.'

They had skated back to safe ground.

Suzie took a deep breath. The pale blue sky of the summer evening was almost cloudless. A blackbird burst into song from the apple tree. The garden grew and flowered and fruited around them. Tragedy had happened, but only to someone else.

Usually there was the discord of competing music from two upstairs rooms. This evening, Tom's was silent.

Suzie sat before the computer, trying to arrange in her mind the story she wanted to tell. What did she believe now about Thomas Loosemore? That the respected churchwarden was not the same person as the militiaman who had thrown the Reverend Chambers downstairs? That he was, but that the hot-headed young man had matured into a sober, godly middle age, his violent past put behind him? If so, had that manslaughter been a gnawing ache on his conscience, a regret for a past he could never undo?

Or had she been wrong all along? Was it that first moment of discovery in the church at Southcombe, when she had thrilled to find her ancestor's name on the churchwardens' board, which had been a sham? Had he never been the man she imagined him, that upright, authoritative figure, moving down the aisle with the eyes of the packed congregation of his fellow villagers on him, smiling at the door with a word of greeting to them, supporting his rector in the care of the parish? She had seen him as something more than a simple son of the soil. A yeoman farmer. A solid, red-faced, genial man, high in the esteem of the village.

But suppose he was not so genial? How violent had been that deportation of the gypsies from his parish? What part had he played in it? She thought of accounts she had read of unmarried mothers, dressed only in a shift, or even naked, being whipped through the streets as a lesson to others. It was no shame for a bride to be with child at the altar, but if no husband could be found for her in time, the wrath of the Church and community descended on the unfortunate young woman. Had Thomas Loosemore ever done that in his year of office? Had he relished that part of his job?

She knew nothing about his character. Those were violent times. Civil war brutalizes people. Was the death of Arthur Chambers an act of sudden passion, out of character, or had it been a defining moment which shaped Thomas Loosemore's subsequent view of himself, telling him: 'This is the kind of man I am. I'm capable of killing'?

How had the other villagers looked at him after that? With respect? With fear? Why had they chosen him to be their churchwarden?

She was suddenly aware of Nick standing behind her.

'No rush. You can finish what you're doing. I just wondered how long you're likely to be on the computer. If you need it all evening, that's OK. I've got plenty more I can do in the garden.'

'No, you have it.' She got up from the swivel chair. 'Honestly. I can't get started tonight. I've just been sitting in front of the screen trying to make up my mind what to write, and not succeeding.'

'What's the problem?'

'It's Thomas Loosemore. You know, the one I found on the list of churchwardens in Southcombe church. Only . . . I haven't told you this before, have I? I found out something else about him. Something not so good. Just after the Civil War, about ten years before he was churchwarden, he was in the militia – or at least, someone called Thomas Loosemore was. Apparently, he dragged the rector down the stairs of his parsonage by his hair, and the poor man fell and cracked his skull.'

'Fatally?'

'Yes.'

'Great stuff.'

'What?'

'Aren't you always telling me that the difference between genealogists and family historians is that the former are set on proving they're related to a lord, while the latter shout "Yes!" and punch the air when they find one of their relatives was hanged for stealing a sheep?'

'This wasn't just stealing. He killed someone. His own rector.'

'So? There was a war on, wasn't there? Or had been. You've always said you have to keep an open mind in this sort of research, and take whatever you turn up.'

'I know, but . . . what's bugging me is that it's Thomas Loosemore.'

'So? What's the big deal? A guy four hundred years ago.'

'Three hundred and fifty.'

'Whatever.'

'Don't you see . . . *Thomas Loosemore.*'

An uncomprehending silence.

'It's why I was so pleased when I first found him. It's what we christened Tom . . . Thomas Loosemore Fewings.'

She sensed Nick stiffen. His blue eyes darkened as he stared back at her.

'You surely can't think . . . There's this guy in the seventeenth century, who kills a man, and because he just happens to have the same name as our Tom. . . . So *that's* what you were getting at in the garden! But that's preposterous. You can't be seriously suggesting that there's any connection between what this guy back in history did and our Tom now.'

Her hand hit the keyboard unheedingly. 'Of course I'm not! It's got absolutely nothing to do with this Julie business. Anyway, I don't suppose Thomas Loosemore meant to kill his rector. He was just doing his job, booting him out of the parsonage because he was a Royalist. If he was in the militia, he'd have been acting under orders from the County Commissioners. They'll have got a Puritan minister to take his place. I'm sure when the man fell downstairs it was just an accident.'

Nick stared at her in silence for a long while. He turned on his heel.

'I'm not sure what you're saying. I'll be in the garden.'

She stared after him unhappily. How could he possibly accuse her of suspecting Tom of any involvement in a girl's death?

What *had* she meant?

EIGHT

Nick had driven Millie to school. She had not protested. Tom chose to walk.

Suzie stood at the bus stop, glad of the morning's work ahead of her. She had slept badly. As long as the connection in her mind between the two deaths had remained unspoken, she had been able to deny it. For a week, she had been convincing herself that the only reason she was upset by the story in Walker's book was the loss of the role model she had wanted to offer Tom. But Nick's accusation had put her unease into dangerous words she could no longer ignore.

Of course she didn't suspect Tom of having anything to do with Julie's death, even accidentally. Of course she didn't! It was unthinkable. And then to have pushed her into a ditch and left her.

Yet in the slow small hours of the morning, lying beside Nick in the darkened bedroom, she had felt the shadow of that earlier manslaughter creep over her. Even though it was only a *What if?* In the too-bright morning light she knew that the question should never even have entered her mind.

And of course it would not have, if it had not been for a chance discovery in an old book in the Local Studies Library.

This was ridiculous. It was the commonest of names. Thomas. The only surprising thing was that she had not found a Thomas Loosemore before this. It was almost inevitable that as she followed the surname back in time she would stumble across one sooner or later.

It was not inevitable that the first Thomas should have been *this* man, *this* story.

With a mixture of panic and relief she realized that the blue-and-white bus was almost at her stop. Belatedly she put out an arm to hail it. This was what she needed to take her mind off such thoughts, the familiar routine of administering her charity's local office. Tom and Millie would be at school, Nick busy with plans, clients, builders. Whatever had happened by the towpath last week, the everyday demands of daily work would enfold them all and insulate them from thinking about it.

She climbed on board and let herself be carried into the city.

The charity concert was coming together. Suzie made notes while she phoned. The hall was booked. The railway band had agreed to play. The local soprano who had done so well on television could manage the date. She put the receiver down while she checked the list of calls she still needed to make.

Almost at once it rang again. She picked it up, with a superstitious annoyance that her run of successes had been interrupted and might not be regained.

'Suzie? Is that you?' It was Nick's voice.

She did not need to hear more for the surge of panic to begin. Nick never phoned her at work.

'What's wrong?'

'It's Tom. He rang me from school. The police want to question him again. They're taking him down the police station. I've said I'll meet him there. I just thought you'd want to know.'

The little office, with its poorly lit window, seemed to grow darker.

'I'll be there as quick as I can.'

'No. I was just keeping you in the picture. There's no need for both of us to go. I assume that, since he rang me, I'm the one he wants to be there.'

She fought down the pang of inappropriate jealousy. She and Tom were always so close.

'But what for? Why are they taking him to the police station? They've questioned him already. You said yourself, he can't have anything more to tell them.'

'Julie wasn't dead then. I mean, they didn't know she was. It's probably because it's a murder enquiry now.'

'But they can't think that Tom . . . You were nearly cross with me yesterday when you thought . . .' Her voice was rising.

'Of course not. But I guess they have to be thorough, eliminate all the possibilities. They know Tom was dating her only a fortnight before. Look, I've got to go. He sounded pretty scared. I'll let you know what happens.'

The line went dead. She looked down at her desk. The list

of names and telephone numbers swarmed before her eyes. She could not make sense of them. They shifted on the white page like an army of stinging ants.

She felt sick. She pushed her chair back and went to the cloakroom for a drink of water. She leaned her forehead against the cool mirror. Her own words came back to haunt her.

'But they can't think that Tom ...'

Was this all her fault? She *had* been on the verge of thinking that, however much she had tried to deny it. All week, she had struggled with the problem of the militiaman Thomas Loosemore and his dead rector. She had so wanted to believe that he was not the same person as the godly churchwarden, or that the fatal injury had not been intended, or that the incident had been distorted out of all proportion by the partisan author of *The Sufferings of the Clergy.* And all the time, she had been masking her real fear: that if her seventeenth-century ancestor Thomas had been guilty, then . . .

No! She screwed up her fists. She must not let herself even imagine that. Her laughing Tom? It wasn't possible that, even by accident, he could do something like that. Even more ludicrous to imagine that he would bundle the body into a weed-covered ditch and leave it to rot.

Stop it. Stop it.

She checked her frightened face in the mirror and hurried back to the office. Nick might ring again at any moment. It would be all right. Some little question that needed clearing up. They would clap Tom on the shoulder. 'That's all right, sonny. You're in the clear. Off you go back to school. Sorry to have bothered you.'

Of course they had to check every possibility. It was just routine.

The office was too cramped. The filing cabinets, the shelves of leaflets, the campaigning posters crowded in on her. She longed for fresh air, for the calm of the cathedral close, but she could not leave the phone. She should have told Nick to ring her mobile, which she normally kept switched off, instead of the office number.

She sat, chill and unmoving, in front of the black computer screen, unable to do any work.

It was nearly an hour before the phone rang again. She grabbed it up, gripping it hard to prevent her hand shaking.

It would probably be from someone at one of the charity's care homes or their London headquarters.

It was Nick again.

'I'm taking him home now. He's a bit shaken up. Can you be there? I need to get back to work, but I don't think he should be left on his own.'

'They haven't arrested him?'

'Good grief, no. You didn't think they would? But I gather it wasn't a pleasant experience. From all accounts they didn't pull any punches, even if he is only a kid.'

'You weren't there at the interview?'

'They wouldn't let me in. Like they said last time, at seventeen you count as an adult.'

She put down the phone.

Seventeen. How old was the militiaman Thomas when he raided the rectory? He might still have been a teenager.

I must be quick. Nick will need to get back to work. I mustn't keep him waiting.

And he would wait until she got home, she knew that. Nick was the conscientious, concerned father.

In a confusion of haste, she gathered up her belongings and crammed them into her handbag. Reading glasses, spectacle case. Had she brought a jacket this morning? She grabbed it from the hook and rushed into the shop.

'I'm sorry. I've got to go. Tom's been sent home from school.' As the two women behind the counter stared at her, she suddenly realized how ominous that sounded. Hastily she added, 'He's not feeling too well. Can you answer the phone if it rings? Tell them I'll get back to them tomorrow.'

Did she imagine Margery gazed at her longer than was necessary before her worried face softened into her usual warm smile. 'Of course. You go on. We can cope, can't we, Janet?'

The smile of the spare, fair-haired woman beside her was thinner. 'You usually leave the answerphone on for the afternoon.'

Blood flooded Suzie's cheeks. 'I forgot!' She looked back at the office door, torn between embarrassment at her stupid mistake and the need to dash for the bus.

Her confusion did not escape Janet. 'It must be very

upsetting for you, this terrible business about poor Julie
Samuel. Tom being her boyfriend, and all that.'

How did she know that?

'He wasn't!' Too quick, too sharp. 'He only had a couple
of dates with her. Nothing serious.'

'Oh, pardon me. I hope you didn't think I was implying
anything. Only you're bound to feel more involved than the
rest of us.'

'Go on,' said Margery. 'Get your bus.'

Suzie escaped into the street. She took a deep breath of the
traffic-fumed air. The noise of cars climbing the hill past the
shop made it hard to think. She began to walk quickly uphill,
hardly remembering if this was the right direction for the bus
stop. What had Janet meant, behind that guarded smile? Was
everyone in the town now discussing her family behind her
back?

Through her confusion she saw that her bus was stopping
on the other side of the street. Of course. Idiot! She dashed
unheedingly through the traffic to catch it.

'Oi, ticket, please,' called the driver, as she stumbled past
him along the aisle. She looked back at him uncomprehend-
ingly, before she realized that she had forgotten to show him
her season ticket.

She sat on the edge of her seat, willing the bus on. It seemed
to crawl through the rows of shops, past the red brick terraces
of the Victorian houses, and out into the newer housing estates
with their well-tended gardens. She sprang to her feet, rang
the bell too early, so that the driver pulled up at the stop before
the one she wanted. Impatiently, she waved him on. The doors
had hardly swung open again before she jumped down on to
the pavement.

The tree-shaded avenue was far too long. Its green canopy
had no charm to relax her today. Nick's car was in the drive.
Her key fumbled for the lock.

He was already in the hall, car keys in hand. 'Sorry to dash.
I've got an important lunch meeting with a possible new client.
Tom's in there.' He nodded towards the sitting room.

He kissed her cheek. Then he was gone.

She recognized in him the same nervous haste that had
driven her homewards. She knew his rapid departure was not
lack of concern for Tom. Quite the opposite. He had cared

enough to sit waiting for that difficult interview to finish, though there was nothing he could do and she had offered to go. He had brought Tom home afterwards, and he had stayed until she arrived. Tom wasn't a little boy; he was seventeen. What had Nick feared might happen if he was left alone?

She stepped into the sitting room, conscious as she did so of the strangeness of this. In summer, family life was mostly lived at the back of the house: in the big kitchen, on the cushioned cane furniture of the conservatory, or out in the garden. The children spent many hours in their own rooms. This carpeted sitting room had a more formal feel nowadays. They used it less often, even for entertaining friends. It was mostly a place to watch a different television programme from the one that was on in the conservatory. That Tom should be in here heightened the feeling of abnormality.

He was sitting on the sofa. He looked, she thought tenderly, too big for it. His knees jutted awkwardly and he seemed not to know where to rest his arms.

Then her eye was caught by the can of beer on the coffee table, the empty glass tankard rimmed with froth. Nick must have given it to him. There was another on a table beside the armchair. Was this Nick's idea of therapy, alcohol in the middle of the morning? They offered the children a glass of wine at the weekend, if they were eating in. It was not something they encouraged on school days. She could not remember Nick sharing a beer with Tom before.

Tom did not turn his dark head to her. He was staring moodily at the window. Her heart was wrenched to see how old he looked in profile, the muscles of his face tense, the mouth downturned.

'How was it?' She came into the middle of the room, where he could see her, since he would not turn to her. 'Dad said they gave you a hard time.'

'Did they have to come to school?' he exploded, rounding on her. 'Couldn't they have showed up here before I left this morning, or rung, even? I'd have gone down to the station, no problem. Did they have to send a flipping marked police car up to the front entrance, and march me out between two uniformed guys, as if I was being arrested? What's everyone going to say when I go back to school?'

She sat down abruptly in the armchair. 'Oh, Tom, I'm sorry!

I was so worried about the police questioning you, I never thought of that side of it. But it's all right now, isn't it? You haven't done anything. Nobody's arrested you. You'll just have to tell the other kids what really happened.'

'Oh, yeah? I was "helping the police with their enquiries". We all know what that means.'

'But you were, weren't you? I mean, now that they know Julie's dead, they have to find out everything they can about her movements. And you want to help them, so that they catch the killer.'

'Of course I'd want to, if I knew anything. Which I don't.'

She could see inside him the little boy who wanted to burst into tears and run into her arms. Was he too old? Could she cross the hearthrug to him and put her arms around him? Was it too late?

She hesitated too long. As a compromise, she moved to sit on the sofa beside him. She thought he moved aside further than was necessary to make room for her. She put a tentative hand on his knee.

'You must be horribly upset about Julie.'

'She was a little bitch.'

The word shocked Suzie. It was several seconds before her brain accepted it.

'Why?'

'Boasting to her friends that she'd scored with me. That she'd won a bet she had with them that she could do it with me.'

'Is that what the police said? And you really didn't?' She regretted the question as soon as she had spoken it.

'I said no the first time they asked, didn't I?'

Was that a flash of anger or pain in his eyes?

'I'm glad about that. But you took her out.'

'A couple of nights clubbing. Big deal.'

It was difficult to frame her lips to ask the next question. 'So why did the police want to see you again? Didn't they believe you?'

'How do I know? They asked me enough questions. I told them what they wanted. That ought to be good enough for them.' He sprang up violently. 'Look, I've had a bellyful of being interrogated. I don't have to go all over it again.'

That hurt. 'I'm sorry. I'm really sorry, Tom. Is there anything

I can do?' The moment when she could have cuddled him was long gone.

'There's nothing anyone can do. She's dead, and that's all there is to it.'

'They can catch her killer.'

'It won't bring her back, will it? Nothing's going to change that.'

A shudder went through him. He stalked out of the room. She thought he would go upstairs to his bedroom, but she heard his progress through the kitchen. There was a burst of music, suddenly loud, then the volume was lowered. When she tiptoed after him, Tom was sitting hunched in one of the conservatory chairs, staring at a game show on the television. She did not think that the movement of the contestants was what he was seeing.

It was bedtime before she realized she had missed her usual afternoon for family research.

NINE

Suzie slipped on a pair of high-heeled shoes, then rejected them in favour of flat but elegant sandals. She studied her strapless dress in the mirror.

Nick glanced at her. 'Their house is by the river. There are probably gnats.'

She searched in a drawer and pinned a stole of lilac gauze around her bare shoulders.

'Will that do?'

'Fine.'

His tone was businesslike. She waited for him to come behind her, to place his hands on her shoulders. She wanted to feel their warmth through the delicate fabric, for his smiling eyes to meet hers in the mirror.

Instead, Nick flicked the black waves of his hair into place. 'Ready?'

He walked ahead of her to the bedroom door. She followed him, feeling oddly like a scolded child. Nick's suspicion of Suzie's fears had brought this coolness between them. Since Tom's visit to the police station, neither of them could bring themselves to discuss what was weighing on their minds.

Suzie put her head round Millie's door. She was sprawled on her bed with her headphones on. There were books and papers scattered beside her, but she did not seem to be studying them.

'We shouldn't be late back, but I shall expect to find you in bed.'

An earpiece shifted fractionally. 'Yeah. Have fun.'

'Bye, Tom,' she called on the landing.

There was no answer. She hesitated. Should she open his door? She decided against it and walked on to the staircase.

Nick was waiting for her in the car.

'Are you sure it's all right now, leaving Millie alone?' she asked.

'She's not alone. She's got Tom.'

The car jerked into life.

*   *   *

The country lanes smelt of hay and diesel through the open windows of the car. It was a balmy summer evening but the tractors were still at work.

Three centuries ago, Suzie thought as she looked around at the hedgerows, this road would have been impassable to wheeled traffic. Thousands of feet and hooves had worn out a hollow deep beneath the level of the fields. Tangles of wild rose and honeysuckle flowered overhead. In winter, it would have been a morass of mud, out of which the laden pack-ponies wrenched their hooves with difficulty. A hot summer would bake those hoof prints into hard ridges and holes, on which the traveller could easily turn an ankle. Today, they coasted smoothly downhill over tarmac.

'So that's the barn conversion. Not bad.' Nick's tone had lightened. He was eyeing the house ahead with a professional, if competitive, interest.

Alice and Jonathan's new home, with its old stone walls and large modern windows, stood in a meadow on the upper reaches of the river, just where it emerged from a wooded gorge. Gorse flashed on the hilltops in the evening sun. Down here in the valley, the shadows had fallen early. Mature oaks spread their branches over the pasture beyond the minimalist gravel garden with its dwarf conifers.

Nick parked the car. Jon was already coming to meet them, releasing the sound of jazz from the house.

'Well done. You managed to find it without getting lost?'

'No credit to me. Suzie's the navigator. She spends half her time poring over maps of the county. She'll probably tell you she's got several generations of ancestors here. She usually has, wherever we go.'

The coldness had gone, in company. Nick sounded his usual humorous self.

Jonathan turned his smile on Suzie. 'Bitten by the old family history bug, are you? Seems to be quite the thing these days. I'm afraid I haven't got time for all that. The future's too interesting.'

'It's just my hobby,' said Suzie. 'You know about my day job. I spend half my time planning for old people's futures. But their past is really important to them, too. If anything, it's bits of their present that start falling away.'

'That's me put in my place. I should be planning for my

own old age, shouldn't I? But I'm enjoying life too much now. And who knows, I may not be around long enough to need an old folks' home. Live fast, die young. Gather ye rose-buds, and all that.'

He was shepherding them through the house, expensively finished and furnished on the inside as well as outside. They emerged on to a patio overlooking the river. About twenty people were gathered there, glasses in hand. Smoke was rising from the barbecue.

The rush of the water was suddenly loud, the notes of the jazz distinct. The chatter had stopped. It seemed to Suzie that everyone's head had turned their way. Smiles were fixed, animated gestures arrested.

Alice broke the silence. She came forward, earrings swinging, and waved at the drinks table. 'What will you have? Chardonnay, claret, fruit juice, or there's some elderflower cordial Jonathan made himself. You can see the bushes he picked them from over there.'

'How very rural. I'll try some,' Nick said. 'I'm driving.'

Suzie accepted a glass of white wine.

The conversation had started again. Did she only imagine people were clustered in tighter huddles, looking across at them furtively as they talked?

'Let me introduce you,' Alice said, steering them towards a youngish woman, comfortably large, with Nordic-looking plaits round her head, and a middle-aged man with tortoise-shell glasses, in a baggy corduroy jacket. 'Have you two met the Fewings? Nick's an architect, and a rather exciting one. Specializes in eco-friendly buildings. We should have got him to design this one for us, shouldn't we, but we came across it ready done-up. And Suzie's a charity administrator. Meet Bernard, who's in charge of advertising for the local rag, and Clarice, who's a super-mum. Six children under eight, including twins.'

'Gosh,' said Suzie. 'That sounds like a handful.'

'Kids. Who'd have 'em? I always intended to stop at two, but it just seems to have become a habit. Still, there should be enough of them to look after us when we're in our dotage and the pension funds have gone broke.'

Someone had caught Nick's elbow and drawn him away.

'You've got kids yourself, haven't you?' Bernard peered at

her over his glass. 'Is it true your son's been involved in this dreadful Julie Samuel business?'

Suzie's heart fell.

So I was right. They were discussing us. Discussing Tom. Everyone knows.

What did they know? There was nothing to know. What did they suppose?

'Bernard!' Clarice nudged her partner. 'You're the bloody advertising manager for the paper, not a reporter. Stop digging for a story.'

'I was doing nothing of the kind. Just sympathizing. It must be rotten when something like this happens to a kid, and it's not just a stranger, but someone you actually know. Sorry, *knew.*'

'We didn't know her,' Suzie said. 'Tom only went out with her a couple of times. We never met her. Well, our daughter Millie knew her by sight from school. But they weren't in the same class.'

'Still, your Tom must be cut up. But he'll be in the clear, won't he? Wonderful what they can do with forensics these days. Eliminate the innocent, as well as trap the guilty.'

'They'd broken up before it happened.' There was an edge to Suzie's voice. 'They were only dating for less than a fortnight.'

'There you are, then. Nothing to worry about. Here, looks as if Jonathan's ready with the barbecue. Can I pass you a plate, Suzie?'

How many times have I got to go through this? How many strangers or casual acquaintances – like these people I only meet at Alice and Jon's, all wondering the same thing? 'Those Fewings, their son, you know. Mixed up in this murder case. Must be dreadful for the parents. Of course, it's much more likely to be some pervert, stalking girls on their own. But you never know. After all, don't they say that most murders are committed by someone known to the victim?'

It was unfair.

She escaped from Bernard, and picked without appetite at the kebabs, spare ribs and salad. As the evening wore on, no one else raised the subject. But she imagined she could read it in the careful looks they gave her, the sympathetic tone of their voices, even when they were discussing the city's new shopping centre or the violence in the Middle East.

She helped herself to gooseberry fool from the buffet and drifted away from the crowd to stand beside the river. It ran dark but clear over the stones. She caught the quiver of a fish twisting away.

Jonathan spoke behind her. 'Lovely, isn't it? We're so lucky. Our own little bit of history.'

'I thought you were sold on the future.' She made an effort to smile.

'Yes, well, I'm not a complete philistine. Best of both worlds, that's what I think. I was really chuffed when we found this old place, and with the car, we're only half an hour from the city. Of course, when the kids come home from uni, they'll complain it's too quiet. Not a lot of night life out here. Well, there is, actually. We can hear a barn owl screeching most nights. Not bad, eh, for a barn conversion?'

'How are the children?'

'Search me. Do yours tell you what's going on? As far as I know, none of them is in prison or pregnant. Be thankful for small mercies, I say. Your two all right?'

She looked up in surprise. Was that just a conversational gambit, the good host putting his guest at ease? Did he really not know the gossip? Or didn't he share the prurient thrill of being associated, however slightly, with someone mixed up in a murder case, which she had sensed all too keenly in the bespectacled Bernard?

'They're both a bit shaken up by this Julie Samuel thing.' It was a relief to broach the subject herself, to talk willingly about it to someone, not to have to fend off unwelcome prying. 'We've gone back to taking Millie to and from school, just in case. Until he's caught. And Tom's obviously upset, because he dated her a couple of times. Nothing serious, but when it's someone you know . . .'

'That's tough. Still, kids get over these things. They've got the rest of their lives in front of them. He'll be applying for university next term, won't he? Any idea where he wants to go? What's his subject?'

'He wants to do law. We're trying to persuade him he doesn't need to do it for his first degree. That's a bit narrow. Something like PPE at Oxford would be good, but I'm not sure he's good enough to beat the competition.'

It was wonderful to be talking about Tom normally, to hear

Jonathan assigning what had happened to the status of a temporary tragedy. Nothing that could affect the rest of Tom's life.

Next evening the inquest verdict was on the local television news. The sound floated thinly from the conservatory into the kitchen as they sat around the table. Normally, Nick would have insisted on switching it off when the food was served. Mealtimes were for conversation. But not today.

'Turn it up,' risked Suzie, with a worried glance at Tom. Millie slipped from her chair and darted into the other room to adjust the volume.

Tom sat with his eyes downcast, his body rigid. Only his fork played with the food on his plate. They were all tense, listening.

'. . . *unlawful killing.*'

'It couldn't really be anything else, could it?' Nick said. He returned to his pork chop, as if the matter was settled. 'It'll have been a murder enquiry from the moment they found her.'

'I told you. He broke her skull,' Millie pointed out.

'They still have to catch him,' Suzie said. She was annoyed to find her throat dry.

'Shouldn't be too difficult nowadays, with DNA testing.'

'If they test the right person. It might be someone the police have no reason to suspect.'

'They took mine at the police station.' Tom's voice was tight. 'And they've been round to any other guys at school she went with.'

'It said she was sexually assaulted.' Millie's eyes were large. 'Does that mean what I think it does?'

'*Yes.*' Too short, too vigorous. Suzie was stamping the thought dead.

'This may not be his first crime,' Nick said. 'They'll be looking for other cases that follow a similar pattern.'

'Do you mind?' said Tom. 'Could we change the subject?'

There was a sudden hush. Mouths hung open in a half-formed question or answer. Nick's face showed guilt and remorse, as her own must. It was not like Tom to admit to weakness, vulnerability.

'I'm sorry,' Suzie breathed.

'Well, at least it means you're in the clear,' Nick said. 'Even if they don't catch the guy right away, the DNA evidence will eliminate anyone else who's been involved with her.'

'Nick!' Suzie protested.

'Thanks, Dad,' said Tom bitterly. 'You need proof I'm innocent, do you?'

Suzie felt a flash of self-justification. Nick was as good as admitting to Tom that the police had been right to treat him as a suspect. He had been unfairly cool with her because she could see a parallel between Tom's story and Thomas Loosemore's.

It made her feel marginally better to see Tom's anger directed against his father, not her.

Not that that old story of Thomas Loosemore had anything to do with this, of course. She was safe in the twenty-first century, where laboratory tests could now establish the truth beyond reasonable doubt. Tom had been adamant he hadn't had sex with Julie. There was nothing to fear.

It was too quiet for a Friday evening. Suzie nerved herself to knock on Tom's door. There was no answer. She opened it quietly.

Tom was seated at his desk in front of the window, doing homework. He turned, unsmiling.

'No Dave?' She forced a smile to accompany her question.

'No.' His curt reply did not invite further conversation.

'He's usually round here on Friday nights, or you're at his house.'

'Well, he's not here today, is he?'

'Obviously not. Is there a problem?'

'You should ask him.'

She sat down on the bed. 'Oh. That means there is.'

'Not on my side, there isn't.'

'So what's wrong with Dave?'

He shrugged. His voice took on a mocking, artificial tone. 'He's a bit tied up this weekend. There's something at home his Dad wants him to help with.'

'But you don't believe him.'

'Do you?'

She stood up and rested her hands on his shoulders, kissed the top of his head. 'Oh, Tom, I'm so sorry. Is it this Julie business? Because the police questioned you? That's ridiculous.

Dave knows you better than anyone. He must know you packed it in with her long before she went missing. He can't believe you had anything to do with it.'

'He hasn't said that's what he thinks. He's just suddenly too busy to come round here. He looks sort of sick every time he looks at me.'

'Oh, Tom.' She hugged him. 'Just when you need your friends.'

He turned from her arms back to his homework.

'No skin off my nose. I'm behind with this coursework, anyway.'

TEN

Nick looked up as she came into the conservatory with her cup of coffee. 'The weather forecast's not too good for tomorrow. It doesn't sound like walking weather. I've promised to take Tom out for some driving practice in the morning. It's been such a good summer, it'll do him good to try driving in the rain. But if there's another village you want to follow up, we could go out there for a pub lunch afterwards, and spend an hour or so looking at the church in the dry.'

She tried to put gratitude into her smile. Nick was making an effort to mend the gap between them. He didn't want her to think he was rejecting her family quest completely, just her link between Tom and Thomas Loosemore.

'As a matter of fact, I think there's a meeting of the Family History Society tomorrow. Hang on, I've got the magazine somewhere.' She rummaged in the rack under the coffee table. 'Yes. *A Grievous Time: the Effects of the Civil War on Local People*. I'd rather like to go to that one, if you don't mind.'

'Suits me. I could do with an afternoon in the shed to strip down the lawnmower. It's been running hot lately. I've been putting it off for a wet day. We can still have lunch at the Riverside Inn on the quay, if you like. We don't need to drive halfway across the county.'

'That would be nice.'

He dropped her off on the pavement in the rain, outside a Methodist church hall at the quieter end of the shopping centre. As she walked into the welcoming bustle, she felt a revival of her enjoyment in a hobby that had recently threatened to turn sour on her. There was a queue at the table where volunteers with a laptop were conducting searches for a baptism, a marriage or a burial from their indexes. Another table bore an inviting spread of booklets on subjects such as *Life in the Workhouse, My Ancestor was a Bastard, Investigating Criminal Records*, and a selection of old maps.

Beside it was a smaller table, with books which she assumed were by the afternoon's speaker. The tallest pile bore in large letters the same title as his talk: *A Grievous Time*. No doubt the author would be selling signed copies afterwards. She tried to edge nearer, to see what else he had written, but the crowd milling in front of the stalls was changing direction. People were moving forward to take their seats. She followed the flow.

As the Society's Chair worked through her list of announcements – a coach trip to the National Archives at Kew, the annual day conference in the autumn, an appeal for more volunteers for transcription projects – Suzie looked around her with appreciation. This room had an appropriately historical feel. It was not the usual featureless church hall, whose only artistic embellishments were wall posters. The panels behind the dais were carved in an ecclesiastical style that would not have disgraced a parish church, let alone a Methodist meeting room. It bore witness to a painful separation, the splitting of the Methodists from their parent Church of England. John Wesley, she recalled, had never meant to found a separate church and considered himself an Anglican clergymen to the end of his days.

She brought her attention back to the present. That must be the speaker, seated beside the chairwoman. A youngish man, with a head of fair curly hair. The hair snagged her attention. She was not good at remembering faces, but she was sure she had seen those blond curls before. Where?

'Well, that's enough from me.' The chairwoman turned her beaming smile on their guest. 'And now it's my great pleasure to welcome the Reverend James Milton, rector of Southcombe, who's kindly come along to talk to us about the effect of the Civil War on the lives of ordinary people in our county.'

Suzie sat bolt upright as the audience clapped. Southcombe. Of course. The eager young rector coming into the church, with the light from the open door behind him turning his curls to pale flames, just as she was complaining to Nick how the Victorians had stripped away everything from the earlier centuries that she had come looking for. Nick had talked to him. For her part, she realized guiltily, she had not even bothered to learn his name. While she had seethed at his enthusiasm for Southcombe's remarkable Victorian artist, it had never occurred to her that he knew enough about the Civil War to write a book on it. She wished now she had not been so quick to jump to conclusions.

He gave his audience that radiant smile she remembered, which had so irritated her then. Today, she warmed to it.

'Every day, we turn on our televisions, and we see news of Iraq, Sudan, Sri Lanka. Communities torn apart by civil war. How many of us remember as we watch their heartbreak that our own country, our ancestors, once suffered that particular bitterness of war within national boundaries, neighbour against neighbour?

'That's how it was here in the middle of the seventeenth century. It's easy to make broad generalizations about communal loyalties. The cities, the wool towns, the sheep farming areas in the north of the county and the ports were mostly for Parliament; the crop-growing regions of the south and the more remote villages around the moor favoured the King. But it was always more complicated than that. Communities, even families, were split. We read of brothers embracing for the last time, before going out to fight for different armies.'

Suzie could not help thinking instantly of the young Puritan militiaman, Thomas Loosemore. He was from a sheep-farming, wool-spinning area. Did that mean he had the blessing of his parents for his revolutionary cause? Or did the old folks prefer the ways of the Catholic-leaning Royalists?

What little she remembered of the Civil War from her schooldays was mostly the names of battles: Edgehill, Marston Moor, Naseby. The rather joyless figure of Oliver Cromwell, forming his disciplined New Model Army to beat the king and rule the Commonwealth afterwards as Lord Protector. She had a mental picture of Charles I hiding in an oak tree, and something about the noble bearing with which he went to his execution. Nothing local.

James Milton showed her a different side to the war: the people who watched in fear while armies marched across their county. First, thousands of Royalists on their way east to support the King. Then the Roundheads coming west to drive them back, only to be defeated in their turn. Cities seized by one side, and recaptured by the other. A beaten Royalist army retreating west, wreaking vengeance on the rebellious wool towns as they went, for the wool trade was strongly aligned with Parliament. They had wrecked the weavers' looms, depriving whole communities of their livelihood. Further south, though, Royalist villagers had shot dead an officer of the Roundhead troopers who came to seize the weapons they were stockpiling for the King's cause, and then had auctioned his horse and gear at the village inn. A mob of Parliamentary villagers had ransacked the house of a Royalist squire. He made her see for the first time small farmers, like her ancestors, watching helplessly as their crops and livestock were seized by whichever army needed to feed its men. Some officers were scrupulous about payment, more were not. And what food could money buy, when the whole countryside was ravaged and looted?

'Worst of all, a byword for savagery, was Lord Goring's Horse, the Royalist cavalry that cut a swathe of devastation across the county, looting, killing and raping as they went.'

Goring's Crew had passed through Southcombe.

The scene swung into focus in her mind. Throughout the war, Southcombe's High Church rector had remained stubbornly loyal to his King. When the victorious Puritans demanded a stiff fine from him, he retorted that he would only give them enough money to buy a rope to hang themselves. He had not just cheered Goring's cavalry through his parish; he had wined and dined Lord Goring and his officers at the rectory.

What, wondered Suzie, had happened to Thomas Loosemore's family in those dark days of civil war? Had his parents seen their farm looted, their barns emptied, their animals butchered? Might he have had a sister, a young wife, even, who fell prey to those undisciplined Royalist predators? How could she know what might have fuelled the anger with which Thomas later seized the rector by his hair? Justice, he must have thought; justice for the common people at last.

Had she been too quick to judge him?

But, a fairer part of her mind told her, there had been no time for justice for the Reverend Arthur Chambers. What Thomas's anger had done in a reckless moment was irreversible.

She joined the queue afterwards, waiting to buy a copy of James Milton's book and have it signed.

When her turn came, he looked up at her, with warm blue eyes, his pen poised. 'Is it for anyone in particular?'

'For me, Suzie, with a z.' She smiled shyly. 'We've met before. I came to look at your church in Southcombe. *We*, that is. My husband and I. I was looking for my ancestors in the seventeenth century, but I was cross because the Victorians had cleared all the earlier stuff away. And then I found his name, my ancestor's, on the board of churchwardens' names. Thomas Loosemore.'

'Yes, I think I do remember now, though I spent most of the time talking to your husband. Loosemore? Not the Thomas Loosemore from Walker's *Sufferings of the Clergy*? The chap who killed the Royalist rector?'

'I'm afraid so. At least, I think it's the same. Would he be the Thomas Loosemore who lived at Wayland and was church-warden ten years later?'

'Your guess is as good as mine. I expect you know there's a gap in the parish registers around then. Could be the same. Or father and son. Cousins, even. Have you tried finding what date he was baptized? We've still got the earlier registers.'

'Not yet . . . I . . . well, it got a bit complicated.'

He glanced past her at the patient queue. 'Look, why don't we talk about this later? If you're not too busy, we could have a cup of tea somewhere quieter. I could tell you what I know about the parish in those days. And you may have turned up things I haven't. So far, I've been more concerned with the broader picture of the community than following up particular families. But sometimes an individual's story can shed illumination on the whole. Have you got time?'

'Yes. Yes, fine. No, I don't have to hurry back. Thank you.'

She took the book from him and moved aside. There were other books on the table by James Milton. A slim, glossily illustrated volume about the Victorian Celia Montague, who had so beautified Southcombe church with her art in the nineteenth century, for all Suzie had raged at the makeover. Thumbing through the photographs, Suzie had to admit her talent and the botanical detail of her flower paintings. Another book was devoted to Lord Goring's cavalry, *Goring's Crew*. A map traced their route across the county, while the text reported their ravages. She wanted to buy that, too, but the author was busy now with other customers. She put it down while she waited.

He was a man of wide sympathies, evidently. Wider, she thought guiltily, than her own.

It took time for him to finish signing books. He spent as much time talking to every other buyer as he had with her. She watched with sudden disappointment as the last copy of *Goring's Crew* disappeared into another member's handbag.

'Tea, dear?'

Absent-mindedly, she took the cup someone offered her, before she remembered that she was having tea with James Milton.

There seemed something slightly illicit in escaping with the speaker, when so many other people wanted to talk to him over the tea the Family History Society provided. But James lingered long enough to sell and sign most of his stack of books. He waved aside the proffered tea cup – *more sensibly than me*, Suzie thought. Yet even when he rose from the table, he listened attentively to people and answered questions, or nodded politely to enthusiasts anxious to impress their own views upon him. *He's good at this*, she thought, watching him. *Well, I suppose you have to be, if you're a minister of religion and everyone wants to offload their problems on to you. On the other hand, not all of them are this good at it.*

He waited until the crowd was thinning before gathering up his papers, packing the last books into a holdall and taking leave of the organizers. Suzie was waiting for him at the door. The rain had stopped, leaving the pavement slick and shining.

'There's a church down the road that's been turned into a community centre. They do a nice cup of Fairtrade tea and home-made cakes.'

'Fine,' Suzie said.

She sneaked a glance sideways at him as they walked down the street, past the small, low-price shops at this poorer end of the town. He was younger than Nick, but older than Tom, and fair, where they were both dark. Not as handsome in his bone structure as her two, a little plump in the cheeks. It was the vigorous hair that made him memorable. It sprang from his scalp as though it wanted to take wing. She felt a disconcerting desire to run her fingers through it.

The converted church was set back from the road, across a graveyard which had been turned into a garden. It was post-war, golden stone.

'You've heard about this church, have you?' James threw a grin at her.

'I know it was bombed in the Second World War. Such a shame. It was dedicated to our local saint, Juthwara, who had her head cut off. There was a shrine to her inside, wasn't there?'

James rubbed his nose. 'Yes, well. To tell you the truth, the bishop took the bomb as a gift from heaven. It meant there'd be one less historic building to keep up out of diocesan funds. But unfortunately the vicar was rolling in it. He insisted on rebuilding the place out of his own pocket. Trouble was, he didn't leave them any money to keep it up, nor, it has to be said, much of a congregation. People were moving out to the suburbs. So now all sorts of good causes have set up shop here instead, and the best bit is this café.'

He ushered her into its steamy warmth.

'This is a bit like the old Church House every parish used to have,' she said, as she hung her raincoat over the back of her chair, 'where they used to brew church ales to swell the funds.'

'I'd never thought of it like that. I see it more as an outreach opportunity,' he said, looking round. There were grey-haired ladies, who might have had business at the Mothers' Union office, down-and-outs, making a cheap cup of tea last the wet afternoon. 'Fancy a flapjack? I can't resist them.'

Suzie had an embarrassed moment of indecision. Should she offer to pay her share? She began to draw her purse out of her shoulder bag, but he waved it aside. 'Have this on me. Let's blow my massive fee for the talk on tea and cakes, shall we?' His smile danced like his curly hair. He carried the tray to their table.

'Now, what was it we were going to discuss? When I've just done a talk, my wits go on strike.'

'I'm sorry! I shouldn't be bothering you with my own research straight after a meeting. I expect you just want to get in your car by yourself and drive home.'

What is 'home', she wondered. Does he have a wife? Children? Almost certainly the old rectory, where Thomas threw the parson downstairs, is an upmarket home now for someone on a higher salary than James Milton. They'll be living in a modest, three-bedroomed house, like any other young family.

He grinned at her, stirring, she noticed, a generous spoonful of sugar into his tea. 'No, honestly. It's not every day I meet someone who's as keen on our local history as I am. My parishioners are used to me boring the socks off them with my latest discoveries, but there are only one or two of them who are genuinely interested. So, what have you found out about the good people of Southcombe?'

She told him how she had traced her family back to Joshua Loosemore in the 1670s, but had drawn a blank about his parents because the baptismal register was missing for the critical years. How excited she had been to discover the name of Thomas Loosemore on the churchwardens' board, with the name of his farm. How likely it was that this was Joshua's father.

And then the shock of reading the story of Thomas Loosemore, the militiaman, guilty of the death of his rector.

'It really helped me,' she said, 'your talk today. I could see for the first time how it might have happened. All the terrible things that had gone before, and Arthur Chambers welcoming Lord Goring, while all around him his parishioners were suffering from what Goring's Crew did.'

'This is really important to you, is it? You need to ex-onerate old Thomas? Funny how personally people take what their ancestors did. I had an American lady come to visit the church, on the family history trail, like you. A Southern Baptist, from the Bible Belt. She was keen to find the name of her several-times-great-grandfather, because the records only showed the mother's name. She asked me, in all innocence, what was meant by "a base child".'

'Oh, dear. How did she react when you told her?'

'Well, I stopped short of saying, "It's another name for a bastard". I didn't think she was up for that. But in the end it didn't do any good, pussyfooting around it. When she real-ized her ancestor was an unmarried mother, she turned red in the face and bawled me out. I'm afraid I shattered her self-image as the descendant of morally correct English Puritan stock. You'd have thought I'd just told her the woman had passed on some disgusting hereditary disease.'

'That's what St Augustine thought original sin was, didn't he? Transmitted down the generations by sexual congress?'

'You read the Early Fathers?' His eyes sharpened with surprise.

She blushed. 'Not exactly for bedtime reading. But I got into early Church history a bit, going back into our Celtic origins. Pelagius, and all that.'

'The British heresy. We have to roll our sleeves up and co-operate in our own salvation, not just sit back and expect Christ to do everything for us. I think I'm a semi-Pelagian myself. But back to Thomas Loosemore, and why it's important to you that he's not just a mindless thug.'

'It's because of my son.' It was a relief to admit it in words at last. 'Thomas Loosemore Fewings. I was so excited that I could tell him something about another Thomas Loosemore in the family. The churchwarden. And then it all went wrong.'

'How old is Tom?'

'Seventeen.'

'And was *he* excited about the churchwarden?' His eyebrows lifted.

'Not really.' She smiled wryly. 'You're right. It was just me.'

'I bet he perked up more at the murder story, or man-slaughter, anyway.'

She coloured. 'I haven't told him about that yet. You're right. I felt a bit like your Southern Baptist lady. It was a shock. Only then . . .' To her astonishment, she found herself telling him the whole story: of Julie Samuel going missing, of Tom being questioned, of his dates with her, and his severing of the relationship, of Julie being found dead by the canal.

'Yes, I heard about it on the television. Nasty case. It makes you shiver to think that there's a man like that walking around such a beautiful cathedral city. You start to feel that nothing's sacred, nowhere's safe.' He was still for a moment, then he looked up sharply. 'But you can't really think your Tom had anything to do with it, just because of something that happened three hundred years ago?'

'That's what my husband says. No, of course I don't. At least . . . I do all this research into my ancestors, and I find out all sorts of facts about them. But I don't *know* them. Short of diaries or letters, I'll never really know what sort of people they were. And I start to wonder . . .' She played with her teaspoon. 'How well do I know anybody, even my own family? Surely every mother whose son goes wrong must think, "My boy would never have done something like that". Then, in the dark hours in the middle of the night, I think, "Am I kidding myself?"'

This time, the silence was long, while he looked hard at her. 'Is this something you've shared with your husband?'

'No, not really. If I even hint at it, he gets really angry. Well, not angry. Nick's too nice for that. But stiff and cold. Disapproving. And of course, he's right. It's stupid to think there could be any connection. I *don't* think it. But I still can't get rid of the feeling. Like a shadow hanging over us.'

'Look, you're right. It's stupid. There's no way I could believe that a normal seventeen-year-old like your Tom would do that to a girl. It's not credible. But it's not stupid to realize how little we know about each other. We have to leave room for the unexpected, and we need compassion. Like the way you're trying to understand why Thomas Loosemore might have done what he did.'

'Yes, thank you. It sounds so silly now, confessing it to someone else.' She raised her own eyes to his with a smile. 'I suppose that's part of your job, confessions.'

'Not so much nowadays,' he grinned back. 'The good old Church of England doesn't go in much for that, except on the Anglo-Catholic wing. The standard issue General Confession in church every Sunday morning is enough for most people. Still, yes, in my line of work, people do tell me some surprising things.'

She longed to ask him for examples, but dared not. Probably he wouldn't tell her, even under the cover of anonymity.

The conversation moved away to safer ground. He told her of account books he had seen, detailing the time when Roundheads had been billeted on Southcombe in the wake of the Royalists.

'At least they gave the villagers IOUs. Whether they ever saw the colour of their money is another matter. I'm sure Wayland Farm was down there somewhere. Are you on email? If you give me your address, I'll look it up and send you the details.'

'Thanks. And thank you for the tea ... and the flapjack.' She sensed that her time was up. He was ready to go. She had had a generous share of his attention. All the same, she felt regret. She had no right to detain him longer, but she would have liked to.

'You'll have to come back to Southcombe and take a look at Wayland. It's down in the valley below the church, just before the ford over the stream. Have you been there yet?'

'No. I only discovered the name of the farm that day we met you in the church. I haven't been back.'

'Give me a ring if you're coming. I can probably supply you with another cup of tea.' He grinned again, boyishly.

I, she thought. *If he was married, it would be natural to say 'we' when inviting someone to his home.*

'And bring Nick with you, of course.'

ELEVEN

She burst back into the house with a lighter heart. Flinging her raincoat on to the hook, she swept on down the hall, looking in every room. No sign of Nick, nor of the children.

'Nick?'

Millie appeared on the landing, towelling her hair. 'He's still in the shed. Don't think it's going well.'

'Oh, dear. Where's Tom?'

'Out.' Millie turned back to her room.

Some of Suzie's gaiety deserted her. After all, what had happened? Well, plenty. She had discovered a whole lot more about the Civil War in Southcombe. It changed the picture. She had enjoyed a cup of tea and a flapjack with the personable rector. She had an invitation to go back to the village and find out more. She allowed herself a little smile. More about Thomas Loosemore? About James Milton?

The garden had the freshness of sunshine after rain. Droplets hung from the sapphire petals of delphiniums, from the heart-shaped leaves of currant bushes, from the spears of grass, sparkling joyfully. She could almost sense the earthworms revelling in the damp, well-composted soil. Blackbirds sang, more tuneful than any nightingale.

The shed was at the far end of the garden. The door was open.

Her presence darkened the interior. She had to peer narrowly to see inside. Nick was squatting on the floor before the lawn-mower, with an assortment of parts laid out around him. More components were ranged on the bench-top, where the plant pots had been pushed aside.

He did not raise his dark head immediately. He was concentrating on assembling a bolt, a washer, and a larger part she could not name, trying to fix them together. He swore.

'Having problems?' she asked, in what she hoped was a sympathetic voice.

'What does it look like?' He still did not look up.

Her enthusiasm would have to wait.

'Have you had a cup of tea?'

'No.'

'I'll bring you one, shall I?'

No answer. She felt the struggle that was going on inside him, between the reluctance to admit that the job was beyond him and the need to be comforted while someone else put it right.

She went silently back to the house, and brought him a mug and a plate of chocolate biscuits. He sighed and thanked her. When he pushed back a waving lock of hair from his forehead, it left a streak of black grease. She hesitated. Would it be tactless to say the obvious?

'You could always take it round to the garage. They'd fix it for you.'

'In bits? Like I'm the sort of idiot who takes a machine apart and can't put it back together again?'

'You're not an idiot. You've done repairs before. It's only this time.'

'I laid out everything in the right order, so that I'd get it back the same way. I'm sure I did.'

'It all looks very organized to me.' She cast a glance over the array of parts on the bench and floor. 'The problem's probably that you've laid them out on a flat surface in two dimensions, but you have to put them together on a three dimensional machine.'

He took a second chocolate biscuit and lifted himself from the floor to a stool, cradling the hot mug in a dirty hand. She sensed a temporary, if gloomy, relaxation; a break from the problem.

'You seem very chipper. I take it you had a good time.'

'Yes, it was great!' Her face flowered into an eager smile. Then she restrained it. Now was perhaps not the right moment to launch into an enthusiastic account of Goring's Crew and their possible effects on the life of a young seventeenth-century farmer. 'I'll tell you about it later.'

Nick was staring down at the floor, not listening. Suddenly, he slammed down his mug, leaped off the stool, and was down on hands and knees at her feet.

His fingers criss-crossed the assembly of parts. She hardly saw the difference in the things he picked up, or the order in which he put them together, but they seemed to snap into place, the spanner tightened. He sat back on his heels and laughed, slapping his knee.

'Idiot! I knew it couldn't be that complicated, even for someone like me. You were right. It wasn't just left and right and over and under, it was a question of front and back too. I should have done enough work on two-dimensional plans of 3-D buildings to see that. You're a genius!'

She beamed, embarrassed, unable to think of anything to say.

'If I wasn't so filthy, I'd kiss you.'

'I'll hold you to that, later.'

She began to gather up the mug and the plate. 'Another biscuit? To celebrate.'

He took two.

She stood, still longing to talk about her own afternoon. But Nick was busy again. She looked at the bench behind her. There still seemed a good many components to restore to their places.

'I'll leave you to it, then. Will you be finished by teatime?'

He was intent on his task again, the parts of the machine slipping together, the floor clearing. Soon he would begin on the ones on the bench. She stepped out into the garden.

A fist of cloud had obscured the sun again. As she walked back to the house, the apple tree dripped on her. There was more rain in the sky.

She went up to Millie's room.

'Is Tom coming back for tea?'

'Search me. You don't think he discusses his Saturday evenings with me, do you?'

Suzie rinsed the mugs and upended them on the drainer. So Tom was out. Not, from what he had said yesterday, with Dave. That was not so unusual on Saturdays. Tom was a chameleon. Dave was his closest buddy, the one who was in and out of the house, or else Tom at his. But there were others, Tom's Saturday-night friends. Dave, she recalled, didn't have girlfriends. It was impossible to imagine him out clubbing, even at the under-18 venues. Tom had hooted with laughter at the suggestion.

She smiled sadly as she dried her hands. She had always found Dave's companionship with Tom reassuring. He was a

good influence, studious, well brought up. It was the wilder
lads Tom mixed with on Saturday nights she worried about.
But they, it seemed, had not rejected him, as Dave had.

Suzie lay on her back in bed that night, noting a cobweb she
had missed in a corner of the ceiling. Her face relaxed. She felt
more at peace. Nick's back was turned to her, so that he could
read in the light of his bedside lamp.

'I feel a whole lot better, after today.'

'Mmm?' A longish pause. 'Why's that?'

'The meeting this afternoon. You were so tied up with your
lawnmower, I didn't have a chance to tell you about it.'

She sensed that she did not have Nick's full attention, but
she went on, nevertheless. 'It was about the Civil War, and
you'll never guess who was the speaker. It was James Milton.
I didn't recognize his name from the programme, but he turned
out to be the rector of Southcombe . . . You remember, the
one who showed you the painted tiles in his church?'

'Oh, yes. Him.'

She turned on her elbow, but saw only Nick's shoulder
in its blue pyjama-top. 'He was talking about the ghastly
things that happened in the Civil War, and how it affected
local people. Not just battles and stuff you read about in
history books, but all the taxes people had to pay to one
side or the other, and the way they took all your crops and
farm stock to feed their troops, and you were lucky if you
got paid for them. And how the Royalists marched across
the county after they'd lost to the Roundheads, and beat up
the towns and villages they passed through. They broke the
weavers' looms and trashed their cloth, so they'd nothing
to live on, and they spoiled the farms, and very probably
the women as well.'

'It still happens. That's what war's like.'

'But suddenly it all made sense. Thomas Loosemore
dragging the parson downstairs. I knew the rector was an out-
and-out Royalist, but I didn't know he'd entertained Lord
Goring lavishly when his cavalry were passing through
Southcombe. And Goring's Crew were the worst of the lot,
apparently. The villagers would have known all about those
two knocking back the claret together, while Goring's men
were doing unspeakable things in their village.'

Another pause. Probably Nick was reading to the end of a paragraph before answering.

'And that makes you feel better, does it?'

'Well, yes. Of course, Thomas Loosemore shouldn't have been as violent as he was, and I'm sorry the rector died. But you can see how he must have felt. Most of the village will have hated the rector for not taking their side and not kicking Lord Goring out of his house. And after the war, here was Thomas's chance. He was in the militia. He'd got his orders from the County Commissioners. It was his job to evict the old rector from the parsonage. Can't you imagine all the bitterness he'd felt coming to the boil once he'd actually got his hands on Arthur Chambers? Who knows what Goring's troopers did to Thomas's family, to his sisters, or his wife, even.'

'A lively imagination's certainly a help with family history, by the sound of it. You should turn it into a novel.'

'But this is important. To me, anyway. I felt really bad about it when I found out Thomas Loosemore had killed somebody. Because we'd given Tom his name. Now it's starting to make sense.'

Nick did turn over then. She heard his book fall on the floor behind him. His eyes were close to hers, too dark, too accusing.

'You're not *still* carrying on with that nonsense, are you? Because some guy called Thomas killed a man in the Civil War? You don't *really* think that has anything to do with our Tom? For heaven's sake!'

'No, I *don't*. I was just trying to tell you. I feel heaps better now. Now that I know Thomas Loosemore probably had a reason. He wasn't just a thug.'

'Did you think for a moment that Tom was?'

'No, of course not!'

She was lying. This was the nightmare that had been haunting her, that she had dared not admit to anyone until this afternoon. That her beloved son might not be what she had thought he was, but a violent young man she had never really known.

Nick sensed it. He rose up in bed, blocking out the light, suddenly a tall menacing figure. His loud voice and his harsh breathing were too close to her. 'That's appalling! I've put up with this obsession of yours for months. I've driven you round to every out-of-the-way village you were interested in. You've shut yourself up in the study for hours with the computer, when you could have been talking to your own children. And now it's driven you so insane, you think your own son is a murderer? You're his mother, for heaven's sake!'

'I don't, I don't! That's what I was just *telling* you.'

'And what exactly have you told me? That you feel a whole lot better about our Tom, because of something you've found out about your great-great-something-grandfather? So you're admitting that you *did* suspect him. And just because you now think your Thomas Loosemore killed his man accidentally in justified anger, does that mean you think that's what happened with Tom and Julie Samuel? That Tom did it, but because he got carried away for some good reason, so it doesn't matter? You're crazy!'

'Hush. Keep your voice down. Millie will hear.'

'And what are you going to pin on *her*, if you happen to find another ancestor called Millie? If it turns out she's a prostitute, or a convict transported to Botany Bay, will you decide that that makes our Millie guilty, too? Are you taking leave of your senses?'

Nick threw himself out of bed. She did not know if he was about to storm off to the bathroom or to sleep in the spare room bed.

Suzie's body was racked with dry sobs. It was less because he was being unfair than because she feared he was right.

'You're deliberately misunderstanding me. Tom would never do anything like that. I know he wouldn't.'

'So why is this wretched Thomas Loosemore so important to you?'

'I don't know! I don't know! I just felt he was.'

There was the sound of the front door opening and then thudding shut.

Nick turned to face her. 'That's Tom. He's home. Shall I invite him up here, so that he can hear what his mother suspects about him? See what he's got to say for himself? Can he plead a gang of Royalist cavalry, or their modern equivalent, made him lose his rag? If so, she'll understand. He may be a killer, but he had a good excuse. Shall I tell him that?'

'No! No!' She buried her face in the pillow and wept.

*   *   *

'Would you like to use the bathroom first?'

Suzie had expected a quiet coldness from Nick next morning. Last night had been so uncharacteristic. Hot anger was not Nick's style. Instead, he seemed exaggeratedly considerate. Was this the nearest he could bring himself to an apology?

She considered his dishevelled Sunday morning self in pyjamas, his thick, dark hair rough from sleep. She longed to run to him, to hug and be hugged, but could not quite bring herself to do it. The short space of shaggy blue carpet had become an unbridgeable sea.

Was she the one who should be apologizing? Her stomach churned. Couldn't he see how upset she already had been, how she was just beginning to make sense of it, before he had shouted at her last night? What she had needed was comfort, not criticism. She wanted his laughter to drive away her irrational fears, not his anger.

She could see that this morning he was making an effort to be patient, courteous. Yet being magnanimous was itself an expression of moral superiority. It was not an apology. To him, she was still the one at fault.

'No,' she said, not quite managing a smile. 'You go ahead.'

James, she reflected, had sympathized with her.

The exaggerated politeness between them lasted all week. Each afternoon Suzie returned from the office to the empty house. There was housework to do, flowers to deadhead in the garden, food to prepare. But at some point she would normally have sloped off to the study, settled herself in front of the computer and spent an enjoyable hour writing up her latest research, turning it into a story about real human beings, or combing the Internet for fresh information.

After her talk with James, she had intended to log on to the Access to Archives website and see if she could find any documents relating to the Loosemores which might shed more light on the family. But she found herself curiously reluctant to reopen that subject.

Instead, she stood in the study doorway and felt her insides tighten. She realized she no longer wanted to find out more. What had been a fascinating hobby, even an addiction, had become a burden. The thought of sitting in that chair, clicking the mouse, seeing the screen spring to life, brought a tightening of her stomach. The fact that she knew this was unreasonable didn't help.

She was not sure whether it was Nick's anger that had revived this feeling of revulsion, or something deeper that would not go away.

She let her mind stray back to last Saturday, sitting in the café with James Milton. It had all seemed so sensible then. James had taken her fears seriously, but he hadn't blamed her. He had made her feel better.

She turned away. She must, in any case, set out soon to meet Millie from school. Since they had renewed their vigilance, her afternoons were shorter.

It was not over yet. It would not be over until the police caught Julie's killer.

It would never be over for Julie's parents.

And what about the rest of us? she wondered as she combed her hair and picked up her shoulder bag. How long do we keep this up? Taking and fetching our teenage daughters on the school run, setting a curfew on their movements, insisting that they never go anywhere alone. How long before the lack of any development lulls us back into normality? How long before Nick and I let Millie behave as before?

The thought still haunted every parent. Was it a serial killer who had murdered Julie? If so, would he strike again?

TWELVE

The car slowed long before it reached the gate. Suzie lifted her head from the rose bush she was trimming. She watched Tom negotiate the gate posts with exaggerated care. As he inched the car up the drive she could see his face through the windscreen, tight-lipped.

It wrenched her heart. This was not her Tom. Almost from the first he had handled the car with a breath-stopping panache, which had stopped just short of folly only because his confidence in his natural ability seemed to be justified. She had no doubt he would pass his test first time.

Now, he positioned the car in the garage as if afraid he might be misjudging its width. He walked into the house without looking at her.

Nick got out more slowly. He hesitated at the garage door, then came towards her. Suzie felt a rise of panic. They had hardly spoken to each other all week. Nick was slow to anger, but also slow, it seemed, to forget. All she'd had from him was exaggerated politeness.

'How was it?' she said, a little breathlessly.

'Not good. Lucky he didn't kill someone.'

She heard the catch in his breath, as he realized what he had said. To cover their embarrassment she went back to snipping roses.

His voice came more muffled. 'I'm sorry.'

She looked up. He had his back to her and was pulling abstractedly at an unopened bud. 'I think . . . we're both a bit worked up at the moment. Even though we know Tom's got nothing to worry about,' she said.

'You're sure of that now, are you?' It hurt. In spite of his apology, the accusation was still there.

'Of course I am!' She *was* sure, wasn't she? She hurried on. 'I know he's innocent. I just wish he hadn't been mixed up with Julie Samuel so soon before. It complicates things.'

'He's taking it badly. I've a feeling it wasn't quite as casual as he wants us to believe.'

'I know.'

There was a difficult pause.

'I wish I didn't have to go away tomorrow.'

'Nonsense. A weekend's break will do you good. And you said it's an important presentation. A chance to showcase your latest ideas.'

'You're sure you'll be all right with the kids?'

'Yes. Why ever shouldn't I be?'

'It's a difficult time.'

'We'll manage.'

If they had been having this conversation in the house, she could have gone into Nick's arms and let him make his apology real with the closeness of his body. They were both too embarrassed to embrace here in the front garden. She could not tell if it had just been words.

Early next morning Nick kissed her goodbye in the hall. The embrace seemed genuine.

'I'll be back Sunday evening, around five, if the roads are clear. The conference finishes at lunchtime. I'm sorry you won't get your Saturday outing.'

'That's all right. If I feel withdrawal symptoms coming on, I can always take myself out somewhere on the bus.' Her voice was light.

She felt the warmth of his jacket pressed against her face. The tightness of his arms around her awoke stirrings of guilt. Should she tell him what she was planning? Perhaps not. The rawness of their quarrel was still too painful. If it was starting to heal, it was better not to risk reopening that wound.

'Have you got your sponge bag?' she said instead.

'Yes. At least, I hope so. If you were a dutiful wife, you'd have packed my bag for me.'

'If I did, you'd tell me I'd chosen the wrong shirts.'

'Fair enough.'

They were both attempting to get back the lost lightness of tone.

He rumpled her hair and kissed her again, more briefly, finally. The car hummed down the drive and turned into the road.

She watched him go, aching for the things she had not said to him. If he had not needed to be at the conference this weekend, things might have gone back to normal after his apology. Tom having a driving lesson. Nick taking Suzie for a pub lunch and then family history hunting in the afternoon. She would not have needed to make these other arrangements without him.

The house seemed quiet, empty. She wandered back to the kitchen, tidied away the remains of their early breakfast. The children were not up yet. It would probably be mid-morning before they drifted downstairs, sleepy-eyed, with uncombed hair. Lunchtime before Millie, at least, was fully conscious.

She glanced at the clock. There was a bus to Southcombe at half past eleven. There were only five a day. She would need to be at the bus station in good time. She must just hope that Tom and Millie would be awake so that she could tell them where she was going and what they should and should not do while she was gone. Especially Millie.

She could have warned them last night, she thought as she ran the water into the washing-up bowl, but it had not seemed prudent. They might have let slip something casually to Nick. Not that going to Southcombe on her own was a secret, of course. She would tell him afterwards. She scrubbed at the cereal dried on the inside of a bowl. But it might be better not to make it sound too planned, too deliberate. Just a spur of the moment thing, she could say.

It had been more than that. The need for someone to soothe this hurt. Someone who would reassure her that the link she had made was irrational, and yet not judge her because, in the tangle of her emotions, she was making it.

Why should Nick object? James Milton had offered to show her Wayland Farm. Surely it was reasonable enough that she should take him up on the invitation?

Her hands stilled. She stared unseeingly across the garden. Thomas Loosemore was still too sore a subject to mention to Nick. Unnecessarily, of course. James had told her to put that nonsense about Thomas and Tom out of her mind, and she had, hadn't she?

A little voice of conscience told her she had not.

Just the same, there had seemed no need to tell Nick that she had rung James yesterday. She remembered those uncertain moments, listening to his phone ring and wondering who would answer it. Would it be a woman's voice, his wife? How would she explain herself? There would be no need, of course. She could just ask to speak to James. It must happen all the time with a busy clergyman, women parishioners wanting to talk to him. If he wasn't in, she wouldn't leave a message; just say she'd ring again.

But it had been James who had answered. Only a split second of surprise before he had remembered who she was, then a warm welcome. Yes, he could spare her some time on Saturday afternoon. He'd be delighted to show her Wayland Farm. He hadn't made much progress yet on more information about the Loosemores, hadn't been able to put his hands on those accounts of billeting soldiers he'd promised her, but there were things he could tell her in general about the village at the time when her ancestors lived there. No, she wasn't taking up his time. He'd be delighted to share a personal enthusiasm with her. He'd look forward to her visit.

James was the one person who had taken her fears seriously and then put them in their proper place. She needed to hear that again.

She stood with her hands around a cold coffee mug and felt the glow of his proffered friendship.

The bus wound through the lanes. It was strange to be sitting high up like this, and not in the passenger seat of a car. She could look out over hedgerows that were usually barriers shutting out the view. The farmland rolled away north to the grey smudge of moorland. Fields that had once been full of dairy cattle stood largely empty. No one wanted to get up in the early morning to milk cows nowadays. Here and there, sheep dotted the grass. Centuries ago, this county had led England, and perhaps the world, in its wool trade. In every cottage, women would be spinning and carding the yarn, whenever their other work allowed. Not for nothing was an unmarried girl called a spinster. She imagined these lanes busy with packhorses taking the wool to the weavers to be turned into serge or kersey, and then the cloth to the tuckers and fullers to finish it for market. Not all of the mills along the rivers were for grinding corn. They had turned the wheels of the cloth industry, too.

The old magic was returning. It gave her a warm feeling

of belonging to ride through this countryside and relive its
history, to people it with generations of her ancestors.

Today, there were only five passengers besides her on the
bus. A middle-aged woman loaded with shopping, an elderly
couple carefully dressed, as if on their way to a formal
occasion, and a pair of teenage girls with unnaturally black
and blonde hair. She puzzled over what they could be doing
travelling, not into the city but out of it, at this time of the
morning. Perhaps they'd been in town clubbing all night, or
on a sleepover.

After half an hour Southcombe came into view, its church
tower prominent on a hilltop and its houses spilling down the
slope.

She got off at the pub. There was the remnant of a village
green, a bench with a memorial plaque, shaded by a chestnut
tree. She looked around. Had there once been a blacksmith's
forge here?

She had not told James how and when she was coming,
only that she would meet him on the green at two, and that
Nick would not be with her. She had not liked to say that she
was coming by bus, which would get her to the village at
twelve. Since she was on her own, he might have felt it
incumbent upon him to invite her to lunch. She did not want
to impose on him.

The Lamb Inn would do her very well. She had eaten here
last time with Nick. She stepped inside, into the familiarity
of oak beams, rows of tankards, blackboards with today's
specials. She found a small table by the huge fireplace, which
was laid with logs, unlit on this summer day.

Two hours to wait. She ordered half a pint of cider and
lingered longer than was necessary over the menu, before
ordering warm focaccia with crispy ham, toasted Gruyère and
olives.

When the meal came, it was very enjoyable. She could not
help a wry smile at the thought of all the thousands of past
customers who must have sat where she did now and what
they would have made of her foreign food. But perhaps it was
not so very different from theirs, after all. Bread and cheese
and bacon.

Would women have sat drinking cider, as she did? Or was the
ale house only for the men? In any case, Southcombe was far

from the coaching roads. Any stranger would have been eyed with curiosity, even suspicion. Now, the landlord's cheery welcome told her, visitors were an essential part of the rural economy.

Times changed. One day she would be a name on someone else's family tree, to be investigated, recorded, and placed in her twenty-first-century social context.

She sat on the bench under the chestnut tree. The memorial plaque on it read: IN LOVING MEMORY OF MORRIS WEEKES 1905–1986. In his old age, Morris Weekes might have appreciated a seat like this to sit and watch the world go by, but it had come too late for him. The Lamb Inn had two outside tables with wooden benches. The narrow cobbled footpath around the green did not allow room for more. Even these might not have been there in the 1980s. Eating outside was a spin-off from foreign travel. Had Morris Weekes ever been on a package holiday to Spain?

He was born both too soon and too late for outdoor living. Go far enough back before electric lighting, and far more activity was carried on out of doors. She looked around her. Those cottages ringing the green would have had benches outside, simpler than the slatted one she sat on, or the women would have brought a chair out to sit in the brighter daylight shelling peas, spinning wool, darning, knitting. Their small, many-paned windows would have let in little light, set deep in thick cob walls. Today, she noticed, many of those cottage windows had been replaced with large panes of double-glazing.

Had this green been bigger once? That row of modern houses opposite – low, simple, white-walled, attempting to blend modernity with the old – had probably been built across one end of it. Had there been a local outcry at the loss of the village's traditional place for sports? Maybe not. There was probably a modern recreation ground with a pavilion in a field on the outskirts of the village. Low-cost new houses meant more opportunities for young couples to stay on in their village, while Londoners bought up the old cottages at sky-high prices for second homes. A village like this needed families to keep its school and shop going.

The sun went in and it was suddenly dark under the branches.

She hadn't thought about rain when she had agreed to meet James here. But the wide leaves of the chestnut canopy would shelter her.

There was something both surprising and reassuring about his choice of meeting place, in the middle of the village, in plain view of everyone. Would tongues wag? The rector meeting a woman who, though no longer young, was still . . . well, personable. Her cheeks grew unexpectedly warm. She glanced down at the smoky blue of her Indian cotton skirt, the magenta silk blouse and the embroidered blue jacket she wore. Clothes made in peasant style, but not to be worn by peasants. Were they too delicately urban for a walk to the farm?

Was there a reason why he had not invited her to meet him at the rectory?

She hadn't seen him coming. He was halfway across the green, dismounting from his bicycle. A bike? She had not anticipated this. She had thought that they might either walk companionably through the lanes, or that perhaps he would arrive in his car and offer to drive her there.

'Hello,' he smiled. The hand that attempted to tidy his curly hair merely ruffled it. 'I hope I haven't kept you waiting.'

'Not at all.' She was getting to her feet, reaching for her bag, unnecessarily flustered. 'It's good of you to give up your Saturday afternoon for me.'

'Not a bit of it. My day off's Tuesday, actually. There's usually too many events I need to be at over the weekend. None this afternoon, as it happens, but I've got a call to make out beyond Wayland Farm, so I thought I'd bring the bike for exercise. You should be able to find your own way back, no trouble.'

A little dip of disappointment. So there would be no tea at the rectory afterwards.

She wondered if she should tell him that she must catch the half-past four bus, but decided against it. He probably assumed she had a car in the pub car park. If she told him about the bus, he might protest that her visit could have waited till another Saturday, when Nick could have driven her here.

Why hadn't she waited for another week?

She had wanted this meeting, without Nick.

The sun had come out again, lighting his blond hair around

his face in front of her. The village centre drowsed in a post-lunch quiet. There was, after all, no one about to comment on their meeting. Unless there were watchers behind those deep-set windows.

They set out across the green.

THIRTEEN

James and Suzie took a lane that led past the new houses, and then angled down the side of the hill. As the road cut deeper between the hedge banks, older gardens rose above them, bright with dahlias and red-flowered runner beans.

'Did I tell you Wayland Farm's a listed building? It's not much to look at on the outside, but it was a grander place in medieval times. They found some smoke blackening on the roof rafters, so the main room was probably once a hall that rose the full height of the house. It was about the seventeenth century before they decided that private bedrooms might be a good idea and put in an upper floor.'

'I wonder if the Loosemores lived there then.'

'Probably not. Landed gentry apart, farming families moved around more than you might think. They didn't often stay on one farm for more than a century.'

'Pity. I was starting to have visions that they might have been a bit grander once, even if they were yeoman farmers in the seventeenth century. By the 1800s they were down to agricultural labourers. At least, my branch of the family was.'

'The good old "ag labs". There are rather a lot of them in everybody's family tree.'

'Except that when I went to find the grave of one who died in 1888, it wasn't what I thought, the humble plot of a horny-handed son of the soil. It was right beside the path to the church door, with a railing round it. Apparently, in later life, he gave up labouring and took on the village shop. So, in local terms, he was a somebody when he died.'

'Here?'

'No. Over in Possington.'

'I'm told they still have a rather fine rood screen in the church there. That, at least, escaped the dreaded Victorian restorers.'

She laughed, embarrassed by his reminder of her outrage at his own church's makeover.

They were dropping lower now. At a bend in the lane, the

valley showed itself below them. Level meadows lay beside
a watercourse among willows. Oak woods climbed the opposite slope.

'That's the Twisted Oak river. It forms the boundary between
the parishes of Southcombe and Nympton Rogus.'

'So your patch stops there.'

'Good heavens, no. I've got five parishes to cover. Nympton
Rogus is one of mine, too.'

'Five? How on earth can you get to five services on a
Sunday morning?'

'I don't. Southcombe has a morning service every Sunday;
Nympton Rogus alternate Sunday afternoons. We have lay
readers who take the service at the other three when I can't,
and I get over to take communion once a month. But yes,
I do five services most Sundays. An early-morning communion somewhere, a family one at ten o'clock here, matins
somewhere else at eleven thirty, an afternoon service, and
an evensong.'

'On your bike?' He was wheeling it alongside her, with
increasing difficulty as the gradient steepened.

'Not usually, I'm afraid. I need the car for all my ecclesiastical gear.'

'Yes, of course.' She had a wild vision of him cycling down
this hill on his way to Nympton Rogus in cassock, surplice
and damask chasuble.

'We're nearly there.'

The changing angle of the road showed below them a clump
of trees, between which nestled a rambling complex of farm
buildings. The house itself, washed in primrose yellow, shone
softly in the afternoon sunlight. It stood secretively with its
almost windowless back to the road.

Suzie felt a tightening in her throat. This was where the
Loosemores had lived. Joshua and Loyalty probably, and
before them certainly Thomas and his as yet unknown wife.
They were not just names in an account book, or on a board
in the church. They had fed the fire to send wood smoke up
that tall brick chimney above the thatch, had crossed that yard
to milk the cows and tend the horses, had carried corn and
root crops into those barns and outhouses to ensure their
survival through another winter.

And stood helplessly by as the king's soldiers raided them?

She tried to imagine a troop of cavalry cresting that ridge
from Nympton Rogus or riding up this valley from the city.
Had the Loosemores been eagerly partisan, throwing in their
lot behind the Parliamentarians? Or had they turned in on
themselves, here in this quiet combe, thinking only of how to
hide the cheese in the dairy, the pigs in the meadow, the harvest
of the cider house?

James was speaking to her, but she had missed most of it.
'. . . cup of tea.'

She turned a vague smile on him, hoping he would read it
as assent to whatever he had been proposing.

The road had levelled out. They were at the gateway to the
long farm drive. A wooden plaque, sliced from a tree trunk,
read 'Wayland Farm'. Belatedly, Suzie remembered her camera
and fished in her bag for it. Too late, she wished she had
photographed the panoramic view of the farm from above.
Perhaps she could do it on her way back. Would there still
be that seductive gleam of sunlight on its yellow walls?

Three black and white sheepdogs came bounding from the
farmyard, barking to announce their arrival. James propped
his bike against the wall and held out the open palms of his
hands to them. They wagged their tails furiously, accepting
his overtures of peace. One sniffed around Suzie's skirt.

A red-faced farmer in brown overalls was coming to meet
them, drawn by the noise.

'Afternoon, Rector. Afternoon, miss.'

'Bill Yelland,' James introduced them. 'Suzie Fewings. She
was a Loosemore before she married.'

'Oh, aye? There was still some of them around Southcombe
when I was a boy. I used to go to school with Jackie
Loosemore.'

'Did they live here as recently as that?' Suzie put in eagerly.

'Not *here*, if you mean Wayland. This farm's been in my
family since my grandfather's time. Don't know as my boy
will want to take it over, though, when I'm gone. There's
nothing for us in farming now. 'Tis all filling in forms, and
no money to show for it. And he's happier messing about with
machines than mucking out animals. Like as not he'll sell up
and it'll be some fancy gent from London as lives here.'

'Where did the Loosemores live, then?'

She heard herself dismissing the grief of this man for a

vanishing way of life, a family tradition that would end with his death. Too late to catch back the narrowness of her own self-centred search.

'Duck's Cottage. You must have passed it on the corner at the top of the lane.'

She had been looking at the newly built houses. She had not given much attention to the cottages on the other side of the road. Perhaps it was one of those whose gardens had showed above her, rich with well-composted vegetables and bright with flowers, the work, not so long ago, of some distant cousin of hers many times removed.

Her interest today was here, in this farmhouse, these particular Loosemores, three and a half centuries ago. She was willing the farmer to say what he did.

'Would you like to come inside, then, see the house?'

'Could I? Oh, thank you, yes.'

They followed Bill Yelland round the corner of the house. The back wall, pierced by only the occasional small window, was very different from the south-facing front. Here, many more windows looked out across the farm to the river. Little pink roses sprawled over the porch, pretty enough for her to see why they had become such a birthday-card cliché. The sweeping thatch occupied more space than the walls beneath it. The bedroom windows close under the eaves looked like eyes having difficulty opening.

The hall was stone-flagged, scattered with rag rugs that looked home-made.

'Mother?' Bill Yelland called. 'They'm here.'

The door to the kitchen opened, letting out a smell that might have been laundry or boiled pudding. Mrs Yelland was larger than her husband, her ample figure spilling over the confines of her apron. Her eyes were smiling, directed at James rather than Suzie.

'You'll be ready for your tea, Rector, after cycling all this way.'

'Walking today, Jean. Mrs Fewings hasn't got a bike.'

'Pleased to meet you, I'm sure.' She was shyer, turning to Suzie.

'It's very good of you to let me come inside and see the house. Is it all right if I look in the kitchen?'

'The kitchen? I don't know why you'd want to bother with

that. 'Tis nothing much. I've never had it fitted out like these modern ones. My daughter's always telling me I'm behind the times. "Mum," she says, "you ought to get rid of that awful old sink. It's a disgrace."'

She stood aside, but only a little, as if reluctant to let Suzie past. Suzie had to edge round her.

This kitchen must surely have been altered since the seventeenth century, but it still had an air of history. The red tiled floor. The Rayburn stove set into what had once been a massive fireplace, radiating warmth. The large wooden table in the middle of the room. Rows of pans hung on the rough, whitewashed stone wall.

Stone, not cob, Suzie's mind registered, to support the big chimney stack at this gable end.

'Well, come you through to the sitting room and I'll bring you a cup of tea.'

This invitation must have been what James had been trying to tell her.

She followed the men across the hall. The room was low-ceilinged, beamed. Faded chintz covers draped themselves over comfortable-looking armchairs. Window sills set into the thick walls were low enough to sit on. Old photographs of the Yelland family took up much of the wall space. At some point, the fireplace, once as large as the one in the kitchen, had been reduced to a smaller compass of black leading and brown tiles. A basket of dried flowers took the place of flames.

It was soothing, old-fashioned, perhaps more Edwardian than anything else.

She took the offered armchair and looked up at the low planked ceiling.

'Is this room the one you were telling me about? The great hall, before they put a ceiling in to make bedrooms?'

'"Great hall" might be overdoing it,' James laughed. 'This was never a manor house. But yes, this room and the one next to it were one big open living space, from floor to roof. Funny how we're going back to that idea. Nobody seems to want separate dining rooms any more.'

'But bedrooms have to be a good idea.'

'And studies, for people like us.'

They drank strong tea and ate Mrs Yelland's rock cakes. Suzie was comforted by the hospitality, the room's cosiness.

But somehow she felt the history she had come looking for was eluding her. She did not believe Thomas Loosemore had lived in a room quite like this.

She was aware of time passing. She sneaked a glance at her watch. Half past three. Her bus would leave in an hour. How long would it take her to climb back up the hill she had so easily walked down?

'I'm really grateful to you,' she said, putting her flowered cup down. 'It's been so good of you to let me see inside the house.'

'You haven't seen the old dairy yet,' James said. 'It used to be the other half of this hall.'

As she stood up, Suzie noticed for the first time the wall behind her chair. She had walked through the door without turning round. Panels of black-stained oak ran the whole length of it, with a narrow bench seat.

'Yes,' James said, as she stopped to stare at it. 'Sixteenth century. It would have been here in your Loosemores' time.'

Suzie fumbled in her bag. 'Would you mind if I took a photograph?' she asked Mrs Yelland.

'Go ahead, dearie.'

'There's a bit of carving somewhere,' Bill Yelland put in. 'Yes, here, see, on the bench-back.'

Suzie craned forward to look. In one place, the thicker wooden border linking the panels had been chiselled into a fan of foliage.

'That's a date, isn't it?' said James, peering over her shoulder. 'Look, in the middle of those leaves.'

He brushed past her to trace his finger over the grooves of the carving. She was aware of the fairness of his head against the black wood, of the warmth of his body, close alongside hers.

'1574.'

'There's something else,' she said, trying to control her voice. 'It's not just foliage. Aren't those initials?'

He bent closer, then realizing he was obstructing her view, stepped back. 'See what you can make of them.'

She stooped where he had, then turned to him, her face glowing. She met the delighted laughter in his own eyes.

'GL. It is, isn't it?'

'I think so.'

'So were the Loosemores here in 1574? Could this have been Thomas's father?'

'Grandfather, more likely. GL. George Loosemore, perhaps? It's a distinct possibility.'

Another name. Another generation. The succession of Loosemores stretched out behind Thomas and in front of him.

Whatever Thomas Loosemore had done, he was only one in the long line of her family. There had been George, if that was his name, before, and Joshua after, and so many more. Now there was Suzie Loosemore, as she had been before she married Nick, standing here, where her ancestors had stood. These were her people. Hundreds, even thousands more had gone to make her and Tom and Millie the people they were. Some had been yeoman farmers, others labourers. They had been great and humble, hard-working and idle, honest and devious. Each new generation inherited genes that gave them the potential to become any of these things. It took more than a name to decide one's destiny.

At the farm gate, James mounted his bike, still resting one foot on the ground. He smiled at her and Suzie felt a rush of gratitude to him for giving her this afternoon, this visit, this new piece of the total picture . . . for his smile. It had given her the comfort she needed.

She tried to put her gratitude into the extra shine of her answering smile, the warmth of her voice. 'Thank you so much. That was . . . special. So much research is following a paper trail and having to use my imagination to fill in the scene. That was solid reality today: the farmhouse, especially that carving, even the muck in this yard.'

James raised his fair eyebrows. 'I should have thought there was still plenty of scope for the imagination. There's not that much about Wayland that's obviously sixteenth or seventeenth century, is there? The basic structure's still there, but it's over-laid with generations of later stuff.'

'I suppose so . . . But to touch that carving. It was like the day I got the churchwardens' account book out at the Record Office and saw Thomas's own handwriting. There was even some of the sand he'd used to blot the ink.'

'Not a microfiche? You were lucky.'

'Yes, wasn't I? Even the archivist was surprised. I suppose

they have to photograph them. With so many of us chasing information now, the originals would never last. But it's not quite the same, is it? Images on a screen.'

'Or a transcript on the Internet.'

'It seems churlish to complain. It means someone can sit at their computer in Australia now and find out what their ancestors were doing in Nether Wallop in 1660. That has to be good.'

'Only . . . I know what you mean. We're in danger of losing touch with the reality. It becomes more like solving clues in a detective novel. You still get a cracking good story, but . . .'

They exchanged smiles, like fellow conspirators. *He knows*, she thought. *He's done this himself, researching his parishes for his books. He understands how I feel, in a way Nick never could, however kind and tolerant he's been about my hobby, until now.*

'On the other hand,' James went on, 'without all these wonderful people photographing and transcribing stuff, we'd never even know about the existence of some terrific information. Last week I tried Googling the FitzRoberts of Nympton Rogus and I came across this Proof of Age in 1485. It had to be established that Anne FitzRobert was old enough to take her inheritance with her to her marriage. A string of witnesses gave evidence of why they remembered the day she was born. It gives a marvellous snapshot of one day in the life of a fifteenth-century community. One guy remembered it because it was the day he fell off his horse and broke his arm. Another said he'd been a young lad who'd started work with the FitzRoberts that day and Anne's father gave him a penny. Jane Miller had good reason to remember it because she was hired as the wet nurse. And someone else told how he rang the church bell to celebrate the news and it broke.'

Suzie laughed her appreciation. She looked past him to the wooded hill where the road wound up to Nympton Rogus. *How long can we stand here talking like this*, she thought? *Why doesn't he go?* A youthful, irresponsible part of her longed to prolong the pleasure of these moments, the sun making the leaves more gold than green, the ripple of the river glinting across the meadow, the tall brick chimneys of Wayland Farm among the elms. But a more practical part of her was scared at the thought of the time which must be slipping round on her watch. The half past four bus was the last one back.

'I'm sorry, I . . .'

'Well, I suppose I . . .' they said together, and laughed.

'Thanks. Thank you again.'

'I hope I haven't made you late.'

She allowed herself to look at her watch at last. 'No, it's OK. I've got half an hour to get back to the village before my bus goes. That should be enough.'

'You came by bus? Why didn't you say? Look, if you miss it, give me a ring. I can always get the car out and run you into town.'

'Oh, no, I wouldn't dream of it. You've been so kind already. I'll be fine. A bit of brisk exercise will do me good.'

'Right you are, then. I won't keep you if you think you can make it. Mrs Tucker will be wondering where I've got to as it is.'

His bike wobbled out on to the road, and then set off more determinedly in the direction of the bridge. He turned to wave.

She watched him go, torn between basking in the afterglow of his presence, and sharp regret at his leaving. She sighed, and turned for the hill. It would need to be a fast climb.

FOURTEEN

The rest of the weekend drifted on peacefully. It seemed strange to be serving up a traditional Sunday lunch, and Nick not there to eat it. She need not have cooked it, she realized too late. Nick was the one who wanted the weekly roast and two veg, and insisted that the children be home to share it. She could have done something easier today – smoked salmon and salad, perhaps, or chops, burgers even. The children would not have minded. They might even have preferred it. Instead, she had cooked pork *boulangère*, the joint roasted juicily on a bed of sliced potatoes and apples.

She had at least one satisfied customer.

'This is good, Mum.' Tom lifted his eyes from a forkful of meat and crackling, and grinned at her. He had a gift of putting such warmth into the crinkling of his eyes. It was good to see him smile again.

'Fat,' Millie complained, poking hers around her plate. 'Disgusting grease, all over everything.'

'I'm sorry,' said Suzie. 'I didn't think about that. But at least it's tasty fat.'

'It'll be your fault if I get diabetes before I'm twenty.'

'Go on,' said Tom. 'There's hardly enough of you to see, if you stand sideways.'

'What's that supposed to mean? I've got no boobs?'

'No. You're just elegantly slim.'

His sister scowled at him with unmollified suspicion.

The slow afternoon passed. Suzie fiddled with things in the garden. Her ears were alert for the sound of Nick's car in the drive. Around five o'clock, he'd said. But the traffic might be better than he'd expected.

She still felt the pain of the quarrel between them, brief though it had been, the belated apology which had not quite cancelled out his accusation. What if Nick had had an accident? What if she never saw him again?

If she was honest, she had been in the wrong, of course she had. It had been unforgiveable of her even to hint that

Tom could have had anything to do with Julie's death. Just because of his name? She should have seen from the start that it had been nothing but stupid superstition.

She snapped the secateurs forcibly at a stem, and realized too late it was not bindweed but her favourite clematis. She brushed away an angry tear.

No. She was to blame. Nick was right. She had let this family history thing get totally out of proportion. She must tell him so, not just let things drift on as though she were the injured party, and he was the only one who needed to make an apology.

At four o'clock she came inside and changed her gardening clothes for a green linen dress. She made up her face carefully, something she rarely bothered to do unless she was going out, then dabbed perfume on her wrists and neck.

She wandered about the sitting room and the conservatory, plumping cushions, tidying newspapers. On an impulse, she went back into the garden and cut some lilac for the dining table.

He's only been away for the weekend. Why do I feel as though it's been a month? I can't wait to see him.

Or was she feeling guilt for her pleasure in yesterday's outing?

At last, the whisper of tyres on the drive. The gentle slam of the car door. She was on the doorstep before Nick was.

He grinned when he saw her, that smile so like Tom's. She ran to meet him. Their kiss was long and affectionate.

'Hey, you smell nice. I should go away more often.'

'It's good to have you back.'

She was shy now. It wasn't easy to say sorry. She would have to pick the right opportunity. Not now, with Tom or Millie likely to appear any moment. She led him into the house.

'Sit down. I'll make you a cup of tea.'

'Give me a second. I can't wait to change out of this suit.'

Then Tom was in the kitchen, as if drawn by the sound of the kettle filling and the rattle of the cake tin. Nick was greeting Millie on the stairs. She appeared moments later, a pale wisp in the doorway.

'I suppose fruit cake is off your diet sheet,' Suzie said, knife poised.

'Sundays don't count.' Millie caught Suzie's hand and moved the angle of the knife wider. 'There's got to be some rewards.'

Nick came downstairs wearing a dolphin-patterned, short-sleeved shirt and shorts. They were together again on the patio on a sunny summer evening, chatting about Nick's conference on reviving traditional building skills, while indoors the kids argued about the television. There was birdsong in the garden. Through the open French windows came the scent of lilac from the table behind her.

'Thanks. That was just right after the massive lunch they gave us.' Nick pushed away the remains of spinach and ricotta flan and salad. 'Have you checked the email recently? Anything more interesting than twenty-six adverts for Viagra?'

'I haven't opened it today. Or yesterday, come to think of it. Sorry.'

Nick groaned. 'That means the old Delete key will be working overtime. If it's like this when we're supposed to have a spam filter, goodness knows how bad it would be without.'

He took a handful of grapes, levered himself up from the table and moved into the study.

Suzie felt a twinge of guilt. She had spent a long time at the computer yesterday evening, writing up everything she could remember about Wayland Farm while her impression of it was still fresh. She had felt a glow of contentment in reliving the afternoon, a combination of James's shared enthusiasm, the hospitable old couple, the farmhouse guarding its ancient past under layers of accretions, the thrill of finding the initials *GL 1574* carved among the foliage on the bench back.

The minutes ticked by. She toyed with a crossword, her mind half on a television programme about penguins in the Antarctic. They made her smile. She thought they behaved as if comically designed by a cartoon animator, rather than as functional creatures of flesh and feathers, brilliantly adapted to their hostile environment.

The credits rolled. She checked the clock. Nick had been gone a long time. Perhaps there had, after all, been an interesting email that he had needed to follow up.

She felt the warmth of his anticipated homecoming fading into chilly disappointment. This was not how she had imagined this evening. She had rather hoped to coax Nick into suggesting an early night. He had noticed her perfume. Hadn't he interpreted her less than subtle signals?

Why was she taking so much trouble for him this evening?

Because they couldn't just carry on, with the quarrel still simmering under the surface, pretending Nick's apology had mended it. That would be easier, but they needed to be honest with each other. She must be the one to heal it.

Perhaps now was the moment she had been waiting for. Tom had gone out to meet friends. Nick was alone in the study. She would close the door behind her. There was no reason for Millie to disturb them. Now she could make that difficult apology, and mean it. It hadn't been Nick's fault; it was hers. Her arms around him, pulling him close, would make it right again.

She laid the newspaper aside.

The study door was shut. She wondered if she should knock, as she did when the children closed their bedroom doors. But the study wasn't Nick's private territory. Any of the family had access to the computer.

She turned to check her hair and face in the hall mirror. She didn't usually take enough trouble to look nice for Nick. She had convinced herself early on in their marriage that she couldn't fool him, since he saw her unglamorous early-morning self. Now she scolded herself that this didn't mean he wouldn't appreciate an attractive wife for the rest of the day.

She realized how nervous she was when she turned the door handle. Was she going to embarrass Nick by bringing this up again? He must have hoped he had put it behind him when he'd said that difficult *I'm sorry*. There had been no reservation in the kiss he'd given her on the doorstep.

It wasn't enough. The wound might be closing, but not cleanly enough. It would leave a scar. Only she could put it right.

Nick seemed not to hear the study door open. She saw the thick ripples of black hair above his shirt collar, the tanned arms dark against the paler fabric. With a sudden longing to put her arms around him, to rest her face in his hair, she moved forward.

He turned. The lines of his face were tight. There was no expected smile. He seemed to struggle to speak.

'So you haven't exactly been a grass widow while I was away.'

She stared at him blankly.

'I didn't realize I was cramping your style. Couldn't wait till I disappeared round the corner before you were off to your new boyfriend in Southcombe.'

James. How could he know? She scrabbled frantically through her mind to remember what she had said.

'I . . . I told you about him. Don't you remember? That meeting at the Family History Society last weekend. He was the speaker. And afterwards he offered to find out anything he could about my family in Southcombe. Show me Wayland Farm where they lived. I *told* you.'

'You'll have to forgive me if my memory doesn't register every detail of your family history research. That's hardly the point, is it? What made you choose *this* Saturday? It's not as if I'd left you the car. Did he come and get you?'

'I went by bus.'

'By *bus*. Remind me, how often have you taken a bus outside the city? Why do you think I spend my Saturdays driving you all over the county? But not *this* Saturday. Oh, no. This week I'm out of the way and you've got somebody special to meet. You didn't want me tagging along.' His eyes were bright with anger, not tears.

'It wasn't like that! For heaven's sake, James is years younger than me . . . than *us*.'

'James, is it now? Not the Reverend James . . . what was his name?'

'Milton.'

'The Reverend James Milton. Suddenly we're on first-name terms. You hardly bothered to speak to him when you were there with me.'

'I didn't know then what he was like. He's been really helpful. Well, you've met him. You saw the sort of person he is. And you liked him too. You scolded me for being rude to him about his church restoration.'

'But then you've found he has something more attractive to offer you. So now it's "James" and "Suzie". "*Dear Suzie, I so much enjoyed our meeting.*"' He half turned away from her, reading from the screen in a clipped, contemptuous voice. *"'I'll keep my eyes open, and when I turn something up, I'll be in touch, and we'll find another afternoon for you to come over. Yours, James.'"*

Her throat tightened.

James had emailed her yesterday evening, and she had been so busy writing up her visit that she hadn't thought to check. She could have deleted the message . . . But no, why should she have?

'What's wrong? It's perfectly innocent. He means exactly what he says. We met there because he wanted to show me Wayland Farm. And we found something really exciting. I was going to tell you, but you've been shut up here in the study half the evening.'

'Trying to come to terms with this.'

'What is there to come to terms with? You're being ridiculous. He's just a nice young rector with a passion for local history. We've got things in common.'

'Evidently. Not like me. I can't appreciate what you two get so carried away about, can I? That's why you didn't want to wait for a Saturday when I could drive you there. I'd just have been in the way.'

'You're twisting everything. He took me to the farm and there was this lovely old couple, like something out of another century. And they invited me in and gave us tea, and there was this bench in the sitting room with a sixteenth-century carving and the initials GL. And we thought it might . . .'

'Thank you; you can spare me the genealogical details.'

He turned back to the computer, closed James's email and deleted it. He switched off. Suzie stared at the blank screen with a painful sense of loss. If only she had opened it herself. She could have sat at this desk, recalling yesterday's visit, warmed by James's renewed invitation, knowing that it need not be the last time she would see him.

She was suddenly aware that Nick was on his feet. He was close in front of her, still stiff with indignation. She wrenched her mind back from James to her husband.

'I'm sorry,' she stammered. 'I wasn't trying to hide anything. You didn't give me a chance to tell you. And there was something else I wanted to say. The reason I came into the study was to tell you I was sorry.' Her voice was becoming unsteady.

Tears were threatening to fall. She had so wanted to do this differently. By now, she should have been nestled in those bare arms. 'For . . . for being ridiculous about Tom. You were right. It was stupid of me get upset about Thomas Loosemore. The fact that he killed someone has nothing whatsoever to do with Tom.'

His eyes narrowed. Too late, Suzie wished she could call the words back.

'You're not still on about that? You can't get it out of your mind even now, can you?'

'I've just *said*, I only brought it up because I'm sorry.'

'It's a bit late for apologies.'

He walked past her out of the room. Suzie stood there, letting the tears flow now. She subsided into the desk chair. The cloth was still warm from Nick's body. She felt a renewed sense of desolation.

She rubbed the tears away. With sudden defiance, her finger found the ON button. The screen went through its boot-up dance until it steadied on the desktop screen with its moorland photograph. She clicked the email icon, then Deleted Items.

James Milton. Subject: Your visit.

Relief washed over her as she saw his message restored to the screen. She could read it for herself in its entirety.

She lingered over the words, '*Dear Suzie, I so much enjoyed our meeting.*'

A hiccup shook her chest. It was too painful to think about Nick and what she should do now.

Instead, she soothed herself with a different image. A younger man with hair like blond flames. Blue eyes, lighter than Nick's, boyishly enthusiastic about his parish's history. The two of them lingering at the farm gate in the sunshine. A meeting of minds.

She switched on the printer. It clattered out a copy of James's email. She folded it carefully and slid it into the pocket of her linen dress.

FIFTEEN

A coldness settled between them, from which there seemed no way back. They did not speak that night, lying stiffly on the further edges of the bed. There was no kiss as Nick left for work next morning.

Later that day, Suzie was in the bedroom, sorting clothes for the washing machine. She lifted the green linen dress from the back of a chair. Something stiff rustled in the pocket as she held it up for inspection. Her heart contracted. James's email.

She took it out and smoothed it open. *Dear Suzie, I so much enjoyed our meeting . . . I'll keep in touch, and we'll find another afternoon for you to come over . . .*

The words, which had caused Nick such pain, sang to her. Odd, how her perceptions had changed. Just recently the name of Southcombe had become a door she no longer wanted to open, because of the unpleasant thoughts that had come tumbling out from an earlier century into hers. Now, shaping her tongue around it brought a glow which yesterday's hurtful misunderstanding could not quite banish. James Milton had walked with her to Wayland Farm, lingered with her afterwards at the gate. The time he had given her was surely over and above the call of pastoral duty. He must have wanted to spend the afternoon with her, to have someone share his enthusiasm. He was saying now he wanted it to go on. This was not just for her; his email told her she was important to him.

So what should she do now? There was Nick. Poor, jealous, misguided Nick. She sat on the edge of the bed, fingering the printout. She longed to email James back, but how could she explain to him that he mustn't reply? If there was another email, the pointless row with Nick would start all over again. It would be too embarrassing to explain this to James.

Yet . . . Her eyes fell to his printed signature. *Yours, James.* Straightforward, innocent, yet enough to carry the warmth of a sunny Saturday afternoon in the Twisted Oak valley. This was too valuable a friendship to let drop because Nick was

being unreasonable. At the very least, James sounded as though
he might be able to find more information for her. It would
be churlish to turn down his offer.

What about his side? Did James have a wife, back at the
rectory where he hadn't invited her?

What should it matter? He looked to be still in his twenties;
she was in her forties, almost old enough to be his mother.
They were just fellow enthusiasts sharing their discoveries.
Nothing more.

So what now? Should she phone him? On what excuse?
She could hardly suggest another meeting just yet.

She sighed, then started. Looking down, she saw that her
mind had not been as calm and rational as she had thought.
Her fingers had been kneading the paper on her lap, crushing
it. She flattened it out, trying to restore the white sheet to its
pristine smoothness, but the damage was done. It was dirtied,
wrinkled with innumerable creases.

What was she to do with it, anyway? Would it be prudent
to put it through the shredder and consign the debris to the
recycling box? She found herself reluctant to let go of it.
Nick's reaction had not quite succeeded in tarnishing her
memory of that golden day. Besides, she told herself practic-
ally, she might need James's email address in the future,
if she could only find a secure way to communicate with
him.

She stood up, and hesitated. Was it safe to keep it in one
of her dressing-table drawers, hidden under handkerchiefs or
underwear? The thought made her blush. That was the sort
of thing girls did with letters from their sweethearts. James
was not like that. A more appropriate place would be in her
family history files. Just another resource, a contact address
that might come in useful.

Downstairs in the study, she took down the appropriate
folder. There were printed leaflets about the Record Office,
the Local Studies Library and the Mormons' family research
centre, and a handwritten list of recommended websites that
she was constantly adding to. She inserted James's email on
top and was about to put the file back on the shelf when she
stopped. On second thoughts, it was perhaps best for it not
to be uppermost, in case Nick saw the clear plastic folder.
She tucked it in among the rest of the papers.

She replaced the file. It was just a name and address, but it felt comforting to know that it was there.

The doorbell rang at four o'clock in the afternoon. Suzie hurried down the hall to answer it. Two dark heads loomed through the frosted glass.

She opened the door to find an older man in a grey suit on the doorstep, with a taller, younger man behind him in sports jacket and fawn trousers. Shock jolted through her body when they produced police identity cards. In her confusion, she missed their names, seeing instead only the scar on the older man's chin. His smile was perfunctory. This was clearly not an occasion for pleasantries.

'Mrs Fewings? Is your son Tom in?'

'No. He should be on his way back from school. What do you want him for?'

'I think we'll wait till we see Tom, if you don't mind, madam.'

Her indignation was rising. 'You've interviewed him twice already. He can't tell you anything more. He had nothing to do with it.'

'Would it be all right if we come in and wait, madam?'

She wanted to say, 'No, sit in your own car, outside in the street.' But she could not. His manner carried a determined authority. She found she could not resist. The younger officer threw a brief smile at her, but she could not return it.

She showed them into the sitting room and stood at the window, staring out. At least they had not come in a marked police car, conspicuously white, with its bands of yellow and blue. The neighbours would have no reason to talk. She understood why Tom had been so angry about the police who had come to his school to take him to the station in a car like that.

Today he would walk unsuspecting up the road.

Millie arrived first. Two weeks had passed since Julie's body had been found. It had proved impossible for parents to go on escorting their teenage daughters everywhere. Millie had strict instructions to stay with her friends until the last turning into her own road, to say nothing to strangers, not to be inhibited about screaming if anything suspicious happened to her.

She was here now. Suzie saw her halt by the gate, looking curiously at the grey car. Then she came on. As she walked up the drive, she turned her pale, thin face to look back to stare at it again.

Suzie met her in the hall. 'The police are here,' she murmured.

'Why?' Low-voiced, large-eyed.

'I don't know. They won't tell me anything until Tom comes.'

'Does Dad know?'

A little gasp. 'I should have thought of that.' She glanced back at the sitting-room door, which she had closed behind her. 'I'll do it now.'

She went to the study and shut that door, too, for extra security. As her hand went to the phone, she had another thought. Should she ring Tom's mobile to warn him? Her arm hovered, outstretched. Then she seized the receiver and dialled Nick's number.

It was a relief to hear his voice answer. 'Nick,' she said, low and urgent, 'the police are back. Detectives this time. They want to talk to Tom, but they won't say why.'

A moment's silence. Then, 'I'll be home straight away. If they try to take him to the station, stall them until I come.'

'I could go with him . . .'

The line went dead.

She was shaking now. Was it too late to phone Tom?

The sound of the front door opening answered her question. She had missed that moment when he walked up the street and saw the car parked in front of his house.

She ran to hug him. He looked pale, as if he already guessed the reason for it.

'I don't know what it's about,' she whispered, 'but there are two detectives in the sitting room.'

Tom straightened his back. He checked his appearance in the hall mirror, straightened his collar, ran a hand over his unruly hair. Then he smiled at her, rather thinly.

'Right. Lead on.'

Both policemen got to their feet as Tom entered.

'Thomas Fewings?' The older man introduced himself and his colleague; they showed their identity cards again. 'I must ask you to accompany us to Park Green police station, to answer a few questions. You are not under arrest, but we have reason to believe you can assist us with our enquiries.'

'I already have. What's new?' Tom's voice gave nothing

away. He was not exactly casual, but nor did he sound intimidated.

'That can wait for the interview room, sir.'

So there is new information, Suzie thought, her heart thudding. What evidence could they possibly have found that might implicate Tom, after all this time? They had checked his DNA. They must know that it wasn't he who had caused Julie's death, mustn't they?

How had she died? The details had still not been made public.

Her eyes went to the window, willing Nick to appear. To play for time, she found herself gabbling wildly. 'You know Tom wasn't involved. You've done laboratory tests, haven't you? It couldn't be him.'

'Mum!'

'Look, my husband will be home any moment. He'll tell you.'

Mercifully, the car was here now, its green roof sliding past above the hedge top. Nick did not turn into the drive, but stopped behind the police car.

She felt a surge of relief, watching him stride swiftly up the path. His face was grave, his eyes dark. She gave him a frightened look as he entered the room. Nick stood wordlessly looking at the plain-clothes officers.

'Mr Fewings?' The same polite introductions. The same explanation, which was no explanation at all.

'May I come with him? . . . Yes, I know I can't sit in on the interview, but I could bring him home.'

'You can follow in your own car, if you wish, sir. If he wants you to.'

Tom nodded. 'Thanks, Dad.'

I should have offered, Suzie thought. *Tom might need me.*

'Could I come too?' she ventured.

'Better not,' Nick said. 'Stay here with Millie.'

They were gone. The house was resoundingly empty.

Suzie and Millie were both on their feet as soon as they heard the car. The front door opened, then slammed again. They exchanged alarmed glances.

'Get up to your room and stay there,' they heard Nick order.

No answer from Tom. Just the sound of his feet on the stairs.

Suzie moved towards the door from the kitchen into the hall. Nick met her, head on. He halted, as though he had not expected to see her there. Then he recovered himself, walked past her and ran water into the kettle.

'I'll do that,' Suzie said timidly. 'Sit down.'

He ignored her.

Millie stared at him. 'What happened? Why have you sent Tom to his room?'

He did not look at either of them. He was tense, almost shaking.

Suzie made him a cup of strong black coffee and put it down in front of him. He did not thank her, but he subsided into a chair, put his hands around the mug and sat nursing it, his eyes downcast.

'Would you like some whisky?'

No answer to that, either.

At last he said, forcing the words out, 'Millie, would you mind? I need to talk to your mother.'

Millie gave Suzie a scared look, but tried to stand her ground. 'That's not fair. He's my brother. If he's in trouble, I need to know. I'll have to face my mates at school tomorrow.'

Nick half rose from his seat. 'Get out!'

He never shouted at the children. Millie's normally pale face whitened further. She left the room. Suzie heard her running up the stairs. She would probably collapse on her bed in tears. Or burst into Tom's room and challenge him herself.

Suzie stood torn. There were all three of her family in the house, and all needing comfort. She did not know whose need was greatest. Probably Tom, but Nick, at least, had information.

She wanted to put her arms round his rigid shoulders, but did not dare. She sat down opposite him. 'All right, tell me, then. What happened?'

Nick seemed to have to pull the words out of some deep and painful place inside him. 'Tom lied to us. He said he hadn't seen Julie Samuel since that night at the club two weeks before she died. Apparently the police found his DNA on her clothing, and traces of fabric they think are from his own clothes. They discounted it, because they thought he'd been upfront with them about dating her. But it turns out he wasn't. They've discovered that the jacket she was wearing was one she'd only bought three days before she was murdered.'

Suzie heard her own gasp slice through the air. 'So Tom . . .'

'Was with her at least ten days after he told the police he'd broken it off. Not more than three days before . . . He swears it was two days, but how can we be sure? . . . And very close to her. Not a casual encounter.'

'What does that mean? They haven't arrested him. You brought him home.'

'Possibly nothing. Except that he's deceived us, and the police.'

'And Julie's parents.'

Nick looked up, off guard. 'I didn't think of that.'

'But why? If he didn't do it. What had he to hide?'

'I gather that's what the police wanted to know. What *I* want to know. He told me the bare facts, but he wouldn't discuss it on the way home.'

'He must have been scared the first time they questioned him. He's still only a boy, for heaven's sake. It must have been horrible for him to realize that he might be a murder suspect. He probably didn't think they'd find out.'

'He's going to need to think a lot harder now.'

'I'd better go to him.'

Nick started to say something. She thought he was going to stop her. Then he closed his mouth, leaving the words unsaid.

She mounted the stairs slowly, unsure what to say. She tapped on Tom's door. No answer. She opened it.

Tom was lying on his bed. She saw the same rigidity with which Nick was sitting in the kitchen, the same drawn, angry face. They were so like each other in appearance, and yet . . . their physical similarity belied the difference in their personalities. Nick and Tom were separate people. They did not act in the same way.

Suzie sat down on the edge of the bed. She stroked his arm gently and felt it quiver.

'You've got yourself into a mess, haven't you, love?'

'I didn't mean to lie.' His voice was muffled. 'It just came out. And when I'd said it, I couldn't go back on it, could I?'

'But it's out now. And it doesn't make any real difference, does it? Whether you were with her two weeks before she died, or two days, it's still the same. You didn't kill her. Nobody can think you did.'

'Can't they?'

'Of course not. Your DNA was on her clothes. But not on her . . .' She broke off delicately. Then a sudden terrible thought hit her. 'You didn't lie about that, too, did you? You and Julie?'

'Not . . . quite. I didn't have sex with her, if that's what you mean. Not properly. We only . . .'

'Only what?'

'Well, you know . . . "petted", I'd suppose you'd call it.'

'So they might have found . . .'

'I don't know. Can they tell the difference between fingers and . . . the other?'

'If he . . .' They were both struggling to avoid the language of sordid reality. 'If there was . . . fluid, yes, I'm sure they'd be able to tell. And if it wasn't yours . . .'

'No, Mum, honestly.'

It would have been better, she thought, *if you had been honest with us before.*

She leaned over and hugged him. 'This is awful for you, love, but it doesn't change the really important thing. And you must see the police are bound to be angry with you for deceiving them. Your dad is angry.'

'Aren't you?'

'Hurt, but not angry. We all do things we'd rather not talk about. Not necessarily because they're bad, but because they're . . . personal. Maybe too precious to want to tell other people.'

A young rector with a bicycle, chatting by a farm gate.

'I . . .' Tom's voice was shaken by a sob. 'I swore I wasn't going to get really involved with any girl before I left school. But . . . Julie . . .'

'You called her a bitch.'

'When?' He sounded genuinely indignant. 'Oh, that. Yes, well, I never thought she'd go and boast about me to her mates. I thought I was special for her.'

'She doesn't seem to have boasted about your last meeting. It *was* the last, wasn't it?'

'Down by the canal, that Sunday night. Yes.'

'She couldn't have told her friends about that, or they'd have reported it to the police.'

Tom sat up. Something had cleared from his face. His tight features softened almost into a smile. 'You're right. Bless you, Mum! She didn't, did she? Whatever she said when I broke up with her after we'd been clubbing, it wasn't what she thought when we got together again.' His face changed tragically. 'What the hell! She's dead, isn't she? What difference does it make now what she felt about me?'

He buried his face in his arms. She sat, stroking his hair.

His voice was muffled. 'How much of this are you going to tell Dad?'

'How much does he already know?'

'I had to tell him the evidence they'd got on me. Where I was. Where *we* were. When. Not why. Not how we felt about each other.'

'I think he ought to know.'

'I suppose you think the police ought to know. Nothing's private.'

'Not after a murder. I'm afraid not.'

'Nobody's going to believe me now, anyway.'

Something was troubling her. 'You said you met on the canal path.'

He lifted his head again. His eyes were ravaged. 'Now can you see why I didn't want to tell anyone? Yes, why not? It's somewhere you can be more or less private. You can talk, without bumping into too many of your mates. And there are places . . .'

'So why was she there two days later, alone?'

'How do I know? I didn't arrange to meet her there, if that's what you think.'

'I didn't say that.'

'No, but people are going to think it.'

'Let them. You know the truth.' She sat in silence for a while. 'Maybe she wanted to go back. You know, relive what happened between you two.'

Or maybe Julie Samuel realized the canal would be a good place for her to meet someone else, Suzie thought, but did not say.

Nick was standing staring morosely out over the garden. The first flush of summer roses was beginning to fade and drop. Suzie gathered up her courage. She made herself go to him and put her arms around him from behind. She felt his start, and then the stiffness of his body.

'Don't be too hard on him,' she murmured into his neck. 'He was scared. He still is.'

'He'd have had a lot less need to be scared if he'd told them the truth. Told *us* the truth.'

'He has now.'

'When he was found out.'

'But it doesn't change anything. He had nothing to do with Julie's death. The police must have evidence about the man who did it. They'll know it wasn't Tom.'

'You're very sure of that, all of a sudden.'

Her turn to go rigid. Her arms dropped from him. 'Aren't you?'

'I don't know what to think any more. I thought I had an open, loving relationship with my son, my wife. Now I don't know what I believe.'

'You can't think . . . For one thing, it's crazy to still think there was anything wrong in me pursuing the family history trail on my own. But Tom . . .'

'You were having trouble about him yourself, because of some bloodthirsty ancestor of yours.'

'You're right. It was stupid. But that's over now. It's got nothing to do with Tom. It never should have. I don't even know that Thomas Loosemore *was* my direct ancestor. He could be some sort of cousin.'

'But you still let yourself think it. Well, I've had a shock today, and it's made me think the unthinkable. My son's not what I thought he was. The relationship between us isn't what I thought it was. What sort of father does that make me?'

'The best. Tom's a good and loving boy. If you could have heard him upstairs . . .'

'He told you all about it, did he? He wouldn't tell me.'

She knew a little flash of triumph, and immediately felt guilty. So, she was right. What was between her and Tom *was* special.

'It was very private, Nick. He and Julie . . . He really loved her.'

'And I suppose no one has ever killed the person they love?'

'Nick! Stop it!'

He pulled away from her and wrenched open the French windows.

'I don't know what's true any more.'

SIXTEEN

For days they waited, skating around each other, as though too close an encounter might shatter one of them. Nick took Tom out for driving practice some evenings. The relationship between them remained stiff, not friendly. Neither Suzie nor Nick could find the comfort they needed from each other.

The house was too quiet. Dave, Suzie was troubled to realize, had not been near them since Julie's body had been found.

Nothing happened. The police did not contact Tom again. Nick said nothing more about his suspicions. Julie's body was released for burial.

Millie came half running up the path from school one day. Her face was alight with news. It was enthusiasm untypical of a laid-back thirteen-year-old.

'Her funeral's on Friday. They're going to have a big service in the cathedral, so lots of the school can go.'

'At last. I've been feeling for her poor parents, not being able to put closure to it with a funeral service.'

Suzie pictured hundreds of home-going pupils like Millie spilling out across the city. A question mark shaped itself out of the numbness in her mind. 'You couldn't fit the whole school in, not even in the cathedral. How will they decide who goes?'

What she meant was, will the Sixth Form be there? Will Tom go? She shot an anxious look at him, eating cereal on the patio. The French windows were open, but he gave no sign that he had heard.

'Dunno. There'll be all Julie's class, of course. Probably lots of Year Eleven, because they knew her best. Anita was saying they might, like, have a ballot for the rest of us if we want to go, or maybe they'll take a few from each class.'

'Do you want to go? I mean, would you, if you could?'

'You bet. They're bound to have the TV cameras there. They always do, don't they? Like, they show her friends and family telling stuff about her, or reading poems they've written. And the police go along, too, don't they, to see if the murderer shows up? I've seen that loads of time on the telly, like in murder films and stuff. Hey, that'd be really spooky, wouldn't it? Imagine looking round and seeing this weird guy standing behind you, who, like, didn't fit in with everyone else. He'd be staring at her coffin with funny eyes, so it gave you the heebie-jeebies. And you'd know it was him. Yuk!'

'Whoever he is, he probably won't look like that at all. He's more likely to be a perfectly normal-looking man you wouldn't suspect. That's what's so dangerous.'

'But, hey, wouldn't it be great if he was there, and I was the one who spotted him?'

'Shut up,' came Tom's voice from the patio. 'Ghouls. Just because her death was in the papers.'

'Is that supposed to mean me?' Millie bridled.

'Yes.'

'Fine! So we're not supposed to feel sorry for her. How would you like it if your life had been snuffed at sixteen, and nobody cared? All the things she's never going to do. Are we just supposed to shrug our shoulders and carry on as if nothing had happened? Some of us have got feelings.'

Tom got up and walked swiftly through the kitchen.

'That wasn't exactly tactful,' Suzie said.

'Well, he was getting at me.'

Loud music was coming from Tom's bedroom. Suzie followed it. She stood for a few moments on the landing, uncertain. Then she knocked on his door.

'Come.'

He was lying on his back, hands behind his head. He gave Suzie a small, weary smile.

'I'm not saying sorry to her. She's a bloodthirsty little vampire.'

'I think she should be saying sorry to *you*.'

He shrugged. 'It's water under the bridge now. Julie's gone. It's no good thinking about what might have been.'

Suzie swivelled his desk chair round and sat down. 'Stop pretending to be the hard nut. You're allowed to grieve, too.'

'That's not what it feels like, as long as people are thinking I might have done it. Even Dave's hardly talking to me.'

Does he suspect that I was beginning to fear this myself?

Suzie thought. *Does he know that even Nick was having doubts when he found you'd lied? Can he read it in our faces? Perhaps I should go.*

Instead, she said, 'That's over now. We've always known the police had DNA evidence that would prove it was someone else. They'll catch him. It was only because you were stupid enough to tell lies to them that the police came down on you. You were never really in the frame.'

'You could have fooled me when they got me down at the station.'

'Well, it will soon be all dead and buried.' She saw him wince. 'Sorry, Tom! What I mean is, we can start to pick up the pieces of our lives again. It was terrible, but it happened. We have to move on.'

'We?'

She flushed. 'We're your parents. Anything that happens to you and Millie affects us, too.'

He gave her a slow grin. 'Thanks, Mum.'

She wasn't sure if he was mocking her. She stood up.

'You're sure you're all right? Millie didn't upset you?'

'I should be Millie-proof by now.'

Suzie hesitated, then went across and kissed him. 'Let's close the book on it. You'll be starting to apply to universities next term. Concentrate on the future.'

Now his grin *was* mocking. 'That's rich, coming from you.'

She waited for Tom to say something more about the funeral. But on Thursday he ate with them as though this was just a normal evening. Looking sideways at him, she decided the trauma was fading. His face had lost that shocked look. Watching him lifting forkfuls of her chicken korma, she thought he was a little quieter, the usually mobile features a little less ready to break into that heart-stopping smile. Yet he did smile occasionally, if only briefly.

Soon now, she reassured herself, *it will be over. Julie will be buried. Closure for her family, and for us.*

No, it can't be closed until they find who did it.

That's not my problem; it's the police's. Except that I have to keep Millie safe until they find him.

It was not Millie she was looking at. Suddenly, staring at her handsome son, it struck her how ludicrous all this was.

The poor girl had fallen victim to the worst sort of criminal. Her death had all the hallmarks of stranger crime: the teenage girl, the lonely path, the rural spot where her body was found.

She looked at Tom with a sudden rush of love that made her want to jump up from the table and hug him.

He looked up and caught her eyes.

'Are you feeling all right, Mum? You look as if you're about to cry.'

Her face relaxed into a slow, but radiant smile. 'Yes, of course I'm all right. I was just thinking how lucky I am to have you. Both of you.' She shot an apologetic glance at Millie on the other side of the table. 'It must be so terrible for the Samuels to have lost a daughter like that. It's the sort of thing you never get over.'

Tom looked down at his plate. 'They've told us we can go to her funeral if we want to. Tomorrow afternoon, in the cathedral.'

'Lucky pig!' Millie burst out. 'All my class want to go, but they're not going to let us.'

'Are you going, Tom?' Nick asked what Suzie had dared not.

'Yeah. I guess I might.'

On the day of the funeral, Suzie watched apprehensively as Tom came down to breakfast. Her heart turned over. He was so incredibly handsome, with that waving black hair, that increasingly craggy face. It was still a matter of wonder to her how she could have mothered such a son. Of course, Tom had more of Nick's genes than hers. She should have seen that any link with Thomas Loosemore was ridiculous. At one time, that would have saddened her, but not now.

'Morning.' Tom gave her that lazy smile.

'You're wearing your school blazer.'

He plucked at the dark blue sleeve, as if surprised to see it. Sixth formers did not have to wear uniform. The blazer had hung in his wardrobe for nearly a year. The sleeve he was holding was a little short, showing an unnecessary amount of clean white shirt cuff.

'Yes, well. Sort of respectful, don't you think? Denim didn't quite cut it.'

He had not, she noted, unearthed his blue and silver school

tie. The one he wore was black velvet. She did not remember seeing it before.

'You look very smart.'

'That was the idea.'

'Lucky beast,' Millie protested. 'I wish I could go.'

'Millie! It's not a trip to Alton Towers.'

'Better than double geography. And it would be something to boast about afterwards.'

Tom was not joining in. His hand hesitated over the cereal packets, as if he was unsure whether he wanted to eat anything. He poured himself a glass of orange juice, then cut a slice of toast in half and sat fiddling with it, tearing it into a heap of crumbs.

'Eat something,' she said, 'even it you don't feel like it.'

'Course I feel like it.' The smile was too bright, too forced. He emptied shredded wheat into a bowl, sloshed on milk, and began to eat, as though there was no problem.

If only I knew what was going on inside his head. She wanted to put her arms round him and cuddle him. If Millie had not been there, she might have done.

The hands of the clock swept them all on, out of the house. It was time for Suzie to be gathering her own things together, heading for the bus and her office.

She got off just short of the High Street. Across the road, the twin towers of the cathedral rose square above the rooftops. The funeral would be held there at two o'clock.

The notice on the charity shop door said CLOSED, but Margery and Janet were already there and the door was unlocked. She gave them a forced smile as she entered.

'Terrible, isn't it?' said Janet, looking across at the cathedral, as Suzie had done. 'That poor girl. I feel for the parents.' She must have been watching Suzie's movements, the turn of her head, the moment when she had paused to recollect. 'Are you going to the funeral? I'm sure the cathedral will be packed.'

'I shouldn't think so. It's all very sad, but I didn't have anything to do with her.'

'What about your children? They go to the same school as her, don't they?'

'The Sixth Form are going, so Tom is. Millie would like to, but her form hasn't been invited. She's quite cross about missing it. I'm afraid at her age, children can be a bit ghoulish. But Tom's older, more responsible.'

'He's a nice lad, your Tom.' Margery gave her warm, supportive smile. 'I'm sure he and his friends are all very sad about it.'

'Of course they are.'

Suzie escaped past them into her office. It was a relief to hang up her jacket, switch on the computer, check the email, and immerse herself in the morning routine. What was happening across the cathedral green had nothing to do with her and her family. She could put it out of her mind.

It was not so easy. When she stopped for coffee, the thoughts came crowding back. She made mugs for Margery and Janet and took them through to the shop. Normally, if they were not busy with customers, she would linger to chat. But she could not face the inquisitive stare of Janet's pinched face, the probing eyes that suggested there was more Suzie could tell them. The hints about a closeness between Tom and Julie.

It's over, she told herself. *And there never was anything to it. Once the police had interviewed Tom they dropped their enquiries. They haven't needed to speak to him since. He's in the clear. And of course, there was never any reason why he shouldn't be, except for one stupid lie because he was scared. Whatever Tom says, no one even suspects that he might have had anything to do with it.*

Except Janet. She's no better than Millie, wanting to work up some prurient excitement so that she can feel she's involved in a sensational case. I can just hear her gossiping. 'I work with his mother.' She's sick.

Suzie had not brought her own coffee into the shop. She made an excuse about pressure of work and retreated to the safety of the office. Yet the cramped, silent room gave too much space for her thoughts about Tom and Nick.

It was just one o'clock. As Suzie locked the office and came through the shop, Janet was also packing up to go home. A different volunteer would be arriving to help Margery in the afternoon. Suzie wished she had got away sooner.

Janet slipped on a cardigan and reached for her handbag. She turned a feline smile on Suzie. 'I'm going over to the cathedral, to see if I can get in. Are you coming?'

'No, thank you.'

'I thought . . . seeing that . . . Oh, well. Still, I've heard they're putting up loudspeakers, so that those that can't get in can listen to the service on the cathedral green. Better than nothing.'

'Yes.'

Janet hovered in the doorway, looking back as though reluctant to accept that Suzie was not coming with her. At last she shrugged and crossed the road, disappearing through the passage between the shops which led to the cathedral close.

'Don't take any notice of her,' said Margery. 'She leads a quiet life, since her husband died. She's always on the lookout for some colour to make it more interesting.'

'You're very kind about people,' Suzie smiled. 'I'd describe her a lot less charitably.'

'I did wonder if I might slip outside myself while we're quiet, and see if I could hear the service from across the road. But then I decided I can pray for the poor girl and her family just as well while I'm standing behind the counter.'

'I'll say goodbye, then. Thanks, Margery.'

'See you on Monday.'

Suzie stood on the pavement, while shoppers and office workers hurried past her, intent on lunch. The bus stop was not far away, on the other side of the road. A few steps would take her to it. She could be on the bus, on her way home, the distance lengthening between her and the cathedral. There was no reason for her to follow Janet through that opening on to the cathedral green. Of course, she was sorry for the Samuel family. Everyone was. But this funeral was nothing to do with her. She had told Janet she wasn't going.

A long gap in the traffic seemed like a sign. It made up her mind for her. Without knowing why, she stepped off the pavement, crossed the road and walked straight past her bus stop into the opening beyond.

In summer the cathedral close was always busy at lunchtime. It was a favourite place for city workers or tourists to eat their sandwiches, encouraging a population of hopeful pigeons. Picnickers usually occupied the seats and the low stone wall around the green. Already today the grassy space was fuller, although the service would not begin until two. People were moving towards a door in the west front, above which rows of carved saints and apostles stood sentinel.

Suzie assessed their multicoloured, everyday clothing. There was little of the subdued black, grey or purple of those who have been invited to a funeral. These were people like Janet, driven by curiosity about Julie's tragedy, by a sentimentality that wanted to become part of this mourning family.

Reticence stopped Suzie where the flagged path crossed the grass. She was not the sort of person who left flowers or teddy bears where a death had occurred. She would sympathize with the Samuels, but from a discreet distance. This was not her tragedy, her loss. She could not, like these others, pretend to their enormity of grief.

A knell sounded an accusation in her heart: *Never send to know for whom the bell tolls; it tolls for thee.* Perhaps those she was deriding as sentimental or sensationalist understood more of what it was to be human than she did.

Below her, people were now being turned away from the cathedral door. The unreserved seats must be full. Suzie tried to see if Janet was among the rejected, but the disappointed crowd was still thickening in front of the doors. Stewards were trying to usher them away, to clear a space of paving. All around Suzie the cathedral close was filling. People were talking quietly or waiting in respectful silence.

At half past one, solemn organ music began to spill from the loudspeakers. The slope of the grass allowed her to see over people's heads down to that cleared space where more conventionally attired mourners were beginning to arrive. Men in dark suits, women in black dresses or skirts, some wearing black hats.

A sudden pressure in the crowd behind her made her turn her head sideways. Her blood beat faster. A contingent of adolescents in blue and grey school uniform was making its way through the throng down the wide, shallow steps from the street to the west door. She had a glimpse of Tom, sober-faced in profile, then the back of his dark hair as he descended the steps below her. Behind him, she caught sight of Dave's ginger head, stooped uncomfortably between hunched shoulders. Tom was taller than most of the other boys.

Seventeen was hardly a boy. A young man.

The pupils halted outside the door, while a teacher conferred with the stewards. They filed inside.

The deep tenor bell began to toll.

There was a flash of gold chains as the mayor and mayoress were greeted at the door.

As the hour approached, a tremor ran through the crowd, an excited whisper. Suzie made herself look down at the black-clad family emerging from a funeral car. These must be the Samuels. How small and forlorn they looked in that empty space before the towering west front.

They, too, disappeared. There was only the coffin to come now.

A moan rippled across the green as the hearse drew up. With practised skill the undertakers slid the slight coffin on to a light wheeled trolley. A cross of pink and white blossoms lay on the blond wood. Not for Julie the small door where most of the congregation had entered. The great west doors, almost always kept shut, swung open to receive her. *Nothing in Julie Samuel's unremarkable life*, Suzie thought, *would have led her to expect such a funeral as this.*

The loudspeakers began a solemn hymn. 'Oh, God our help in ages past'. Here and there, a few people outside joined in uncertainly. Was Tom singing inside, his deep voice following the printed order of service?

Into her mind came something Millie had said. There were probably detectives in this crowd – inside the cathedral, too, studying who had been drawn to Julie's funeral. She looked around. The serious onlookers were mostly women, but there were a few men. Was the killer really somewhere here, perhaps within a few feet of her? Almost certainly she would not know, even if she were looking full at him. He would probably appear, as she had told Millie, ordinary, even respectable. Sexual perverts could be plausible, deceitful.

What if they never found him? They would have to live with this threat, always under the surface. Somewhere in the locality this dangerous man was living.

Always supposing that Julie had been killed deliberately, that it had not been a tragic accident.

Was it possible that it could have been done by a boy her own age?

No! She had sworn never to think that again.

There was a way out of this fear that was circling round her. One thing could make a huge difference: another murder.

She shuddered violently. What was she wishing? Surely not that? She thought of all the teenage girls inside the cathedral.

The press of people around her had become suddenly oppressive. She was feeling faint. She had been standing for a long time and she had had no lunch. She felt a desperate desire to be somewhere calm and quiet.

With murmured apologies, she worked her way through the ranks of mourners behind her on to the cobbled path that skirted the close. There were fewer people standing here. Some passers-by were threading their way through, intent on other business. Suzie joined them.

There was a narrow lane at the far corner which led to the red sandstone ruins of a priory, preserved amid the development of modern shops. To her relief, there was an empty seat within its cloister.

She could still hear the loudspeakers from the cathedral, somewhat muffled by the intervening buildings. Had she been wrong to scuttle away during the prayers? Should she have been silently joining her thoughts to theirs, while she waited for the next hymn?

The tone of the service seemed to have lightened. There was music now, but it was no longer solemnly ecclesiastical. This was the sort of song a teenager might have enjoyed. Suzie did not recognize it. Almost certainly Tom would. Then, more faintly, came a girl's voice speaking. One of Julie's friends, probably. Millie was right. She would be reading a poem, or telling about the girl she had known.

How well had Tom known her? If he were the one standing at the lectern in front of that congregation, and Julie's family, what could he say to them? What had happened on their first two dates? And that last one by the canal? What did a seventeen-year-old boy and a sixteen-year-old girl do together? What had Tom and Julie done? She had only guesses and fears; half-formed imaginings from Tom's few words. She would never know. She could not ask him again.

Julie's friends thought they knew. Suzie winced at the memory of Tom's initial anger: '*the bitch*'. She wished with all her heart he had not said that. But he had been hurt when he heard that Julie had lied about how far they had gone. Suzie had persuaded him to soften his judgement.

She had to believe Tom.

They were singing again in the cathedral. This time she recognized *Lord of the Dance*. She tried to picture the scene inside. The lofty Gothic interior, the robed clergy. The crowded congregation, girls in tears. A coffin before the altar with a pink-and-white floral cross, a family in black mourning. The funeral of an ordinary teenager, not a saint. Julie Samuel was made special only by the manner of her death.

The uncomfortable thought persisted: Julie's tragedy didn't mean that she had always told the truth.

Was it wrong to think like this, even while the girl's funeral was taking place?

A fragrance from a nearby baker's shop wafted through the ruined priory. She recalled that there had been a tempting array of pies and pasties in the window. She would sit here until the service was over. Then she would get something to eat. It might make her feel better.

SEVENTEEN

She found a place to eat her picnic lunch in the grounds of the castle, far from the crowd now spilling away from the cathedral green. As she ate, she studied the red sandstone of the ruined keep. The crumbling masonry took her back a thousand years, to a time remote from a twenty-first century 'unlawful killing', or indeed a seventeenth-century manslaughter.

Still, there had been, she thought wryly, plenty of bloodshed then too, as the Normans marched their conquering way across Anglo-Saxon England to set up this castle and subdue the city and countryside.

Their? Naturally she identified herself with the defeated English. It would probably be impossible to trace her ancestry further back than the beginning of the parish registers in 1538, but those unknown men and women of the soil must surely have been farming here long before that. For centuries before; millennia, even. She lifted her eyes to the distant hills and then dropped them to the flower bed in front of her, bright with petunias in the reddish soil. A shiver of awe ran through her to feel how deeply she was rooted in this earth.

Yet was she right to be sure that her origins were as entirely English as she was supposing? Shirley at the Family History Society had been telling them how she had just discovered that her agricultural labourer grandfather had been descended, through one line at least, from distant lords of the manor, with pedigrees going right back to the Norman Conquest. She had even found the village in Normandy from which her ancestor came to the Battle of Hastings.

It was not so implausible that some ancestor of 'GL', who had panelled the hall at Wayland Farm and had his initials carved on the bench-back, might have married the daughter of such a landed family. Did that mean that, for her, the 'them' of the Norman keep in front of her was, in some small degree, 'us'?

Did it matter? Would a tiny input of genes from a thousand years ago make any difference to who she was today?

It was, she decided, *knowing* her ancestry that made the difference. It made her see everything afresh, not with the eyes of a student acquiring factual information about social history, but with a personal interest in the lives of the people who had brought her into being. Her existence here in these gardens, eating this pasty, depended on the fact that *this* man, *that* woman, had come together under those historical circumstances, had survived this plague, that war, had raised their children in labouring poverty or yeoman comfort so that one child in particular had not died in infancy but had grown up to become her ancestor. Her life, and Tom's and Millie's, hung on an unthinkable succession of such slender threads.

She brushed the last crumbs from her skirt and at once eager sparrows hopped to dispose of them. She dropped her polystyrene coffee cup and the paper bag that had contained her pasty into the rubbish bin. The afternoon was half over. By now, the crowds would have dispersed from the cathedral close. She was reluctant to go back into those crowded city streets, to see the inevitable headlines of the evening papers: JULIE'S FUNERAL TODAY.

A refuge offered itself. On the other side of the gardens was the Local Studies Library. She could take herself into its enveloping peace for an hour or two. She would need to choose her objective carefully. She was certainly not yet ready to reopen the Thomas Loosemore investigation. She had, however, plenty of other lines to research. The 1901 census, for example. She had found her great-grandparents in the online index. They were somewhere in the vast civil parish of the county's biggest city, but she had been reluctant to pay the fee to access the details at home, and without knowing their address it would take her forever to trawl through the library's microfiches. But now she remembered the library offered free access on its computers to the searchable databases of Ancestry. This might be a good day to fit one more piece into the jigsaw.

Once she had made up her mind to this, she felt immediately happier. She had an objective which was safely removed from the more painful topics of the last few weeks. There would be the satisfaction of rounding out the picture of another generation. It would be like the old times, when family history was an enjoyable hobby, as well as her gift to her descendants.

She walked through the familiar doors, signed in and swung round to the enquiry desk, meaning to ask for access to one of the computers. Then she saw him.

James was leaning over one of the large tables, with a map spread out before him. Suzie felt the blood leave her face, and then flood back. She stood transfixed.

It was ridiculous. She was a middle-aged married woman. She should not be reacting like this to the sight of a blond young man, especially a parish priest.

What is he doing here in the city? Don't be silly. You know he's keen on local history. Of course he comes here for research, just as you do. He can't have known you'd be here too, this afternoon.

He hadn't seen her. She stood, irresolute. Should she go to the enquiry desk, book her computer, carry on as if nothing had happened? That was being foolish. If she saw a friend, any friend, in the library, wouldn't it be natural for her to say hello?

Did it matter that it was James? Why was she making such an issue of it, if their friendship was as innocent as she had protested to Nick that it was?

Before she could decide what to do, James raised his head and saw her. There was a moment's surprise, and then that illuminating smile.

It was the smile that drew her over. She walked slowly across the search room towards him, as confused as a teenage girl catching the eye of a desirable boy.

'Hello, what are you doing in town?' she said breathlessly.

'I had a meeting at the Bishop's Palace. It finished a bit earlier than I expected, so I couldn't resist the temptation to drop in here for an hour. There are a couple of survey maps I wanted to look up. You'll be interested in this one.'

She followed his pointing finger. A river wound its way across the map. She looked at the name penned alongside the buildings on one bank. Wayland.

'What a coincidence!' She lifted her face to him with a startled smile and met in his the laughing anticipation of her pleasure. 'That you should be looking at this just when I walked in.'

'Not such a coincidence when you come to think about it. I wasn't actually looking for Wayland when I got this map out.

What I'm really interested in at the moment is Nympton Rogus.' His hand moved over the map. It crossed the Twisted Oak river and the woods on its northern side, towards a village clustered round the church. 'Wayland Farm is in Southcombe parish, but as you saw for yourself, it's quite a walk from there up to Southcombe church. Did you catch your bus, by the way? I assumed you must have, since you didn't ring me for help.'

'Yes, thanks.'

'Good . . . Well, look at the map. As you can see here, although it's in a different parish, your family's farm is actually much closer to Nympton Rogus. That's why they happen to be on the same sheet. Since you're here, do you want to have a proper look at it? I love these old field names, don't you?'

She bent forward. The words were upside down. She moved around to his side of the table. They stood side by side while she studied the map, her heart beating from awareness of his closeness. She smelled the warmth of his body, and a surprisingly fragrant tang of aftershave.

James's finger was moving now over the fields around Wayland Farm. She tried to concentrate on the field names he was showing her.

'The Marsh. That tells a story, doesn't it? Honour's Piece. Who was Honour, do you think? Is she on your tree? Sawpit Bottom. The Scrimp. Wonderful, aren't they? There's probably a story behind most of them, if we only knew it.'

'Yes.' It was astonishingly difficult to think of anything sensible to say. Then, recovering herself a little, 'I ought to be writing these down, making a sketch of them.'

'No need. I'm having a photocopy made. I can do one of that section for you, if you like.'

'Yes, thank you. Yes, I would. Look, let me pay for it.'

She was gabbling on, afraid he would refuse to take any money, and she would feel she was imposing on him.

He waved her purse away. 'Wait till I've done it. I'll tell you what the damage is then. You're staying around?'

'Yes. I was going to try to find some of my folks on the 1901 census.'

'Don't let me hold you up, then. I expect you'll want to get back before your children come out of school.'

The cold slap of reality. He saw her as the older generation, a mother, not that equality she had felt standing close to him.

'It's all right. They'll be home before me, as it is. Tom was at the cathedral for the funeral. I don't suppose they bothered to go back to school afterwards.'

'Yes, I saw the crowd outside. Terrible business, wasn't it? I hope your children weren't too upset. You said Tom knew her, didn't you?' His smile had faded. He was watching her steadily.

'He'd dated her.'

Conscience nipped at her. Ought she to be home, in case Tom wanted someone to talk to after the funeral?

James's eyes narrowed with concern. 'Yes, I remember you telling me. That must have been awful for him. And for you, as his mother.'

'Yes, it was.'

How much did he remember of that conversation in the café, and how she had tangled an older story with Tom's? She felt a longing to tell him all that had happened since: Nick's anger with her, the police coming back, Tom's lying about that last date within days of Julie's death. Not here. She couldn't tell him in front of the library staff, the other researchers. She couldn't trust herself not to cry. Most of all, there was no way she could tell him what Nick had thought when he'd read James's email.

One question edged out, before she could stop it. 'How did you know my email address? I know I forgot to give it to you so that you could send that stuff about billeting soldiers. I mean . . . thanks for your message. I'm sorry I didn't answer it . . .' She was blushing, confused.

'Oh, simple detective work.' His grin was back. 'Do you remember you once posted a query about Joshua Loosemore of Southcombe to the county email group? I thought of replying to it, but I didn't have anything on the Loosemores then, and you hadn't mentioned Wayland Farm.'

'I didn't know the Loosemores lived there until I visited your church and saw the churchwardens' board.'

'Anyway, I didn't reply to you then, but I saved your email in case I ever turned up any information on them.'

'That's funny,' she said. 'So you already knew about me before we'd even met.'

'Yes,' he declaimed, the corners of his eyes crinkling. 'It was meant to be!'

He's joking, she told herself. *He doesn't mean that seriously.*

She escaped in confusion, back to the enquiry desk. Seated at the computer, she tried to compose her thoughts and concentrate on the search she had come to make. She accessed the Ancestry website and clicked on UK Censuses, 1901.

George and Lilian Loosemore, somewhere in that sprawling port. George born . . .? She had not brought her notes with her, of course. She had forgotten the date, but she could at least remember his place of birth. Rollewood. That should be enough information to pin him down. It was a small village. There would surely not be two George Loosemores of a suitable age, both born there and moving into the city.

She was right. There he was in the index, just as she had seen him on her computer at home. This time, all she had to do was click to see the image from the enumerator's book.

14 Cathlain Street. George Loosemore. Head of household. Age 32. Dockyard labourer. Place of birth, Rollewood.

Living with him were his wife Lilian, children George, Maud, Caroline and Edward. Edward was her grandfather. He had been one year old then. She read the names of his siblings again. What a shame the name Loyalty had dropped out of use. There was no Thomas, either.

Safe. There were no painful correspondences here. George Loosemore had moved from agricultural labouring in the countryside when farming was in decline. He had found himself a different labouring job in the expanding naval dockyard.

George Loosemore? There *was* a connection. Her great-grandfather would not have known that his initials, GL, had been carved on a bench-back by a prosperous farmer in Southcombe, miles from his own birthplace, when Queen Elizabeth I was on the throne.

When she raised her eyes she could see James at the photocopier, discussing with the librarian how to copy large maps. She was grateful that it was he who was grappling with the technology, and not her.

She was still making notes when he came over to where she was sitting at her computer. He held a black-and-white copy of the map in his hand.

'Sometimes the photocopies are clearer to read than the originals. Here you are. Twenty-four pence.'

It was less than she had expected. She got out her purse and paid him the coins, with thanks. She was glad he had not embarrassed her by making her indebted to him, even by so little.

'Well, I'd better be hitting the road,' he sighed. 'I shouldn't really be here. I've a mountain of stuff to do back in the parish, but since I was almost next door I couldn't resist the temptation.'

'Thanks again for the map. I'm so glad I ran into you.' A colossal understatement.

'Perhaps I'll see you again?' It was still there, that open invitation.

'I hope so, if you find anything else. Or I do. Only . . .' She stopped, embarrassed by her own situation now.

'Yes?'

'It's quite silly, but when Nick read your email, there was a bit of a misunderstanding. He thought . . .' Her face was burning. She could not go on. But she had to tell him. The danger that he might email her again about this further meeting was screaming out at her.

James stared at her for a moment. Then he threw his head back and roared with laughter. '"*Vicar seduces married woman.*"' She could see startled heads turning to listen.

'Oh, dear, I'm sorry!' He struggled to recover his composure. 'You know, we're always "vicars" in the tabloid press. They haven't heard of rectors. I trust you put his mind to rest.'

'I tried to.'

His eyes were more serious now. 'I really *am* sorry. I didn't think I might be making trouble for you. But I take it you'd rather I didn't email you again.'

She nodded.

'That's a shame. I thought Nick and I had had a really good conversation in the church. Look, if I find anything, I'll write by snail mail. I'll be sure to address the letter to both of you and I'll issue a formal invitation for you and Nick to visit Southcombe together. Do you think that would be OK?'

'I hope so. Yes, thank you.'

He grinned, more shyly, and took her hand. 'Don't worry

too much, Suzie. It's an occupational hazard for unmarried clergymen. *Ciao.*'

She watched his blond head disappear down the stairs.

So there was no wife at the rectory.

The house was quiet when she got back. Suzie busied herself dusting the hall, sorting through the junk mail in the porch, cleaning smudges from the mirror. It was something of a surprise to step back and see herself reflected in its new clarity, and not just as a blur beyond the marks she had been wiping from its surface. Brown hair falling to her shoulders below a tortoiseshell clip, lightly curling, not yet touched with grey. Large hazel eyes. High colour in her cheeks between finely carved bones. She smiled tentatively. Was this what James Milton saw? This still-attractive woman? Or just the researcher with her notebook, a mere repository for information?

She had been more than that to him. He did, at the very least, welcome her as a listener, someone genuinely interested in his own enthusiasm. She fingered the delicate ear peeping from her drawn back hair.

Nonsense. She stood back and straightened her shoulders. She was married to Nick. Happily married to a good, kind man . . . She caught her breath. They had not been so happy together recently. They were both under strain. That was it. Nick had hidden his fears about Tom better than she had, but they must have been there all the time.

It was over now. The police interviews, the funeral. That was all behind them. They could all get on with their lives again, as though it had never happened.

The woman in the mirror frowned at her. No, that wasn't possible. Tom's hurt was real and it would be lasting. Nick's suspicion, once spoken, could not be caught back. And she was having to learn to trust her own son all over again.

Her thoughts strayed back down the path she had forbidden herself.

How had the reality struck Thomas Loosemore, when the news of his old rector's death found its way down the hill from the village to Wayland Farm in the valley? What had his congregation thought as they sat in the old pews under their new Puritan minister? How had they looked at Thomas, knowing that it was his hands that had given the fatal push and sent Arthur Chambers tumbling downstairs to his death? Did they think that it could have been any one of them, in the aftermath of anger and hurt which lived on, even when the whirlwind of the Civil War had swept past them? Were they already doubting their own righteousness in the communal shock of the beheading of their anointed king? Was it a relief to the villagers to place the blame for one death, at least, on Thomas, and not themselves?

The telephone rang beside her, startling her.

'Mum?' Tom's voice sounded surprisingly cheerful. 'I'm round at Greg's place for a game of chess or three. Staying for supper. That OK?'

'Yes, of course.' Then the significance caught up with her. 'Did you say Greg's? Not Dave's?'

There was a short pause.

'Like I said, Dave's busy these days.'

'Still?'

'Apparently.' His tone was brusque now, covering pain.

Suzie tried to recall who Greg was. A tall, gangling lad with a loud laugh.

'I'm sorry. I liked Dave.'

'So did I.'

'I expect it will blow over. Anyway, thanks for ringing. When will you be home?' She wanted to say, 'Are you all right, after the funeral?' But she was afraid to voice her concern.

'Dunno. Ten?'

'Haven't you got homework to do?'

'We missed maths, because of the funeral. Bet she sets us a double dose on Monday.'

'All right, then. Don't be late.'

'It's Saturday tomorrow.'

She put the phone down. The silence echoed. What time was it now? Quarter to five.

A cold shock ran through her. Where was Millie?

She stared at the telephone, willing it to ring again.

Self-accusation was scrabbling at her mind now. She had come home from the library later than usual, still sparkling from her chance encounter with James. She had been almost singing as she sped up the drive, expecting to find the children home before her.

The house had been quiet. No school bags tossed on the hall floor. No dirty crockery in the kitchen. No music from the bedrooms.

Yet she had been glad, rather than worried. It had given her a few moments' peace to recover her composure, to switch herself into the more staid role of wife and mother. She had taken the photocopied map into the study and placed it in her Southcombe folder. Then she had changed her mind, taken it out again and spread it, instead, on the kitchen table. This time, she had resolved, there must be no secrecy, no revelation about their meeting left too late. She would tell Nick straight away that she had bumped into James in the library. She would show him the map of Wayland Farm, point out the evocative field names, discuss how the place had changed over a century and a half.

She had pushed aside the thought that Nick might not want to hear about that.

Then, unaccountably, she had gone back to the study and taken James's email from her resource folder. She had smoothed out the crumpled paper, read his brief words again, though she knew them by heart, then replaced it carefully between other papers. Silly, really. Nick had already seen it. But he had tried to delete it before she could read it.

She had made herself a cup of tea, and sat at the kitchen table, dreaming in front of the map. It had not occurred to her to wonder why no one else was home yet. Where Millie was.

The house seemed suddenly cold, though outside it was still another pleasant summer day. Suzie stared at the telephone on the hall window sill, willing it to ring. Then she moved decisively towards it and snatched up the receiver. Her hand hovered over the keypad, while her mind scrabbled frantically trying to remember Millie's mobile number. It was several panicked seconds before it occurred to her that it was programmed into the phone. She pressed M, OK, and heard the other phone ring. A sigh of relief. At least the battery was not dead. No one answered; the voice mail did not cut in. The mobile rang on, singing its jaunty tune over and over.

Slowly it dawned upon Suzie that she was hearing the sound, not just through the receiver, but also floating down the stairs.

She dropped her own phone and leaped up the steps two at a time. Millie's bedroom door was slightly ajar. She flung it open. Amid the jumble of discarded clothes, magazines, unwashed mugs on the floor, the small silvery mobile sat beside Millie's bed, carolling away. As she looked, it stopped. A black lead ran from it to the charger.

Wherever Millie was, whatever had happened to her, she had no phone.

Don't be silly, Suzie tried to tell herself. *Your generation grew up without mobile phones. We managed all right without being in constant contact with family and friends.*

But Millie could still have used somebody else's phone. Tom had rung from Greg's house. Millie could have phoned from wherever she was. If she *was* at a friend's house and not . . .

Oh, God. I have to tell Nick. She ran downstairs again.

From his office, Nick was calm, reasonable, almost his normal self. 'Look, it's not five yet. She's hardly an hour late. I expect one of her mates has invited her to go off and do something interesting and it didn't occur to the silly girl to ring you. She'll be home for supper, or she'll let you know when she remembers. She's a good kid.'

'But only a week ago, you were running her to school because we were afraid a psychopath was on the loose and I was fetching her home. I should have been there, but I stopped doing it. It's my fault.'

'Getting hysterical isn't going to help. We couldn't keep her wrapped up in cotton wool for ever. Other parents were doing just the same. I'll be on my way home in ten minutes, anyway.'

'Should I ring the police?'

'I don't imagine they'd take you seriously yet. If she's not home for supper, it'll be different.'

'But anything could happen between now and then. She could be lying somewhere bleeding to death.'

'Suzie! Get a grip on yourself.'

'Don't you care?'

'Of course I care. She's my daughter too.'

'But you don't seem worried.'

'I'm concerned. Of course I am. And I'll have something to say to her when she does get home, for being inconsiderate.

I'm just trying to keep my feet on the ground and not let my imagination run away with me. Look, I know as well as you do that there's a very small chance that something bad has happened to her, but it's far more likely that there's a more mundane explanation. A teenager too busy with her own affairs to think that other people will be worrying. Have you tried her friends' houses?'

'No. I didn't think . . .'

Suzie slammed down the phone and scrabbled through the directory. She tried three numbers. No result. At the fourth number, the response was rapid, eager. 'Is that you Tamara?'

'No, it's Suzie Fewings. Millie's mother.'

'Is Tamara with you?' Suzie heard the breathless hope in the other woman's voice.

'No, I'm afraid not. I was ringing to see if Millie was at your house.'

'She hasn't come home? Nor has Tamara.'

In the shock that followed, Suzie could not decide whether it made her fear worse to have another parent share her anxiety, or whether it was better to know that Millie might not be on her own.

'Nick says it's no good telling the police yet.'

'I already tried that. They weren't exactly unsympathetic. They did say they realized how we must be worried, after what happened to Julie Samuel. And to let us know if she still wasn't home in a couple of hours. Look, do you mind? I'm a bit desperate to keep the line open, in case Tamara rings.'

'Of course. I'm sorry.'

'Ring me back if you hear from Millie. And I'll let you know if I get any news.'

The line went dead. Suzie stood shaking. She put the receiver down.

Should she ring the police herself? Let them know there were now two girls missing? She didn't need Nick's permission. Her hand reached out, less surely than before, then stopped. Nick was right. The police wouldn't take her seriously yet. Especially now it looked as though the two girls had gone off together. Surely there was safety in numbers?

She looked at the clock. It seemed impossible, but it was still less than two hours since Millie should have been home.

Anything could have happened to her in an hour. How long had it taken Julie's killer to do what he did?

She was being ridiculous, melodramatic.

No, she was not. They had not yet caught the murderer. He was still walking the streets, watching young girls. Watching Millie.

Her legs would not support her. She subsided into the chair beside the mirror and stared into the cold terror facing her.

EIGHTEEN

Nick was home. Suzie knew from the fierceness with which he embraced her and from his strained face that he was far less calm and unconcerned than he had sounded on the phone. It was as though there had never been any coldness between them.

'Any news?'

She shook her head.

Like her, he hesitated in front of the telephone, tapping his fingernails on the window sill. Then he picked up the receiver and dialled. She listened anxiously, trying to gauge how seriously the police were taking Nick.

'What's Tamara's surname?' he mouthed.

She wrote it on the pad beside him.

He put down the receiver. A deep cleft in his forehead drew his dark eyebrows together. 'They're trying to play it down, but I think that was just for my benefit. "*If the two girls are together, sir, there's probably nothing to worry about.*" But they've put out an alert for their guys to keep their eyes open. If she's not back for supper, they'll consider starting a search.'

Supper? Suzie's dazed thoughts seemed to travel a great distance to another world where she chose recipes, prepared food, cooked meals. What had she been meaning to do for this evening? Her mind was blank.

'I expect there's something in the freezer.'

Nick looked at her curiously, not understanding the chain of jumbled thoughts between his statement and hers.

'I could do with a whisky, but I'd better keep a clear head.'

Suzie put the kettle on and poured them tea instead, but she stared at her own full mug and had no appetite for it. The thought of food was even worse.

I must make an effort, she told herself. *If Millie comes home, she'll want a meal.*

If. The little word was too dangerous, too conditional.

She opened the freezer and looked dully at the packets inside. Something on the second shelf triggered a memory.

Pizza. Hadn't Millie complained that Tom had come home late for a meal and been allowed to help himself to a pizza, while she had had to eat the ragout Suzie had cooked?

She got out the box and stroked away a film of frost. Pepperoni. Did Millie like that? She thought so. She laid it on the kitchen counter. There was nothing to do now but wait.

After a while, her slowly moving brain made another decision. She began to prepare a salad.

The front door opened at quarter past six. Millie tumbled into the hall, white-faced.

Suzie tore from the kitchen and Nick from the study. Millie hurled herself into Suzie's arms.

'Mum, Mum, there was a man. He was horrible.' She was shaking, heaving with sobs.

Suzie led her into the kitchen. Nick had the kettle on and was spooning sugar, which Millie hated, into a mug.

'It's all right, love.' Suzie was cradling her.

'Where on earth have you been? Tell us what happened,' Nick ordered.

Millie looked up, red-rimmed eyes huge in her scared face. 'Tamara and me were coming home from school. You know you said we weren't to walk on our own? Well, we'd got to the park when we saw this gang of girls from Year Ten in front of us, and one of them turned round and Tamara said, "Oh, my God, it's Becky Drew. She threatened to do me over at lunchtime. She hates my guts. Quick!" And she grabbed me by the arm and pulled me through the gates into the park.'

'Millie! You know we told you not to come home that way.'

'I know, I know. But Tamara was really scared. I'm sorry!'

'Couldn't you have waited out of sight, and then gone out on to the street again after they'd passed?' Nick asked.

'Tamara was afraid they'd come after her, so we ran. And we were about halfway across when this man stepped out of the bushes.'

'What man? What was he like?'

'That's what was so horrible, afterwards. He looked sort of . . . nice. Older than you, Dad, with a tweed jacket and glasses. He didn't look like a dirty old flasher, or anything. And he said, "Steady on. What seems to be the problem?"'

Sort of friendly, like. And Tamara said, "There were some girls chasing us."'

'But they weren't, were they?'

'No, but we had to explain why we were running, or it would have looked daft.'

'And then?'

'He said, "I'm an off-duty policeman. I'll see you young ladies across the park, if you like.'

'You didn't let him, did you?'

'No, of course not. Well, we tried to say we were OK now, and we didn't need him. But when we started walking fast towards the other gate, he came with us.'

'Was anyone else about?'

'No, and we'd just got to that bit where the path goes through that shrubbery thing by the pond, so we couldn't see very far. And however fast we walked, he went faster too, and he kept, like, talking to us from behind all the time, trying to sound nice and friendly. But we didn't believe him now. And then I looked at Tamara and she looked at me, and we started to run again. Only then Tamara tripped and she came down really hard and twisted her ankle, and before she could get up he was kneeling down over her, and trying to make out like he was really concerned. And he started feeling her leg.'

'Didn't you scream for help? I told you to.'

'No. Mum, I was really petrified. I couldn't think straight. And then this man said he'd get his car and take her home. And he went off in a hurry. And as soon as he'd gone, Tamara said, "Have you got your phone, because mine ran out at lunchtime." And I felt in my bag, and I couldn't find it, and then I remembered I'd put it on charge last night and I forgot to unplug it this morning. So then I said to Tamara, "Look, we've got to get out of here before he comes back." And I got her up and put her arm round my shoulder, and we sort of hobbled along, but we were frightened he'd come back with his car before we got out of the wood, so we turned down this side path and looked for somewhere we could hide.'

'Millie!'

'You weren't *there*, Mum. It seemed like the best thing to do. And we found this big tree, with a sort of hole at the roots, and we got in there. And then I thought I heard a car. And I knew it must be him, because people aren't supposed to drive across the park. And then the engine stopped and we could hear him calling for us. And it was awful, because he sounded, like, really concerned. I thought, what if he really is a policeman?'

'You didn't go out to him, did you?'

'No. We just sort of crouched there, and hoped he wouldn't find us. And we could hear him crashing about in the bushes, getting closer. Only then, someone else must have come along, and there was some sort of argument about the car.'

'Didn't you go out and tell the other person?'

'Dad, I didn't want to see that man ever again. And we'd have had to give our names and stuff to the other one, and then the horrible one would know who we were, and where we lived and everything. And what if the other man believed he *was* a policeman and let him take Tamara in his car? You don't know how scary it is when someone *looks* nice and talks nice, but you know they're not like that inside, because who's going to believe you, when you're only thirteen?' She started to cry again.

'There, there,' Suzie hushed, rocking her.

'We ought to get on to the police, right away,' Nick said. 'They've got to catch him.'

The telephone rang. For a moment, they all looked at each other, startled. Then Nick went to answer it.

'That was Tamara's mother, wanting to know if Millie got home all right.'

'You went to Tamara's house?'

'We waited a long time, because we were afraid he'd still be looking for us. And then Tamara could only walk really slowly. I wanted to go and get help, but she wouldn't let me leave her on her own. So by the time we got out of the park . . .'

'Didn't you ask someone to give Tamara a lift home . . .? No, I'm sorry, that was silly.'

'Of course we didn't, Mum. What do you think? So it was a really long time before I got Tamara home. And her mother was in quite a state.'

'You should have phoned.'

'I know, but I wasn't thinking straight. I just wanted to be *home*.' And she burst into tears again.

'Tamara's mother's rung the police,' Nick said. 'They'll be coming round here, too.'

'Did you get the number of his car? Could you describe it?'

It was strange to see another policewoman, a plain-clothes detective constable this time, in the same armchair, questioning Millie, not Tom. This one was sympathetic, but insistent.

'We never saw it. I told you, we were hiding under the tree.'

'So you didn't see the other man who spoke to him about it?'

'No. Sorry.'

Millie described again the man who had stepped out of the bushes as well as she could. Another constable made notes.

About 50 or 60 years old. Medium height, balding, with short grey hair. But his moustache had a touch of ginger about it, unless it was a nicotine stain. His glasses, Millie thought, were tortoiseshell.

'Or were they orangey? It's really hard to remember. I didn't want to look at him. We were so scared.'

He had been quite smartly dressed. A sort of yellowy-green tweed jacket. She couldn't remember the colour of his trousers, or his shoes.

'A bit posh, from the way he spoke. I thought, if he was a policeman, he wouldn't be just a bobby on the beat . . . Sorry . . . More like an army officer or something.'

'What makes you say that?'

'Dunno. Just the way he held himself. Sort of, like, straight in the back.'

'Thank you. That's very helpful.'

After that, Nick and Suzie went with her to the police station, where Millie helped them put together an Identikit picture of the man. Tamara was there too, her ankle bandaged. The girls exchanged scared, silent looks.

When it was over, Millie went to bed early, with hot chocolate and her winter pyjamas, though her shivering had nothing to do with the temperature of the evening. Suzie sat with her until she fell asleep.

She came down to the conservatory and slipped on to the sofa beside Nick.

'Is she all right?'

'No, I don't think she is. She's not even boasting about what a story she'll have to tell her friends tomorrow. I don't suppose she'll ever really forget it.'

'Thank God it wasn't worse. If I could find the pervert, I'd kill him with my own hands.'

Suzie hesitated. 'The awful thing is that, when I was worrying about the police questioning Tom, I caught myself almost wishing there would be another murder, so that he'd be in the clear. I know that's terrible. But I never thought it would be . . .'

'We don't, do we? I mean, we get alarmed enough to take precautions, but we never really let ourselves imagine it actually happening to our own children. We couldn't bear it. There was an awful second or two when it entered my head, but I couldn't allow myself to really think it. Not till now.'

'But it didn't happen. Not the worst.'

'It could have. If the girls had believed him. If they'd got into his car.'

'They didn't.'

'I could kill him,' Nick said again.

Suzie stared into the darkening garden. 'It's sort of odd that it should happen today, of all days. It was Julie's funeral this afternoon.'

'Was it?'

'Don't you remember? Tom was all dressed up in his school blazer and black tie.'

'Oh, yes. Well, he's well out of it now. At least Millie's given them a good description. They know who they're looking for. If it was the same man.'

'What do you mean?'

'We don't really know, do we? Whoever killed Julie may not be the only sexual pervert on the loose.'

She shivered. 'You mean . . . if they catch the man who did this to Millie, it might not necessarily solve the other thing? That's stretching coincidence a bit, isn't it?'

'Unless he was aiming for a copycat murder.'

'Nick, don't!'

'I'm just being realistic. If Millie had gone with him . . .'

She went to him and hugged him tightly. 'It's all right. She's upstairs in bed. She's OK.'

'If I ever get my hands on him . . .'

She was back in his arms, but the world had not become safer.

They were still waiting up when Tom came home, considerably later than ten. He strode whistling down the hall and grinned when he saw them. He looked much more dishevelled than when he had set out for school that morning. The blue blazer hung from one shoulder. The black tie had gone. It was as though he had consigned the funeral to the distant past.

Suzie studied his face as Nick told him the news. He whistled again, with surprise this time. He ran his hand through the dark waves of his hair. She saw him struggling to change from his carefree Friday evening expression to one of appropriate concern.

'Gosh, poor kid. That's rough.'

She took a breath of relief. She had not seen in his young face any realization that this might exonerate him. His concern was entirely innocent, genuinely for Millie. And immediately she felt appalled, because the thought of exoneration could not have occurred to her unless a part of her mind still had a lingering doubt about his innocence.

Was the shadow of Thomas Loosemore *still* lying over her?

Then she remembered the painful anger in Nick's face because he had not been able to protect Millie from this man. *I'd kill him.*

The old question came back to haunt her.

What had happened at Wayland Farm when Goring's cavalry had ridden down on Southcombe, when the Reverend Arthur Chambers had entertained Lord Goring and his officers at the rectory? Had that same expression been in Thomas Loosemore's face as in Nick's? That same helpless rage?

'You should go to bed, Mum,' Tom said, ruffling her hair. 'I didn't mean to keep you up. You look shattered.'

NINETEEN

I t seemed strange to wake up on Saturday morning and look out on the garden. The early sun lit up the colours of red roses and purple clematis, as though nothing had happened.

She went softly along the landing and put her head round Millie's door.

'Would you like breakfast in bed, love?'

Millie nodded. Her face seemed even paler than usual. She looked smaller, cowed somehow, hunched on her pillow. Suzie went to her and hugged her.

After breakfast, Nick set to work in the garden. Suzie stood at the sink, watching him. She was relieved to see that he appeared to be working normally, digging and hoeing weeds. There was none of the furious activity that might have expressed still-smouldering rage. *He's in control of himself now*, she thought, *whatever he feels inside. We're civilized people; we'll leave retribution to the police.*

She washed the last of the breakfast things and rinsed the glasses. They had made no plans for the day. They could hardly go out and leave Millie alone. Unspoken between them was the certainty that this was not the time for a family history expedition.

Still, her thoughts strayed back to Southcombe. What was its rector doing this morning? Her mouth softened in a smile as she tried to picture him.

Suddenly she checked, staring at the wet glass in her hand. She hadn't yet told Nick about her meeting James in the library. She had been determined not to keep it secret from him this time. Not, she justified herself, that she had ever meant to conceal her bus trip to Southcombe; she had just delayed telling him too long. And now what had happened to Millie had driven yesterday's encounter completely out of her mind. Anyway, how could she have introduced something so trivial after that? It remained unspoken.

This was a new day. She and Nick had to get back to normal,

somehow. She ought not to wait any longer. She hung up the tea towel and took off her apron.

A thrush was singing in the apple tree. Suzie made her way past it along the curving path to the vegetable plot. Nick was bending to deal with a deep-rooted dandelion. He straightened up and looked at her expectantly, evidently assuming that she had come to deliver a telephone message.

At once, she felt embarrassed. She should have waited until coffee time, introduced it into normal conversation. Coming down the garden to tell him gave the event an importance it did not merit. But she was here now.

'I met James Milton yesterday.' She was speaking too quickly.

'Who?'

'You know. The Southcombe rector. The one you talked to about the paintings in his church.'

'So?' He looked at her blankly.

Did he really not remember how angry he had been about that email?

'I bumped into him in the library. I'd gone to check on something in the census and he was there looking at the field survey maps.'

A frown was tightening Nick's face. 'I don't understand you. Our daughter's just escaped from someone who's probably a murderer, and all you can think about even now is your bloody family history.'

The shock was like a blow to her face. It was not like Nick to swear. She felt the blood mount in her cheeks.

'You were cross with me before because I didn't tell you I'd been to Southcombe to meet him, though I would have done if I'd had time. So I thought I had to tell you about yesterday, even though I only bumped into him by accident. I didn't want to keep any more secrets from you.'

He looked at her doubtfully. She could see his natural fairness warring with deeper feelings of hurt. Was it only because he was so upset about Millie? It struck her, too late, that he was right. She should not even have been thinking about Southcombe today.

'Thank you for telling me.' He was formally polite. She felt the coldness return. 'Was that all?'

'Yes.'

Telling him had been a mistake. Not now. She had not made it better. It should not have been the first thing she talked about the morning after Millie's trauma. She could see now how it must seem to Nick that her meeting with James was more important to her than it really was.

'I'll go and see what Millie wants to do today.'

She walked across the lawn, towards the house. It *wasn't* important to her, was it? A casual meeting with the young rector?

His hands giving her the photocopied map. His uproarious laughter, startling everyone else in the library. *'It's an occupational hazard for unmarried clergymen.'*

She should not be remembering all this, this morning. She should be thinking only about Millie. What kind of mother was she?

Even so, the thrush was still singing blithely in the apple tree.

As she closed the kitchen door behind her, Suzie was overwhelmed with the sudden desire to tell James everything that had happened. The feeling startled her. Perhaps it was the way clergymen were trained, to invite confidences from their flock. She knew instinctively that he would understand the crosscurrents of her emotions: her thankfulness that Millie was unharmed, murderous rage against the man who had attempted to take her, guilt that she had stopped meeting Millie from school, and the treacherous, treasonable relief that this finally lifted suspicion from Tom. She was too close to confess all of this to Nick. James, she told herself, would listen to her with more objectivity.

Suzie pushed away the accusing thought that objectivity might not be what she truly hoped for from James, that the shoulder she yearned to cry on was more than metaphorical.

She must busy herself with Millie. But when she went upstairs, her daughter's voice was chattering animatedly on her newly charged mobile. Suzie smiled with relief. This was more like the old Millie. She would be ringing round all her friends, revelling in the fact that this time she would be, undisputedly, the centre of attention. She and Tamara would be the stars of their circle for weeks to come. Other girls, Suzie realized with a sick amazement, would probably envy them their experience.

Yet only because the two had come out of it safe. Only because their friends were too young to imagine properly what might have happened. The girls would shriek with horror, they would enjoy the vicarious excitement. They could not begin to experience what a parent feels.

She put her head round the bedroom door and smiled at Millie, waiting for the call to end. But the question she had been intending to ask proved superfluous.

'See you, like, twelve o'clock? Outside Burger King. The whole gang's going to be there. Cheers, Annie.' Millie put down the mobile. Her eyes were sparkling, her cheeks flushed. 'Hi Mum.'

'I was going to ask you what you wanted to do today. I gather I'm a bit late.'

'Yeah. Me and the girls are meeting up in town. Tamara's up for it, even with her leg. We thought we'd, like, brief all the gang so they know who they've got to watch out for. Wouldn't it be great if, suppose, we could be the ones to catch him if he tries anything like that again?'

'I sincerely hope none of them will put themselves in a position where it *could* happen again. If you two hadn't gone into the park when I told you not to . . .'

'*Mum!* I explained. Those bullies were going to do Tamara over.'

'Well, let's not go over that again. Look, promise me you'll stay out of danger in future. I go cold thinking about what could have happened.'

'It was just bad luck I forgot to unplug my phone. I'd have called somebody when Tamara fell over. Honest, Mum. And the girls aren't stupid. They'll stay together.'

'No, Millie. I'm not having thirteen-year-old girls setting themselves up as decoys. Have you forgotten how scared you were last night?'

Millie's expression changed. She shuddered. 'Yeah, well. He was seriously creepy. Yuk! He gives me the shivers just thinking about him.'

'Be careful, then. Make sure it never happens again. To you, or anyone else.'

'Well, if we catch him, it won't, will it?'

'Millie!'

'Sorry, Mum. Just winding you up.'

'I'm not sure I should let you out at all today.'

'Just try and stop me.'

Millie flung off the duvet and began rummaging in her drawers for underwear.

'Shower?' suggested Suzie.

Millie glowered.

Suzie closed the door. There was no sound from Tom's room. He must be sleeping late. She fought back the urge to edge his door open and see his face asleep on the pillow.

Her Tom, her firstborn. The dark cloud had blown away from him. It hung now over a middle-aged man with a balding head and thick-rimmed glasses. Her young, beautiful Tom was innocent.

If this *was* the same man who killed Julie.

She shook her head. Julie Samuel was dead. Nothing would ever put that right. Catching Millie's assailant could not bring her back. Tom had cared about her. He had been to her funeral. He would live with the grief of his loss always.

Suzie took the car to the supermarket for the weekly shop. After all the anguish, there was something comfortingly methodical in wheeling the trolley up one aisle and down the next, list in hand. All the same, her mind was distracted today. She was halfway round before she realized she had missed the lettuce and had to retrace her steps to the fresh produce shelves.

She queued at the checkout, wondering if Millie would still be at home when she got back. She would have liked to forbid her to go out today, but she knew Millie needed the comfort of friends. She would revel in the boost to her street cred that the adventure had given her. Telling her story over and over would help to transform it into a kind of fiction, a well-rehearsed tale. It might, with luck, replace the darker reality Millie would otherwise have to hug to herself in the solitude of her bedroom.

She had been standing in line for a minute or two before the newspaper placard on the end of the counter grabbed her eye. TEENAGE GIRLS ATTACKED.

Her heart turned over with shock. So it was not just Millie's friends now. The whole world knew.

It seemed an agonizing age before it was her turn at the

checkout. She fumbled for her card, could hardly remember her PIN. She sped to the kiosk at the front of the shop and bought a copy of the local paper. She opened it up, oblivious to the fact that she and her trolley were blocking the exit.

Millie's story occupied most of the front page: the man in the park, Tamara's fall. They had printed the girls' Identikit impression of their assailant. The police were appealing for the man who had challenged him about his car to come forward.

Suzie scanned the front page closely. Everything was there except Millie and Tamara's names.

Another headline screamed: COULD THIS BE JULIE'S KILLER? There was a warning to teenage girls to keep away from lonely places.

The chill horror was creeping back. It was not all over, despite the sunshine of this Saturday morning. She had been foolish to think it could be.

She swung the car into the drive and braked sharply. Tom was wheeling his bike out of the garage. He gave her an embarrassed grin.

She let down the window. 'What's with the bike? You haven't used it in months, hardly at all since you started driving lessons.'

'Yeah, well. I thought I'd ride around a bit this morning. Get some exercise.'

'Where are you going?'

He shrugged. 'There's a cycle route through the parks. I might take that.'

The word stabbed her, as though she had pressed a finger that hid a buried thorn. *Parks*.

'Not you, too? You're not going out looking for the man who tried to kidnap Millie, are you? Tom, leave that to the police. You can't do anything.'

'I can look, can't I? The more eyes the better.'

'But he's hardly going to be hanging around in a park today. Not right after all the publicity about what happened to Millie. Look.' She thrust the newspaper with the sketch of the man's face in front of him.

Tom took the paper from her and read it. 'Millie'll be upset that they haven't got a picture of her,' he laughed.

Suzie knew it was true. She switched off the engine and got out.

Tom was frowning down at his bicycle, as though trying to reach a decision. 'All the same, I feel like the exercise.'

She put a hand on his arm. 'It's brought it all back, hasn't it? Just when I hoped the funeral would put a closure to it and we could move on.'

'How can I move on until I know who did it?'

Suzie hesitated. 'It must have been terrible for you when the police were questioning you, as if they thought you might have done it.'

'Yeah, but I knew I didn't.'

She felt again the black guilt that she could ever have come close to suspecting that Tom might have been involved, even if it had only been a terrible accident.

She drew a sharp breath. 'I'd rather you didn't go out looking on your own. Now that they've published his picture, it's not just teenage girls who'll be in danger. Anyone who might identify him will be a threat to him.'

He considered this for a moment. She thought he looked relieved.

'Before all this, I'd have asked Dave to come out with me. The lazy sod could do with some fitness training.'

'Why don't you ring him anyway? Things have to get back to normal between you sometime. Then couldn't the two of you just stay home and play a nice computer game? Zap a few virtual baddies?'

'No, Mum.' Something of the old smile flashed briefly from those intensely blue eyes, though more sadly than before. 'Not now.'

Millie had gone, loaded with warnings about being careful. The house seemed strangely empty as Suzie unpacked the week's food and stored it away. It took a while to realize what was strange. Normally she and Nick would be setting out somewhere by now, driving to lunch at a village pub.

Nick must have felt the same. He came into the kitchen, hands earthy, and stood silently for a while. Then he smiled tentatively at her.

'I don't know about you, but I didn't feel it would be right today, pushing off into the countryside and leaving the kids to it, the way things are. But since they're out anyway, we could still find somewhere for lunch, if you like.

Maybe down on the quay again? Then we could take a stroll along the canal . . .' He caught his breath. 'Sorry. Bad idea.'

She tried to smile back, eager to help him bridge the cold gap of recent weeks between them. 'We could walk down the river bank instead.'

'Right. Let's do that.'

As she got herself ready, it was a relief to have something to fill the time, to stop her imagining things.

The day was clouding over, but they sat outside on the waterfront eating prawn baguettes and watching the mixture of locals and holidaymakers strolling past. Nick, she noticed, was staring hard at them, particularly the men. As she was.

'I suppose he must be a bachelor, or divorced,' she said. 'It's too creepy to think he could be a family man. Imagine him going home to his wife and children after . . .'

'He has to be sick,' Nick said. 'Surely his family would know he isn't normal.'

'We can't assume that. The police's job would be a whole lot easier if criminals looked different from the rest of us. That's what scares me.'

'Point taken. Still, it's men on their own I find myself looking for. And there aren't too many of those about – at least, not older ones. It's mainly youngsters down here.' He looked down at his plate, where prawns had dropped un-noticed from his sandwich. 'And then in the middle of the night I got round to thinking, what if Millie got the wrong end of the stick? What if he really was just a decent guy who was trying to help them? What if the real murderer is laughing his socks off, because the police are on the wrong track now?'

'You don't really believe that? That Millie's scared us out of our wits for nothing? You didn't yesterday.'

'No, I don't. Not in the cold light of morning. The way she said he was fondling Tamara's leg, the fact that he was beating around in the bushes looking for them. No, I may try to make myself feel better about what happened to her, but I can't. It was him, all right.'

Nick paid the bill and they set off along the quayside, past the cavernous arches in the cliff, which now housed shops selling reclaimed timber furniture and locally made glass. The crowds were thinning as they left the city. Suzie tensed,

imagining that the quieter the path became, the more possible
it was that they might see him.

Don't be silly, she told herself. *He could be anywhere. Why
here, why now? He's almost certainly staying under cover
today.*

All the same, they both studied everyone coming towards
them.

The path took them past old mills from the city's industrial past, through elder bushes dark with berries, over the
scuffed grass of recreation grounds, with the river slipping
slowly beside them. Her thoughts went to Tom, cruising the
city's parks on his bike. She wished Dave could have been
with him.

'I should have told Tom that if he did see anyone who
looked suspicious he mustn't approach him. Just phone the
police.'

'He's not a fool. He'll work that out for himself.'

'I hope you're right. What would you do, if you thought
you saw him?'

Nick stopped abruptly. The colour darkened in his cheeks.
'I'd . . . You're right. I don't know what I'd do in the heat of
the moment. Perhaps not what I *should* do.'

'Tom's only seventeen. And you're far more sensible than
he is.'

'Have you got your mobile on you? You could ring him.
Mine's in the car.'

She drew hers out of her bag and selected Tom's number.
There was a pause while she waited for a reply. She remembered the horror of discovering Millie's phone ringing in the
bedroom. Then Tom answered.

'Hi Mum.'

'Tom, darling. Look, Dad and I are worried about what
you're doing. It's a thousand to one against you coming across
him by chance, but if you do, be very careful. Don't, whatever you do, go near the man, or let him see you suspect
anything. Wait till you're out of sight and then ring 999.'

'I'm not a complete idiot, Mum. There's only one of me.
What did you think I was going to do? Surround him?'

A pain squeezed her heart. 'Is Dave with you?' There was
just a chance.

A moment's silence. 'What do you think? No, he suddenly

has family stuff to do nowadays. Look, Mum, I'll be all right. Trust me.'

'I hope so. We've been worried enough about Millie. I couldn't bear it if . . .'

'Give me the phone,' said Nick. 'Tom, look, no heroics. I know how angry you feel. I do myself. But just don't mess up. We've got to get this right.'

He listened, then ended the call and handed the phone back to Suzie. 'He says you're right. It's needle-in-the-haystack time. He'll be home for supper.'

Four hours. Anything could happen in that time.

TWENTY

They were out in the open when the afternoon dissolved into steady rain. It pimpled the surface of the river and made pockmarks on the dusty path.

'Drat,' said Suzie. 'It's been fine for so long, I never thought to bring a raincoat.'

'Looks like we'd better head for a bus.'

By the time they had crossed several fields to the main road they were thoroughly wet. As they waited at the bus shelter, Suzie shivered.

'At least Tom won't still be out in this.'

The windscreen wipers swung their slow pendulum. The bus seemed to take forever to bear them back into town. Then they had to hurry down to the car park above the quay, find their car and drive home.

He's bound to be there before us, Suzie thought. *Millie will be safe in some steamy café with her friends. Tom will be home.*

She hurried to the front door, while Nick put the car in the garage. She felt the emptiness as soon as she stepped into the house. Tom was not there. She ran upstairs, but she knew he was not in his bedroom. She checked the answerphone. No message.

Why did she feel so scared? It was ridiculous to think that Tom, by some unbelievable fluke, should be the one to spot the man.

'He's not home,' she said as Nick came in, the waves of his dark hair flattened wetly against his head.

'Have you tried ringing him again?'

'Not yet. Do you think I should? I'm afraid he might get impatient if he thinks I'm nagging him.'

Nick looked at the clock. 'It's only four. You're probably working yourself up for nothing. He'll be sheltering some-where, if he's got any sense.'

'I expect you're right. I might as well wash my hair. It's dripping, anyway.'

They were trying to be reasonable. She felt the tension in Nick, even while he tried to reassure her.

The burst of spray from the shower drowned out the rain. Water blinded her. The hum of the hairdryer cut off all sound. She would not hear if the phone rang.

She switched off the dryer and sat on the bed in the sudden silence. After a moment, she was aware of faint sounds from downstairs. Nick was watching the sports results.

She sat on, twining the still-damp strands of her hair round her fingers, coaxing curls. She wished there was someone she could talk to about how she felt. Nick was too close, too concerned.

Her eyes strayed to something white on the dressing table. There was a folded sheet of paper there. She knew what it was, though she could not remember how it got there. The field map of Wayland. She last recalled it spread out on the kitchen table. Could that be only yesterday, before she realized Millie was missing? She had no idea when or why she had brought it upstairs.

She picked it up now. It brought a remembered warmth, James's hands giving it to her, the brush of his jacket sleeve, the surprising fragrance of his aftershave.

She spread the map out beside her on the duvet. Wayland Farm, though as it was in the nineteenth century, not two hundred years earlier in Thomas Loosemore's time. But some things had lasted. She had seen them, touched them. The long farmhouse under its sweeping thatch. The great stones at the base of the barn, which had made her marvel at the men who had lifted them. The apple orchard between the house and the river.

What had happened here? To Thomas Loosemore's sister, or his wife? What had been the scene at Wayland in 1645, when Goring's cavalry swept through Southcombe, bitter from their defeat at the hands of Lord Fairfax?

Next second, the reality surged over her in all its violence. The poultry squawking as they scattered before the horses' hooves. Geese honking, dogs barking. Women running out of the dairy, or dropping their baskets in the orchard. Terrified children snatched back from danger. Men too far out in the fields to run home quickly enough. What could they do, anyway, to stop cavalrymen armed with swords and pistols?

The black horse reared over with her with rolling eyes. The face of his rider terrified her more. Even as she turned to run, he was vaulting to the ground. The yard was too small; there was no time. She had no strength.

She was seeing it now in vivid flashes. In the straw of that barn? In the long grass of the orchard? On the floor of the dairy? In the bedchambers under the eaves which she had not been shown?

How did she know so certainly this had happened? The air shrieked to her across the centuries. *What if this is Thomas Loosemore's wife?*

Through her tears she saw another face approaching hers, a far more familiar face. It was twisted now, but she read disgust, not pity. He stood staring down at her dishevelled dress. Then he turned away.

The significance hit her for the first time. All her mind until now had been on Thomas, her Tom's namesake, dragging his royalist rector down the stairs, as so colourfully described by Walker. She had not one piece of evidence about his wife, whose horror was now twisting her own body in desperate denial. Yet it was from this nameless woman, the mother of Joshua Loosemore, that Suzie Fewings, née Loosemore, was descended.

The sounds screamed in her head. She sat shaken by the tumult of her imagining.

Only now did she face the shocking possibility.

Was Thomas Loosemore truly her ancestor?

She made rapid calculations. Joshua Loosemore had had children in the 1670s. She had estimated his birth date in the 1650s. What if she was wrong? Wasn't it more likely that he was a child of the 1640s? What if his father was . . .?

She saw him now: the lace at his throat, the arrogant armour, the luxuriantly curling moustache and pointed beard. Or a coarser trooper, furious with these Puritans who had so obstinately defied King Charles and beaten his army. Was *this* the man she was descended from, and not Thomas Loosemore after all?

She drew her mobile out of her handbag and sat caressing it with her thumb. Then, with swift decision, she took out her diary and found the note she had made of James's number. The television was still on downstairs.

Even as she pressed the digits, she realized that she was not sure what she most wanted to talk to him about. The terrible thing that had almost happened to Millie? Her fear that Tom might do something irrevocable? Or the awful scenes still echoing in her head, which were convincing her that Thomas Loosemore was not, after all, her ancestor, that she was descended from a nameless Puritan woman and one of Lord Goring's brutal cavalrymen.

The decision was made for her.

'James Milton. How can I help?'

'James, it's Suzie. Suzie Fewings.'

'Suzie! I'd been wanting to ring you, but I didn't know if it would be diplomatic, after what you said. I saw about the attack on two girls near you, and I thought how worried you must be. You've got a daughter that age, haven't you?'

'It was Millie.'

'I'm sorry?'

'It was my daughter Millie. She and her friend were the ones that man accosted in the park. He tried to get them into his car.'

'Gosh! I don't know what to say. Is she all right? You must be devastated.'

'Yes, we're both pretty knocked out about it. Millie seems to be OK, all things considered. She was scared stiff last night, of course. But she's out now with her friends, basking in the limelight. They kept her name out of the papers, but all her mates will know by now that it was her. It may be worse when she's alone.

'Only it's Tom I'm worried about now. He went out this morning on his bike, to cycle round the parks looking for this man. I know he won't find him, of course. He's bound to be lying low, after all this publicity. But if he did . . .'

'You're thinking of Thomas Loosemore, aren't you? How he dragged the rector down the parsonage stairs and killed him.'

She caught her breath in a gasp. 'How did you know I was thinking that?'

He laughed softly. 'Most of the conversations we've had so far have been about him. And you're afraid that Tom . . . if he got his hands on this guy . . .'

'Yes. Something like that. It was an accident! I'm sure

Thomas Loosemore never meant to kill him. It was just that all the feelings he'd had to keep bottled up . . .'

'You mean the story I told you, about the rector and Goring's Crew?'

'I . . . Look, James, you've got to believe this. I was sitting here, thinking about Tom and Thomas Loosemore, and suddenly it all hit me. It was as though I was *there*. Those Royalist cavalrymen galloping into the yard, and the geese honking and the children screaming. And there were women. One young woman. And he was dragging her somewhere . . . I don't know . . . into the barn or the dairy. And she fought him, but she couldn't do anything. And he . . . And the men were out in the fields and they couldn't get there in time. But what could they have done, anyway? And the way Thomas looked at her, after they'd ridden off, as though she was soiled goods. And then the baby coming . . .' She was crying.

'Steady on! You were imagining this.'

'It was *real*. I was there, hearing it, seeing it . . . *feeling* it. It was horrible.'

'It's a possible scenario, of course. War's like that, I'm afraid. But you don't know. At least half of family history is speculation. Intelligent guesswork, no more.'

'The baby. It could have been Joshua Loosemore, couldn't it? My ancestor? The one whose parents I came to Southcombe looking for? Her baby could have been Joshua.'

'It's only a hypothesis, Suzie. You haven't got a birth date for him, have you? The registers for the Civil War period are missing. He might have been born years after. You don't even know there *was* a baby from Goring's raid. Or if there was, that he wasn't Thomas's child anyway. You're upset about Millie and Tom. You're working yourself into a state on the flimsiest of theories.'

'It would explain why Thomas was so angry with the rector, wouldn't it?' She paused. 'Arthur Chambers *was* guilty, wasn't he? You said he entertained Lord Goring and his officers with a fine dinner. Only, I suppose, to be honest, they could have forced him to. If they burst into the rectory, demanding food and wine, he couldn't have said no, could he?'

'That's very fair-minded of you, but I'm afraid I can't give the Reverend Arthur Chambers a clean bill of health. He preached a sermon "Against the Wicked who Defy our

Sovereign Anointed King". It castigates the impious Puritans and Parliamentarians in his flock for rising up against their divinely appointed ruler. He calls on them to welcome the King's troops as if they were a host of delivering angels. He was so pleased with it that he had it printed as a pamphlet. I'll show you my copy of it, if you like. No, I'm afraid Chambers welcomed Goring's Crew with open arms.'

'And so Thomas threw him downstairs.'

'Your story fits. But that's all it is, Suzie. A story.'

'I heard her scream. I felt as if *I* were screaming.'

'I'll pray for you, Suzie, if that will help.' He gave a conscience-stricken laugh. 'I mean, I believe it will. You've had a bad fright. First Millie, and now you're worried about Tom. You put your finger on it yourself, though. It's not going to be he who finds this man. Anyway, if your theory's right, your Tom's no longer Thomas Loosemore's descendant, is he? You've broken the link.'

She sat in startled silence for a few moments, absorbing the implication. 'I hadn't thought of that.'

'Look, you're still in shock now. Tom will come home. The police will catch this man. From what I saw on the television, the girls seem to have given a really good description. Then you can go back to enjoying your family history. You must have dozens of other lines to pursue, besides the Loosemores. But talk to me if you need to. I'm always here. I'll be remembering you and Nick, and Tom and Millie in my prayers.'

'Thank you.'

'Bye now. Take care.'

She sat on the edge of the bed, nursing the dead phone between her hands.

Nick's voice sounded from the doorway behind her. 'Who were you talking to?'

She turned, startled into a guilty lie.

'Millie. Just checking up.'

'Not Tom?'

'No. Not yet.'

He walked across to the bed and fondled her hair, a little awkwardly. Her guilt increased. For all the danger of another misunderstanding, she should have been honest about James this time. She could have explained that he was a priest, that she felt the need for his spiritual counsel, which was not entirely untrue. It might have been better to risk Nick's anger again than deceive him.

It was too late now.

'He'll be back,' Nick consoled her. 'Wet and cold and fed up.'

'I could do some home-made soup.'

'I'll vote for that.'

She busied herself in the kitchen with tomatoes and beans and spices. It was good to be here, chopping vegetables, warming herself in front of the stove as she stirred the pan. Had the mother of Joshua Loosemore found such comfort in her farmhouse kitchen, going about the far heavier tasks of the seventeenth century while her body thickened?

Imagination. James had said so. The flimsiest of theories.

But she had shared another woman's terror and pain.

Millie came home first, sunnier than Suzie would have believed possible the day before.

'It was, like, really cool. Everyone wants to talk to us about it. And there's this brilliant boy in Year Eleven, Michael Stansby, and he came up to me in the street and said, "That was you they were talking about on television, wasn't it?" And I went all trembly at the knees, because he's, like, drop-dead gorgeous.'

Tom returned, wet and moody, as Nick had predicted. He did not want to talk.

It was Millie who saw him the following week. Her grey eyes were wide as she burst through the door, the pupils dark and brilliant. She must have run home. The torrent of words struggled through gasps for breath.

'I've seen him! Mum, it was him. He had a cap on, and he's dyed his moustache black, but I took one look at him and my heart, like, turned a somersault. I thought I was going to faint. And I was terrified he was going to turn round and see me, and he'd know it was me and I could tell the police about him, because me and Tamara had got his picture in the papers and everything. And it was like one of those nightmares where you want to run and you just can't move. And then one of the kids' mums walked between me and him, and it, like, broke the spell. And I just ran as fast as I could and I didn't stop running till I got here.'

'It was the same man? You're sure? Was Tamara with you?'
Suzie was hugging her daughter's thin shoulders, trying to
marshal her own thoughts into some sensible order. Millie's
fear was communicating itself to her.

'Of course I'm sure,' came her muffled voice. 'Do you think
I could forget that face, all creepy and smiley? No, Tamara
wasn't there. I was with Carmen, but I just left her behind
and ran.'

'Have you told the police?'

Millie stopped gasping and went still in Suzie's arms. 'No!
I should have, shouldn't I? I just didn't think.'

'Where was this? Outside school?'

'Not *our* school. St Benedict's Primary. He was hanging
about by the wall looking into the playground as all the little
kids were coming out.'

'Beast! Look, I'm going to ring the police straight away.
But you'll have to tell them what you saw.'

'Do I have to? Couldn't you do it this time?'

'No. You saw him. I didn't.'

'OK.' Millie went quiet. She looked younger, uncertain, so
different from the radiant glow with which the awe – even
the envy – of her friends had clothed her at the weekend.

Suzie hesitated, then dialled 999. This was urgent; the man
might still be there. It seemed to take an excruciating time to
be connected to the police, though it was only seconds. More
delay as she identified herself, before she could give Millie's
message.

Then, at last, she felt the relief of being believed, of knowing
a police car was already racing to the primary school. It was
time to hand the phone over to Millie to give more details.

While Millie talked, Suzie got out her mobile and rang
Nick. A greater relief. He would be home straight away. There
was nothing more she could do but wait for them all to arrive.
The police, Nick . . . Tom.

The police arrived first. This time, it was comforting that they
were two she already knew from that first visit: the young,
uniformed Sergeant Lucy Morris, with the black ponytail, and
the fatherly Constable Elton Wall. They sat Millie down in
the sitting room and questioned her minutely on what she had
seen.

In spite of her renewed fear and anger towards this preda-
tory man, Suzie was aware past pains were being smoothed
over. Now it was not Tom who was under suspicion.

She felt a little shudder of surprise. Was this just coincidence? Could James be right? If the intensity of her vision
had any grounds in reality, then the genetic link between Tom
and Thomas Loosemore's manslaughter might never have
existed. In any case, how could she help but look on the violent
young militiaman in a totally different way now?

She felt his rage. If she could get her own hands on that
man . . .

The front door opened. Tom? She sped into the hall.

It was Nick. She had been so caught up in the millrace of
her thoughts that she hadn't heard his car. His face was grim,
and yet lit with a fierce excitement, like a huntsman who has
heard the hounds give tongue. He gripped her arms, hard
enough to hurt.

'Millie's all right?'

'Yes. Scared, but OK. She's talking to the police now.'

The front door swung inwards behind Nick. This time it
was Tom. He looked from one to the other, questioning.

'Is something up? What's Dad doing home this early?'

'Millie's seen that man again. Outside St Benedict's school.'

Tom spun round without a word. He was over the doorstep
in one swift stride.

'Wait! I'm coming with you,' Nick cried.

'Can I drive?'

'No.'

Watching them speed down the path to the car, Suzie knew
that the police in the room behind her would have forbidden
this. 'Leave it to us, sir,' she imagined them saying. Yet she
understood utterly what drove her menfolk. She was feeling
herself that violent hate, that urge for revenge. She was swept
by rage that the man who had already killed Julie, and then
had tried to do the same to Millie, had turned his attention
now to little girls. She found she was shaking with emotion.

The officers had finished with Millie. Sergeant Morris stood
in the doorway, calm and businesslike in her crisp uniform.
Did she feel the same rage as Suzie? Could she?

'That's it for the moment, Mrs Fewings. Millie's been a
great help. We'll get him now, don't worry. But, please, could

I ask you not to say anything about this to anyone else? It's essential he doesn't know we're on to him even though he's tried to change his appearance. If he goes to ground, we could lose him.'

'Yes, I understand. You've warned Millie, I suppose? She's going to find it hard not to tell her friends.'

'That's natural,' the sergeant smiled, 'at her age. But Millie's a bright girl. She understands the need for it.'

Suzie looked past her into the sitting room.

The older constable rose from the sofa. 'Was that your husband I heard in the hall just now?'

'Yes, and my son Tom.'

'Could I have a word with them, too? Make sure we're all singing from the same hymn sheet.'

'I'm afraid they've gone out.'

Both officers stiffened. 'Why?' asked Sergeant Morris frostily. 'They'd only just got home. I hope they're not planning anything stupid.'

'I think they hoped they might catch the man before he got away.'

'We've got half the police in the city out trying to do just that. It would be a very bad idea for your husband and son to get involved.'

'I couldn't stop them.'

She hadn't tried.

TWENTY-ONE

Nick and Tom did not find him. They returned tired, tense and angry.

Next day, Nick insisted on driving Millie to school again. Suzie set out to the bus stop. Halfway down the tree-lined road she found her steps slowing. Could she really sit at her desk this morning as if nothing had happened? All over the city now, children would be flocking to school. Was the man with the dyed-black moustache there on some crowded pavement, watching them closely, singling out a possible unaccompanied child? How could she busy herself with fund-raising and requests for care home roof repairs, while he was still out there, free to attack again?

As she turned into the greater noise of the main road, it took an effort of will to tell herself that the police were out across the city, that they were far better equipped to handle this than she was, that the elderly people whose charity she worked for also needed her attention.

The bus journey passed in a blur, except when they passed a school. Then Suzie peered intently at the throngs of pupils and parents. There were hardly any men. No one she saw raised her suspicion. Each time, her head craned backwards, looking at them as long as she could. Then she slumped round in her seat, frustrated.

Doubt troubled her now. Could Millie really have recognized him? Was it likely that her attacker would risk capture by showing himself openly, so soon after his picture had appeared all over the city, even with the feeble disguise of dyed hair and moustache?

A new question gnawed at the back of her mind. Could she even be sure that this was Julie's murderer, and not just some sad, dirty old man?

She clenched her fists until the nails dug into her palms. He had terrified Millie.

*   *   *

Margery greeted her in the shop with her usual understanding smile. Suzie had confided to her the previous day that Millie was the girl who had been accosted in the park. She could trust Margery.

But not Janet. The memory of the avid curiosity in the other woman's sharper face disgusted her. She could not have trusted Janet to keep the news to herself.

Fortunately this was not Janet's morning for helping in the charity shop. Barbara was plumper, easy-going, with a warm country burr in her voice. She made no reference to what had happened. Suzie responded to both their greetings and slipped into her small office behind the shop.

It was, after all, better to have something else to occupy her mind this morning. In a few minutes the hypnotic lure of the computer screen took her over. There was, as always, a string of emails to attend to, as well as the stack of letters in the morning post. She ran her eye over them, assessing their urgency. There was a staffing crisis at Beechcroft House; both the matron and one of the care staff were off sick. She needed to find a temporary replacement. The relatives of an applicant who had been told there was no place available at Four Pines were threatening to sue. These were familiar problems, ones she could deal with.

Lunchtime came sooner than Suzie would have believed possible. She surfaced from the public sphere into her private world with a sense of disorientation. The reality of the situation she had left crept back over her.

It was chilling. She wanted to dive back into that world of repair contracts, staffing agencies and placating letters and pretend that what had happened to her own family did not exist. The renewal of tension made her feel sick.

Margery must have seen her face. She murmured to Suzie as she passed through the shop. 'Try not to worry. I'm sure they'll find him.'

Suzie smiled back, bleakly.

She stood under the clouded sky, wondering. Should she go home as usual, to housework and preparing the evening meal? Or could she instead find an excuse to bury herself in the Local Studies Library or the Record Office, blotting out the twenty-first century?

She was startled to realize that she did not need an excuse.

This was Tuesday, her usual afternoon for research. It had not crossed her mind until now. She had brought none of the files she needed to pursue her investigations. When she tried to think what information she might look for today, her mind went blank.

What else could she do? The school lunch hour was already over. Millie's man, if he was on the streets at all, would have no reason to be lurking outside gates again until the schools finished later that afternoon.

She remained for a long while looking down the hill as the homeward buses passed her. She was trying to remember the wider geography of the city. Where were those schools?

Though she knew it was futile, she began to walk. She could take in half a dozen or more if she took a circuitous route home.

How would a man like that pass the afternoon? Was his obsession so great that he must always be drawn to where young girls might be? Did he fill his hours watching the empty swings in the park, or stand peering through the wire at deserted netball courts? Was he, instead, at home, fuelling his lust with videos or pornographic websites? Or did he perhaps spend his time as normal people of that age did, watching daytime television or tending his garden, out shopping or changing his library books?

Why was she assuming he did not have a job? It was hard to tell from Millie's description whether he would be a pensioner or not. It was possible that he had been in prison for sexual assault before, and no one would employ him. But, no, the police would surely know about that. After Julie's death, they would have visited every man on the sex offenders' register and compared his DNA.

She had reached the bottom of the hill beyond the shopping centre without realizing it. She looked up at the tall brick building in front of her. What she saw jolted her perception. The primary school she had remembered here was now closed, boarded up. It must, she supposed, have been relocated to a greener site on the edge of the city.

She walked on, up another hill. Rows of Victorian houses accompanied her on either side. There was nothing interesting here. Somewhere, it occurred to her, a few streets behind the main road, there was a park. It would be foolish to pass so close and not check it out.

A handful of toddlers were in the play area, their mothers chatting on a bench. A man in his twenties was shouting encouragement to a little boy and girl as they tackled the climbing frame. She stood watching them for a while, envying their innocence. Happy families, untouched by fear.

She was surprised to find that she was getting hungry. She had forgotten about lunch. She trudged some way on before she found a small row of shops and bought an uninspiring cheese sandwich. She sat on a low wall to eat it. The best of the summer weather had gone. She wished she had a hot drink.

She looked at her watch. Only two o'clock. Girls would not be coming out of school until after three.

A shock ran through her. She should be at Millie's school by then, to walk her back. Just in case.

She began to walk faster. She had lost track of how far she was from home. This was not a part of the city she often visited. Yet she felt urgency driving her. It was not just Millie. It was all the girls that man with the heavy-rimmed glasses might set his sights on. He might be anywhere. She had to find him.

She lingered outside another primary school, hearing the chatter of young voices through the open windows, until she felt a growing guilt that she herself might be an object of suspicion. Further on was a secondary school. The site seemed vast. She could not get near the buildings. The main gate was fastened. She saw only distant figures of boys and girls on the athletics track.

The next park she came to was deserted. Uneasily, she scanned the bushes by a stream that ran through it.

Now the first mothers, some with babies in buggies, were beginning to trickle along the streets to meet their children from school.

Nowhere was there a man in glasses with a black moustache. She should not have expected that there would be.

As she followed the mothers towards yet another primary school, a police patrol car passed her.

Of course. They would be out in force, watching just such places as she was.

It was a moment before the implication struck her: the police did not think it ridiculous that the man might still be on the streets.

It was only ridiculous to think her amateur efforts could

have any bearing on his capture. Hadn't she told Tom just that? But today she felt what drove Tom and Nick: it was righteous anger, the passion for justice, the determination to rid the world of the possibility that any other girl could be harmed by him.

No. It was, if she was honest, something more animalistic than that. She began to understand the ferocity of a lynch mob.

Yet when she followed the mothers to reach the school ahead there were no police uniforms in sight. Well, she corrected herself, there wouldn't be, would there? They would want to catch him in the act, not scare him off. If they were here, it would be in plain clothes.

She scanned the waiting crowd. Mostly female, of course. A few young fathers, and here and there an older man she assumed must be a grandfather. Some of these certainly wore glasses, but none had a moustache, of any colour. Was it possible that he had shaved it off now?

Her mind went to the middle-aged constable who had come to the house to question first Tom, and then Millie. How would he seem to her if she saw him waiting outside a school out of uniform? As the arm of the law, or as a suspect?

She studied all the men. There was a spotty youth who looked too young and unconfident to be a father, except that he was nursing a crying baby against his shoulder. Was he, she wondered, on shift work, or unemployed while his wife worked for the rent?

It was the older men she must concentrate on. One of them stood chatting to a group of mothers. They seemed to know him. He must be a regular on grandparent duty. Hardly an object of suspicion.

Could she spot a police officer here? That young woman, standing a little apart from the rest, rather neatly dressed in a crisp green shirt and well-pressed beige trousers? She seemed to be observing the people around her carefully. The woman's eyes shifted to rest thoughtfully on Suzie.

Under their scrutiny she blushed guiltily. She was wasting her time, confusing the situation further. She should leave it to the professionals. She ought to be home. Had she left herself enough time to get to Millie's school before the end of the longer secondary school day?

She walked away fast, knowing how odd this must seem –
if it was indeed a police officer watching her – that she had
been waiting outside the school and then changed her mind.

She was being silly. The police were not looking for a
woman.

Suzie hurried across the main road and plunged into a maze
of Victorian terraces. Instinct told her that if she could steer
a course diagonally uphill it would bring her eventually to the
estate where she lived.

The layout of the narrow streets, at right angles to each
other, frustrated her. They ran either straight uphill or along
the contours. She was continually crossing them, turning
corners, changing direction, trying to thread her way across,
as well as up the slope.

The terraced houses ended suddenly at a red brick wall. An
open gate showed her a walk arched over with wisteria. Lawns
and flower beds bright with petunias lay on either side. She
could cut across these gardens more easily, but would there
be another gate up in the far corner where she needed one?

There was no one about. She took the risk. In the distance
she could hear the high voices of children released now from
school. A few shrill calls sounded nearer. She came round a
yew hedge and found herself at the edge of another children's
playground. There were the usual swings, roundabouts, low
slides, a modest climbing frame. Nothing out of the ordinary.
Four small children were throwing themselves on the equip-
ment, while two mothers, one with a buggy, chatted outside
the surrounding wire, not watching them.

And then Suzie saw him. He was standing on the far side
of the enclosure, on a path between two yew hedges. Their
dark height made him look smaller than he probably was. He
looked exactly as Millie had described him yesterday. A black
cap, pulled low over his forehead. Horn-rimmed glasses. A
black moustache. The face rather jowly, the body stocky rather
than plump. Today he wore a navy blue blazer and a patterned
cravat tucked into a cream shirt. A respectable-looking, somewhat military figure.

A sick shudder ran through Suzie. She knew exactly how
Millie had felt, struck immobile with horror, unable to move.

A second later, rage broke through the barrier of shock in
her mind. She was not Millie; she was Millie's mother.

With an inarticulate yell, she broke into a run towards him. The wire surrounding the playground was in her way. She must race round it. The little children had stopped playing and were staring at her. The two women broke off talking. They were nearer to the man than she was. Couldn't they stop him?

'It's him!' she yelled as she dashed past them.

The man had stiffened. Then he began to run, back behind the yew hedge. She would lose him. Idiot! Why hadn't she stood quietly and phoned the police?

She flung herself round the gap in the hedge and caught sight of him again. He had reached the far side of the gardens, but was now balked by the red brick wall. There was no gate in sight. Suzie tore across the grass, rage speeding her feet. He dodged to one side and sprinted uphill. For a man beyond the middle of life he could run quite fast.

He was halfway up a sloping path now. There would surely be a gate at the top. Above her panting breath, she could hear the noise of traffic from the road beyond. She was closing the gap between them, but not fast enough. She threw herself forward, willing her legs on. She must catch him before he reached the road.

She could see the gate now above her, through a bed of rose bushes. The running man was almost there.

From the right, another figure shot across the grass, leaping a flower bed. Someone tall, lean, in black jersey and jeans. For a crazy moment, she thought it was Tom. The flying form hurled itself at the man with the spectacles, bringing him crashing to the ground. The cap flew off. Exposed to view was the bald head Millie had described, fringed now by short hair that looked unrealistically black.

The older man fought desperately. Suzie was desperate, too. She tore up the slope to reach them.

He was lying still now, with his chest heaving. Handcuffs pinned his wrist to the younger man's.

She did not care. She flung herself on him. The red paisley cravat was in her hands, she was twisting it, choking him. The man's young captor was shouting at her, but she took no notice. His free hand was not powerful enough to stop her. He grabbed a radio from his belt.

Seconds later, a police siren screeched along the road outside the park. Two uniformed officers came running through the gate.

Hands were grabbing her, hauling her off the man. A police-woman was questioning her. The words made no sense.

As the man in the black sweater pulled his prisoner reluct-antly to his feet, reality began to assert itself in Suzie's mind. He was not Tom's age, but a young police officer in plain clothes. He looked shocked.

Suzie could not speak. She stood panting, still held by the strong hands of the policewoman. She was staring at the hand-cuffed man. There was blood on his face. His glasses hung crookedly from one ear. The cream shirt was torn. He, too, was gasping for breath. His frightened eyes flinched from hers.

At last she said, in a harsh voice she hardly recognized, 'I should have killed him.'

'You nearly did,' said the younger man quietly. 'But well spotted. I hadn't got close enough to check if it was him before you spooked him.'

Her choking lungs were beginning to steady at last. Her fury was beginning to fade. She was limp with exhaustion.

It was a surprise to find that Millie's assailant, now he was in front of her, looked more pathetic than sinister. His lip was trembling and he was looking at her with real fear. There should be words of scorn and hate she wanted to say to him while she had the chance. Nothing would come.

'Could I have your name, please, madam?' The police-woman had eased her grip on Suzie's arm, but did not let go.

Suzie turned to her blankly for a moment, before she found her voice. 'Suzie Fewings.'

She saw the woman start. 'Fewings? Was it your daughter in the park last week?'

Suzie nodded.

The policewoman looked across at the arresting officer. 'Just as well we got here when we did.'

There was a second siren outside. Two officers were starting to walk the man with the bleeding face towards the gate. Suzie felt herself being propelled after them, past a bed of blood-red roses.

And then her world went dead.

TWENTY-TWO

She came to in the police car. The black uniformed shoulders of the driver emerged into focus in front of her. It was curious: she thought she must have fainted, but there were no faces leaning solicitously over her. She was sitting upright on the back seat, next to the bulky policewoman. She must presumably have walked to the gate and got into the car with only minimal help. She still felt stunned.

I could have killed him.

Vividly she saw the bespectacled man with blood on his face. She felt again her hands twisting his cravat. Handcuffed to him, the first lone policeman had not been able to restrain her as well. If the others had not arrived so quickly . . .

Like a recurring nightmare came back the image which had haunted her for weeks: an elderly man tumbling downstairs. Blood on the flagstones beneath his skull.

She drew a sharp breath of denial. She had not been the one who had sent the balding man crashing to the path today.

No, but it had been her fingernails which had drawn that blood, her fists which had choked his breath.

She looked up, startled, suddenly aware of the other occupants of the car. She half expected to see the arrested man in the front passenger seat, still with blood in his hair.

Of course he was not there. They must have taken him away in the other patrol car.

The policewoman beside her had noticed her return to full consciousness.

'You all right now? You looked a bit fazed back there.'

'Yes, thanks. I don't know what came over me.'

'Shock, love, seeing him right in front of you, after what happened to your daughter. You went a bit berserk, though. Let's hope he doesn't sue. Best leave that sort of thing to the law.'

'I know. I'm sorry.'

'We'll make you a hot drink when we get you home. Will your daughter be in?'

'Millie?'

'We'll need her to identify him.'
'Yes. Of course.'
It was not over yet.

The car took both Suzie and Millie to police headquarters.
Suzie's own visual memory was poor. She was terrified that
Millie would not be able to identify the man.

She sat in the waiting room, tense and fearful. She had
stood up to accompany Millie to the identity parade, but had
felt a cowardly relief when the policewoman had told her to
wait. She did not want to see that man again. Nor, she
imagined, did Millie.

The minutes ticked by.

Millie came back with the policewoman. Her head was up
defiantly.

'Yeah, no question, it was him.'

A police car drove them home.

Tom was waiting. 'Why the police escort? What have you
been up to, Mum?'

His lopsided grin teased her. Suzie shuddered as she remembered what she had nearly been guilty of in the park. But behind
his grin she sensed tension. Tom would never, she thought, see
a police car again without a shiver of apprehension.

'Mum caught him!' Millie burst out. 'In a park again, lurking
round a kids' playground.'

Tom's eyes flashed with shock and incredulity. 'Julie's
killer? *You* found him?'

Julie? The name jolted Suzie's tired brain. Suddenly the
facts fell into a new pattern. All her anger had been over Millie
and what had nearly happened to her. It was incredible that
the link to a greater tragedy had escaped her.

She was aware of Tom's burning eyes on her.

She told her story: how she had done just what she had
advised him not to do, trailed round the schools and play-
grounds looking for a man answering the description Millie
had given, who was watching young girls. She expected more
teasing from Tom, his mood buoyed up with the jubilation at
her success.

Instead Tom's shoulders sagged. His eyes narrowed in a frown.

'This doesn't make sense. Julie was sixteen, and she could
look older. What would the guy who killed her be doing

hanging round a toddlers' playground? And *that* sort of man? Some old geezer with a bald head and a Hitler moustache? Are you telling me Julie would have been down on the towpath with a tosser like that?' He turned away and clumped upstairs.

Millie and Suzie looked at each other.

'The pig! Is he trying to say I'm lying about what happened to me? Mum, that *is* the man who tried to get me and Tamara into his car.'

'I know, I know. He's just upset.'

'You'd think he'd be over the moon about you catching him.'

They were still hanging up their jackets in the hall when the front door opened again. It was Nick. Millie spun round and threw herself into his arms.

'Dad, you'll never believe what happened! Mum . . .' The whole story tumbled out again, growing more colourful in Millie's retelling.

Nick hugged his daughter. 'That's great, Millie. I'm glad he's finally behind bars. I bet you are, too.'

Then his eyes met Suzie's over her head. He looked, she realized with a start, furious.

'You didn't even tell me? You went after a killer on your own. You saw him arrested. You've been with Millie to the police station. And you never thought to pick up your phone and let me know?'

She was shocked to realize suddenly that she hadn't. 'Nick, I'm sorry. It wasn't deliberate. But it all happened so fast. When I saw him in front of me, I went a bit mad. There was blood on his face. I think that was me. I know I tried to throttle him. They had to pull me off. And then I sort of passed out. I don't think I actually fainted, but next thing I knew, I was sitting in a police car being driven home. The policewoman said it was shock. I'm sorry if I wasn't thinking straight. I should have told you.'

'I wish you had. You know I'd have come like a shot.' Nick's eyes on her softened as he let go of Millie.

Yes, she thought. *However much I hurt you, you'll be there for me when I need you. I don't deserve you.*

If only Millie were not there between them.

'Does Tom know?' Nick said. 'He'll be thrilled that it's over, that they've got him.'

'We told him, but . . .'

'He doesn't believe it's the same man, the pig!' Millie protested. 'He just wants to take the kudos away from me. He's not going to admit that I could have got killed just like Julie.'

'Don't, Millie!' Suzie pleaded.

'They'll soon be able to prove it,' Nick said. 'They'll do a DNA test.'

Of course, Suzie thought. *Then they'll know for certain. Doubt is a thing of the past.*

Life, she supposed, could return to normal now. Millie would still have to testify at the trial, but that might be months off. That might be difficult for her, but given her age, she could probably do it by video link. Reliving her experience would be painful, but much less threatening than if it had been a case of rape. Suzie shuddered and pushed the thought away. It was hard to free her hands of the feeling of wrenching the man's cravat.

Still, the future was clear. She could pick up the threads of her life again. She could even go back to researching her ancestry on Tuesday afternoons. It was not just the Loosemores. She had an ever-increasing number of surnames which still led back to question marks, like the family of Loyalty Turner who had married Joshua Loosemore. Others she had traced back as far as the church records would take her. Even so, there was always more to discover. She might find references to the family in the accounts of the Overseers of the Poor, allowances made to them in times of hardship, or their church rate contributions giving some idea of how well-off they were, perhaps even the name of the farm where they lived. The Access to Archives website might turn up a lease or an apprenticeship indenture. However scant the personal information, she could find out the social, economic and religious background against which these humbler lives were lived, the national picture of the rise and fall of monarchs, of wars and taxes, the local catastrophes of storm or drought or plague. This historical tapestry could always be more intricately embroidered.

She did not even need to wait for next Tuesday. She would treat herself to an expedition later this week.

On Thursday afternoon she stood in the locker room of the Record Office, still undecided. In her hand was a thick file with all the stories of her ancestors so far. Which of them should she choose? Her fingers riffled the pages from her grandparents back through the generations to the Tudors. Most were villagers, a few from the wool towns or the city. Her eyes lingered again over the Loosemores of Southcombe. She had seemed to live their experience of the Civil War so vividly. How much else could she discover about this little family in the years when they had farmed at Wayland?

She smiled wryly. Was this an infection that she could not shake off? Why still *this* family, *this* parish? What more did she think she could discover?

She drew the relevant pages from her file. Her pencils, her purse, some writing paper. She deposited everything else in the locker and made for the search room.

There were red index files for most parish records, black for the Overseers of the Poor. She selected S for both and found Southcombe.

With the Overseers of the Poor, she drew a blank. The accounts began after the Loosemores had left the parish, or at least the branch of the family in which she was interested. The earlier records would probably not have helped anyway. The yeoman farmers of Wayland were not likely to have been a burden on the poor rate and she already knew where they lived.

She turned to the red file. On a previous visit she had seen the churchwardens' accounts in Thomas Loosemore's own handwriting. What else could there be to learn?

She needed to check the file number for the relevant decades, so that she could order the account books from the desk. Instead, she found a square of white paper had been pasted over the reference number. On it was typed 'MFK 9'. That meant a microfiche. She remembered the archivist's surprise on handing over the original account books. '*Looks like it's time we got this lot on microfiche.*'

They had. No longer could she sit with the churchwardens' book in her hands, while the sand with which the warden had blotted his ink sifted down on to the table. Her fingers could no longer turn the actual pages, as his had. Of course, it was inevitable. There were too many people like her tracing their ancestors nowadays. The original sources were too precious, too fragile.

She located the microfiche in a catalogue drawer and took it to one of a row of readers. The screen lit up; she slid the glass plate beneath it. Words sprang to life before her.

It was still the original handwriting, of course, though she was seeing it now at one remove. It varied from warden to warden, a meticulously curling script or an ungainly scrawl. Some of them had had to pay the parish clerk to write it for them. As she scrolled through the years, the entries were at first soothingly familiar, then became repetitive. The journey to the archdeacon's court to take the oath, the provision of bread and wine, minor repairs to the church gate or bell ropes, major repairs to the roof. Women were paid for washing the church linen, farmers with carts for bringing building materials. Then: '*Pd John Corkeram for killing oupes 4d.*' Oupes? She made a note and took it to the enquiry desk.

'What's an oupe?'

The young archivist gave her a dazzling smile, delighted at the chance to air her knowledge. 'Churchwardens' accounts? Payment for killing them?'

Suzie nodded.

'An oupe's what they called a bullfinch. Pretty things. Black back and a red breast. But they pecked the fruit buds in the cider orchards, so it was all-out war. The parish paid so much a head. We reckon the villagers killed thousands of them.'

A lesser kind of slaughter.

Suzie went back to her accounts. There were only the faintest echoes of a more troubled world. '*Pd to seven sea-faring men 1s.*' What voyages did they crew from the Channel ports?

Past violence had not been forgotten, either. Again and again: '*Pd for Ringing the Fifth of November 7s 6d.*' That would be the Gunpowder Plot of 1605, intended to blow up James I, the royal family and Parliament. Thereafter, every November the fifth the whole population was required to attend a service of thanksgiving for his deliverance, with much ringing of bells.

Apart from the bullfinches, there was, after all, little here that she did not already know. There was no further mention of the Loosemores or Wayland Farm. Nothing that made her heart beat faster with the thrill of discovery.

She switched off the microfiche reader, returned the fiche

to its drawer, and moved instead to the card index files of place names. There was a small stack of entries for Southcombe. Most of the dates were irrelevant for her purpose.

Her concentration was flagging. She could use a cup of tea.

She was walking along the corridor past the locker room when she heard the phone, faint but familiar. She checked. It wasn't a distinctive ring tone, but it was like her own. She ran to her locker, fumbled for her key and grabbed the phone from her handbag.

'Yes?'

'Sorry. Did I make you run?'

'James!'

'I haven't caught you at an inconvenient moment, have I?'

'I'm in the Record Office. You were lucky to catch me. I've only just come out of the search room.'

'Sorry. I thought it was a Friday when I met you in the library over a survey map.'

'You remembered?' Why did she feel ridiculously pleased that he had?

'Shouldn't I?'

'Actually, Tuesday's my regular afternoon for research. But I'm all over the place at the moment.'

'Never mind about that. Look, I'm phoning because I thought you'd want to know what I've just turned up. You remember I told you I had a copy of Arthur Chambers' sermon praising Goring's Crew? Well, I got it out and had another read of it. There was something interesting in it that I'd forgotten. I suppose it didn't seem that important when I read it the first time, before I met you and your Loosemores. It explains why Chambers was so particularly hospitable to Goring's cavalry. Listen to this: "*I have the more pride in what these honourable men do in the King's service because mine own son hath made one of their number.*"'

'You mean the rector's *son* was one of Goring's Crew?'

'It looks like it, doesn't it? Think about it. Chambers had been the rector of Southcombe for about thirty years by then. His son must have grown up there. It's a small parish. If the Loosemores were substantial yeoman farmers, they'd have been part of the same social circle as the rector. The Chambers lad must have known young Thomas Loosemore. They may have gone to school together. And then back he comes galloping home, after Fairfax had trounced him and his mates. And his childhood buddy has grown up into a Puritan Parliamentarian.'

'Who's letting his imagination run away with him now?'

'Ouch! Fair point . . . It's just . . . I've been thinking about, you know, your . . . vision. I may have been a bit too dismissive of that. I should know in my line of business that there's more than just three dimensions to life, shouldn't I?'

'But do you really think . . .?

'You don't know who Thomas Loosemore's wife was, do you? But the chances are she came from the same social circle as the two young men. It's my guess Chambers junior would have known her too.'

'And he stood by while one of them . . .'

'Or worse than that.'

She processed this idea in silence. At last she said, 'You mean . . . if he'd been keen on her once and now he saw a way both to punish Thomas and get what he'd always wanted, he might have . . .?'

'Like I said, it's just speculation. But think about it. It's been haunting me ever since I reread the sermon.'

'So . . . it might not have been the old rector Thomas was so mad with, even though he did entertain Goring to dinner. It was the *young* Chambers. The one Thomas couldn't do anything about. The one who . . . took his wife.'

'If your vision was true. It could be.'

She heard again the scream of the geese, felt the woman's horror. Her throat contracted with fear.

'It was real, I'm sure of that.'

'I'm beginning to believe you.'

Suzie walked in a daze to the refreshment room and got a polystyrene beaker of tea from the dispenser. As she sipped it, it occurred to her that, in his excitement, James had said nothing about the arrest in the park, though it had been on the local news. They had even mentioned Suzie's name, though to Millie's disgust she had refused to be interviewed.

She felt a confusion of emotions. What did a wild young Royalist cavalryman have to do with a balding old man with a dyed moustache, loitering in a park by the children's playground?

TWENTY-THREE

When Suzie opened the front door the house seemed startlingly full of young men. There were, she realized after a moment, only two of them. Tom and Dave were on their way upstairs, mugs of tea in their hands, scattering cake crumbs on the carpet. Her spirits leaped as she recognized Tom's best friend.

Tom's voice was loud, laughing. His lean form was ahead, his wavy dark hair almost disappearing above the turn in the stairs. Dave, shorter, but broader-shouldered, followed more quietly. He turned his head as Suzie entered and grinned shyly down at her. His thick tawny hair shadowed his eyes.

'Great cake,' he said, waving a half-eaten slice.

'I'm glad you like it.' She stopped herself from offering him a dustpan and brush.

Dave was back. She read Tom's delight even in his retreating back.

She made her way to the kitchen, smiling. It was good to see the house returning to normal. And Millie was delighted that her assailant had been caught, though understandably nervous about the court case. Still, it was worth the hassle, she had indicated to Suzie, since it would enable her to play the heroine with her friends for weeks to come.

Suzie tidied the kitchen table and wiped up the spilt milk. She could understand something of Millie's pleasure at basking in the limelight, though the police had warned Suzie herself against her giving interviews, in case it prejudiced the trial. She was still a little piqued that Tom had not been as impressed as she had expected with her part in the man's capture. Oddly, he did not seem to share the rest of the family's joy that the murderer was now safely in prison.

She took her file of research notes into the study and replaced them on the shelf. This, she thought happily, was like the old days: the staircase echoing to the tramp of teenage boys, laughter from Tom's bedroom. They would be playing video games, or surfing the Internet on quests that would be meaningless to her.

It was worth the crumbs on the carpet. She fetched the dustpan and brush and swept the stairs herself.

Dave stayed to supper.

'Great fish,' he said. 'Thanks, Mrs Fewings.'

Suzie smiled at him fondly. She had disinterred it from the freezer at the last minute, when she found there would be five to feed. But Dave was a nice boy, well brought up, taught to say thank you.

The two of them disappeared speedily back to Tom's room.

'What about homework?' she called after them.

'Yeah. We'll do it,' came Tom's not entirely convincing reply.

Millie had drifted into the conservatory and switched on the television, while Nick was still clearing the table. Fragments of news commentary floated through to Suzie in the kitchen.

'. . . Inspector Wallace confirmed that the police are still seeking the person who killed Julie Samuel. The man arrested in a park on Tuesday has been charged with a lesser offence.'

There was an indignant howl from Millie. 'A lesser offence! That beast tried to get me in his car to murder me. And he calls it a lesser offence?'

Nick and Suzie were there in an instant.

'Shut up for a minute, Millie. I want to hear this,' Nick said urgently.

But the newsreader had moved on. The screen showed local beehives which were being decimated by disease.

'What was that about?' Nick asked Millie. 'Did you get all of it?'

'Only some rubbish about how the police don't think the man Mum caught is the one who killed Julie. That's crazy. He's got to be the same, hasn't he?'

'Not necessarily,' Suzie said quietly. 'You remember, Tom never thought he was.'

A disturbing recollection was coming back to her of the afternoon in the Record Office, of James's phone call. In Thomas Loosemore's eyes, she was growing more certain, it was not just the old rector tumbling down the stairs who had been guilty, but his son even more so.

'The police will have got the results of the man's DNA test,' Nick said. 'They must have found it didn't fit.'

'That's what you think. It was *him*.' Millie flounced out of the room and upstairs, ignoring the washing-up.

'I suppose it's a form of innocence,' said Suzie, 'wishing she'd really been picked out by a murderer, although I doubt that she'd thank me for applying the word "innocent" to her.'

'She's thirteen,' said Nick, stirring the soapsuds with a dish mop. 'I remember going through a stroppy phase myself. It's Tom I'm worried about. It looks as if there's still no closure for him.'

'He sounds pretty normal at the moment. He's got Dave upstairs. It's like the old times.'

'He doesn't know this latest news, though, does he?'

'It won't surprise him. He never did believe they'd got the right man.'

'So, if not an old, bald paedophile with glasses, then who?'

'I'd rather not imagine it.'

They finished the washing-up in a shared silence. Suzie knew that this time it would not be wise to tell Nick about James's phone call. It would rake over embers best left to go cold. Though he tried to be helpful, Nick did not share James and Suzie's passion for piecing together fragments of their past, their thrill at uncovering new evidence, the disinterring of a long-buried story, like an archaeologist easing a precious find from the soil. Nick would see only two people from the present, a man and a woman, and assume that what drew them together was other than what it really was.

How honest was she being? Her cheeks warmed, recalling the sound of James's voice, their shared excitement. James, it occurred to her now, must have made a note of her mobile number after that call about her shocking vision.

She turned a wine glass in her hand, polishing its already gleaming surface.

'Penny for them?' Nick had emptied the bowl and was drying his hands.

Suzie almost dropped the glass. 'Oh! Nothing important. I was back with family history again.'

'You do have a remarkable capacity for letting the seventeenth century take precedence over the twenty-first. Even now.'

'I didn't know this afternoon that there was this news

to come. I thought it was all sorted, that we could get back to normal.'

'What's normal now?' Nick hung up his apron. 'Tom is always going to be someone whose ex-girlfriend was murdered.'

'His girlfriend . . . probably.' Tom had cared more than he wanted to admit. 'If it *was* murder. The police have never actually said how she died.'

'Whatever. She's still dead.'

'Well, you see, what's getting to me is . . . there was this sermon the rector of Southcombe preached . . . I mean, the old rector in the time of the Civil War.' She hesitated, aware how little Nick would be interested in Arthur Chambers' son, and how she would have to watch her words carefully to make it seem as though this had been her own discovery, not James's.

'Go on.'

It was only then she realized, with a palpable shock, that she had not told Nick about her vision of that terrible day in 1645 when Royalist cavalry came riding into Wayland farmyard. It was so vivid to her still. How could she not have shared it with him?

And then she remembered why. She had been sitting on the bed, with her hair still damp, putting down the phone after recounting it to James. Nick had come into the room and asked, 'Who were you talking to?' She had lied.

'You wouldn't be interested.' Guilt was making her uncomfortable.

'Try me.'

'Just . . . well, there were these two young men in Southcombe then. Thomas Loosemore, who may or may not be my ancestor, was a young Parliamentarian farmer. I've told you about him. And there was the rector's son, who was in Lord Goring's Royalist cavalry. That was the troop that sacked and looted their way across the county after they were badly beaten by the Roundheads.'

'So? Everyone knows the Civil War split communities.'

How could she make him see? What happened that day meant almost nothing without the sound of the children screaming, dishes of milk crashing to the dairy floor, the cruel pressure of a man's body in the straw.

She could see her own face distorted in the wine glass.

'Suddenly, it all seemed real to me: Wayland Farm, the Royalist horsemen galloping into the yard mad for revenge, two young men who'd once been friends, a woman.'

'What woman?'

'Thomas Loosemore's wife. I don't know what she was called. She almost certainly *was* my ancestor.'

'What about her?'

Suzie put down the glass and turned back to the draining board. She began briskly drying the cutlery. 'You're right. I was just imagining it. Anyway, that's got nothing to do with Tom.'

Suzie positioned the ironing board so that she could watch television through the conservatory door. The footage of a polar bear picking its forlorn way across melting ice floes was becoming sadly familiar. She picked up a shirt from the pile.

There were running footsteps in the hall. Millie burst into the kitchen.

'Mum, there's a police car outside!'

Suzie's heart seemed to stop. Surely it was over, wasn't it? They had arrested the man. It took a moment or two before the significance of this evening's newscast sank in. The man she had chased was charged with molesting Tamara and Millie, but not with Julie's death.

But they couldn't still suspect Tom. The police had been through all that: his DNA on her clothes, the fact that he had been with Julie on the towpath two days before. They'd satisfied themselves they could eliminate him from their enquiries, hadn't they?

'Mum! Something's burning!'

She became aware that she had been staring at Millie open-mouthed, her cheeks stiff and cold. Smoke was rising from Nick's shirt under the iron.

'Where?'

Millie pointed to the shirt.

'I mean, where's the police car?'

Millie dumbly led the way to the sitting-room window. Not far off, they could see the roof of the car, with its blue lamp switched off, over the top of the hedge. The greenery was like a barrier, positioning it in a different world.

'What's it doing there?' Millie hissed.

'Probably nothing to do with us,' Suzie said, 'or they'd have come to the door.'

The two of them stared at it, unsure what they were fearing.

'Does Tom know?'

Millie shrugged. 'Dunno. I haven't told him.'

'Don't.'

She went to the study. Nick turned from the spreadsheet on the computer.

'The police are waiting outside.'

'What for?'

'I don't know. Their car's just sitting there. It's parked in front of Number Ten, rather than us.'

Nick followed her. She saw the same disturbance in his face.

'If it's us they want, why don't they just come in and ring the bell?' she said.

'I'll ask them.' Nick, she knew, was trying to sound braver than he felt.

She watched him walk resolutely down the drive and out of the gate. Another head rose into view beside his. A man was standing talking to Nick. He was not in police uniform. Could he be the grey-suited detective who had questioned Tom?

Then the car's engine started up and it pulled away.

Suzie almost ran on to the drive to meet Nick.

'What did they want?'

'He wouldn't say.'

'Should we tell Tom?'

'No, he's got enough bad news to come about Julie's killer. Leave it.'

It was hard to settle back to the ironing.

It was about nine o'clock when Dave and Tom came down the stairs. Suzie had taken over the computer from Nick and was answering her email. A fellow enthusiast was asking about the cholera epidemic of 1832 and Suzie could give him information about the streets of the city worst affected.

Whatever the police had wanted, it did not seem to be anything to do with the Fewings, after all.

The noise of the boys' feet brought her back to the present. She smiled to herself. How did just two of them manage to sound like a herd of kangaroos jumping from stair to stair? She put her head round the study door.

'Finished for this evening? Good night, Dave.'

'Night, Mrs Fewings.'

Dave was a sensible lad. She thought he looked tired. It was another school day tomorrow. He was off home early.

She gave him an affectionate smile. Tom might be rude about his friend's staid behaviour, but she liked him. It was reassuring to know that Tom was closer to him once more than to some of the wilder ones in his year, like Greg.

Tom opened the front door. The boys stood talking on the doorstep. Suzie caught a mention of psychology. It almost sounded as though they might have spent at least part of the evening on homework.

The street lamps were on, though it was not fully dark yet. Dave was going down the drive, his ginger hair flaming in the yellow light.

'You up for the athletics trials next week?' Tom called after him.

'Me? Get real, mate. PE's not compulsory now.'

'Couch potato.' Then she heard Tom's voice rise. 'Bloody pigs! What are they doing here?'

Suzie ran to the doorstep. The police car was back, waiting silently a short distance from their gate. As she watched, the doors opened. A policeman got out on either side. The driver was in uniform, the older man not.

Dave had turned to look. He gave a strangled cry and stumbled forward, as though a knee had given way. In the light of the street lamp his face seemed unnaturally pale. He looked wildly around him, like a rabbit searching for somewhere to run. The two men were walking steadily up the road towards the gate.

She recognized the scar on the chin of the older one.

Tom's eyes moved from the advancing policemen to Dave. He took a few uncertain steps towards his friend.

'What's wrong, mate?'

The plain-clothes officer was in the drive. 'David Bennett, I am arresting you in connection with the death of Julie Samuel. You are not obliged to say anything, but . . .' The words of the caution trailed away in Suzie's mind. After the first horrified moment, her eyes left Dave. She was looking at Tom.

He was as pale and shocked as Dave. He rounded on the police officers, now one on either side of his friend.

'Are you crazy? Dave wouldn't hurt a cockroach, let alone Julie. She was *my* girl.'

Dave was gabbling in terror, 'You can't! You haven't got any evidence. You never took my DNA.'

Tom stiffened. His gaze turned back to the other boy. 'Dave? It's not true, is it? You couldn't have!'

Suzie's fists clenched, her whole body dreading the moment when he took in the truth. History was repeating itself. It was going to happen again. *It must not happen.*

Dave's freckled face was collapsing. Tears were spilling down his cheeks. His head hung, but his wet eyes went up to Tom now, pleading.

'I swear it was an accident, Tom. There was this stone in the grass. I never meant to hurt her. *Help me!*'

Tom lunged towards him. The other boy hung helpless, locked in the grasp of a policeman on either side. His face was right in front of Tom's, the eyes terrified, his jaw hanging slackly.

As Tom's arm shot out, Suzie's scream rang through the evening stillness. 'No, Tom!'

It brought Nick racing into the hall.

It was a second of horror before she saw her dark teenager's hand come to rest on his friend's shoulder. Tom was crying too.

With a sense of unreality, she heard him say, 'Dave, mate! All this time . . . Why didn't you tell me?'

'I was afraid you'd kill me.'

The men led him away.

Suzie walked slowly down the path to stand beside Tom. She put a hesitant arm around his waist. He turned to her, his face questioning, as if surprised to find her there. For a while, he stood silent. Then he brushed his hand over his wet eyes and shook his head.

'Who's going to tell his mum?'

TWENTY-FOUR

'Why did you shout "No, Tom!" just now?' Tom was looking down at his mother with a terrible sadness.

The police had driven Dave away. The Fewings were still standing, shocked, on the driveway.

'Did I?'

'Yes. Like you were afraid I was going to murder the guy, or something.'

'I . . . I suppose I had this horrible feeling that history was going to repeat itself.'

'You mean old Thomas Loosemore? That guy you got so fired up about because he had the same name as me . . . until you found out he killed his rector.'

'You *know* about that?'

'Sure I know. You weren't going to tell me, were you? But Dad did.'

Suzie rounded on Nick. 'Why?'

He held up his hands. 'It just sort of came out. I was giving him a driving lesson one Saturday, and there was this kid, just stepping off the pavement on to a zebra crossing. Tom nearly didn't stop. I suppose we were both a bit shocked. And you'd just been on about your Thomas Loosemore.'

'Who killed someone.' Tom said quietly.

Blood flooded Suzie's cheeks. 'But I never believed . . . I mean, I was worried sick about what you were going through with the police. We all were. And it all became part of the same nightmare.'

James's words: *You're afraid that Tom . . .* It was true the parallel had been haunting her. She stammered her denial.

'But I knew it wasn't real. I mean, I knew it couldn't be you.'

It was the terrible scene in the farmyard that was real to her now, not what had happened on the stairs at the rectory.

Tom raised his eyebrows. 'I'll believe you.'

'Thousands wouldn't,' added Millie.

'It was an accident, anyway,' Suzie said hurriedly. 'It must have been. I can't believe he meant to kill.' Her mind was still on the Loosemores.

'Of course he didn't. Dave's just not that sort of guy. Hell, he never even goes out with girls. How did he get her down to the canal in the first place? Dave and *Julie*?'

Suzie found herself jolted back to the twenty-first century. She put her hand on Tom's arm. 'We never did know how Julie died, did we? The police have never said.'

'Things can go wrong. If he'd never done it before . . . And Dave's the type who'd panic. Hell, wouldn't any of us? The poor guy must have been so terrified he just pushed her body in the ditch and did a runner. And none of us ever thought of suspecting him. The police didn't ask him for a DNA sample like the rest of us. I couldn't understand why he didn't want anything to do with me afterwards. Like he thought it was me. It never occurred to me what the real problem was.'

'You're not angry with him?'

'Me? Mum, I could weep for the guy. When I think of what he must have been going through all this time . . .'

She stared up into the drawn face that looked so like Nick's and saw only grief.

A great weight lifted from Suzie. Another tragedy had happened, but this Thomas Loosemore was not responsible. History did not inevitably repeat itself.

She let out a long, shaky breath and tried to smile. 'Come inside, then, Tom Fewings.'

Next day Tom was quiet. Suzie thought his face seemed longer, the last childish plumpness fallen away from his cheekbones. He looked sad, bewildered. Nick and Suzie did not know what to say to him. This was not the violent rage Suzie had feared in that first horrified moment.

Dave had been released on police bail, but was refusing to take Tom's calls. Tom had, Suzie realized, suffered a double loss. He had lost his best friend; and his impression of what Julie had felt for him could not, in the end, have been the truth.

On Saturday morning Tom sat at the breakfast table, twisting a coffee mug in his hands. Any other weekend, Suzie knew, he would have been out with Dave.

He raised his blue eyes. 'Dad? Any chance I could get in some driving practice today? Maybe not just round the town, but out in the country.'

Nick looked sideways at Suzie, questioningly. She nodded.

'OK, if that's what you feel like. Good idea to take your mind off things. Your mother and I are usually out chasing her family history, but under the circumstances, why not?'

Tom grinned at them both. There was a sudden flash of laughter. 'Oh, Mum's invited. Millie, too, if she wants to come.'

'All of us? Where are you thinking of taking us?'

'Southcombe.'

There was a silence.

'Am I missing something? What's with this Southcombe?' Millie looked from one face to another.

Suzie struggled to explain. 'It's one of the villages where I've traced our ancestors. There was a story there about a Thomas Loosemore. You know Tom's full name is Thomas Loosemore Fewings.'

'You'll like this.' There was a harsh edge to Tom's laughter, but he went on gamely. 'He threw some reverend guy down the stairs and broke his skull. Funny, that. There was a reverend from Southcombe phoned yesterday.'

Suzie shot an alarmed glance at Nick. 'James Milton? What did he say?'

'That he had some news you'd be interested in. Sorry, I forgot to tell you.'

'That's all right,' Suzie said. 'You've got a lot on your mind just now.'

What had James found out?

'But why do *you* want to go to Southcombe?' Nick said to Tom.

He shrugged. 'Looks like there's been a lot of talk about me and Southcombe behind my back. I just thought I'd like to see the place – maybe the rectory where it happened. So when this parson guy rang, I told him we'd come over. Thought we could all meet up for a pub lunch, if that's OK with you, and he could tell you this new stuff he's found.'

Nick and Suzie stared at him, uncertain what to say.

Tom drew a circle with spilled coffee on the table top. His face coloured.

'Oh, and the guy was kind of helpful, about . . . all this.

Seemed like he knew most of the story already. For a god-bod, he seemed a pretty good guy to talk to.'

'You didn't tell me it would be single-track lanes,' said Tom through tight lips. 'What do I do if I meet a combine harvester?'

'Unlikely in June,' said Nick, 'but haymaking machines can be pretty massive these days and there might be the odd caravan. Just reverse till you find a field gateway to pull into.'

Tom's knuckles tightened on the wheel.

They came over the hill into Southcombe, passing nothing more threatening than a Land Rover. There was the parish church, the pub on the green, the chestnut tree, just as Suzie remembered them. Sunlight was dappling the grass as the leaves shifted in the breeze. They got out and stood looking across the valley towards the woods around Nympton Rogus.

'Wayland Farm's down there, beside the river,' Suzie said. 'You can't see it from here. We can go there after lunch.'

There were trestle tables outside the Lamb Inn. Nick fetched drinks and they sat reading menus. Suzie kept glancing up across the green.

She had expected James to arrive on his bicycle, as he had when he took her to Wayland. Instead, he came swinging across the grass on foot, a figure of light, in fawn trousers and a freshly pressed pink shirt. His fair curls rippled in the sunshine. He could, she thought, have modelled appropriately for an angel, if the church needed a new carving.

'Hi, everyone. I hope I haven't kept you waiting. Now, Nick and Suzie, I've met.' He reached across to shake Nick's hand. 'Good to see you both again. Tom I've talked to on the phone. And you must be Millie.' Turning to her, he gave her his radiant smile.

Suzie took one look at her daughter and knew what had happened. Millie's sallow face flushed and she could find nothing to say except a whispered, 'Yes'.

'May I?'

James swung a long leg over the bench to sit between Suzie and Millie, facing Nick and Tom. The scent of his aftershave brought back heady memories. Silly, really, Suzie told herself. She was three times as old as Millie. Nothing untoward had occurred between James and her. His bare arm brushed hers lightly as he reached for a menu.

He and Nick went to the bar to place their food order. She heard him joking with the bar staff inside, chatting with other customers. Of course, it was not just her. As rector, it was his job to be interested in everyone. She and Tom were not the only ones who found this 'god-bod' good to talk to.

The men returned, James steadying a pint of beer. They sat in the sunlight, sipping their drinks, waiting for the food.

Then James turned to Suzie, his smile dancing for her now. 'I've been doing some homework since you last came. You said you didn't have a baptism for your Joshua Loosemore. You weren't sure if he was really Thomas's son.'

'The Southcombe registers for the Commonwealth period are missing. They don't start again till the Restoration of the monarchy in 1660.'

'And you've looked in the surrounding parishes, of course.' His eyes teased her.

'I've checked on the Internet. There's nothing in the IGI for Joshua Loosemore except his marriage.'

'And . . .?'

'Oh, I know there are some parishes that aren't on the IGI. Mostly small ones. I was going to look up the ones round Southcombe in the Record Office, but I haven't got around to it yet.'

'As it happens, I can save you the trouble. I'm not entirely alone in my passion for local history here. I mentioned your problem to a friend of mine. Madeleine's a splendid lady of eighty-two, who's my churchwarden. And no, she hasn't thrown me down the stairs yet, although I'm sure she's been tempted at times. In her spare time she also happens to be the on-line parish clerk for Nympton Rogus. She's got her own set of microfiches for the parish registers, so she can field email enquiries from all over the world. Here's what she found.'

With the air of a conjuror, he produced a folded paper from his breast pocket and spread it out on the table in front of them.

'Here we are. Baptisms at St Budoc, Nympton Rogus: "*1649. Thomas, son of Thomas Loosemore, 6th March.*" The new year didn't begin until Lady Day then, so that would be 1650 on the modern calendar. "*1651. Ann, daughter of Thomas Loosemore, 4th September.*" There's a burial for the poor little soul three months later. *"1653. Joshua, son of Thomas Loosemore, 13th August."'*

The familiar name leaped out at Suzie from the page. She felt her eyes widen as she turned to James.

'"*Joshua, son of Thomas*." It has to be him, doesn't it? But baptized in Nympton Rogus, not in Southcombe. Does that mean his father wasn't the same Thomas Loosemore? Not the Wayland Farm one?'

James's mouth was twitching with a delighted laughter he was finding it difficult to suppress. His merry eyes held hers.

'I told you Madeleine was a splendid lady. That's not all she found. It seems the rector of Nympton Rogus was a literary gent, who liked to enliven his parish registers with memoranda of contemporary events. How about this one?'

He lifted the first sheet of paper to reveal another. His voice took on a register of importance.

'*After the regicides had foully slain our anointed king those ordained priests who had been most zealous in his cause were cruelly turned out of their livings. By the grace of God, I was spared, but my neighbour the Revd Arthur Chambers of Southcombe was so grievously harried that he died of his injuries. Afterwards the guilty parishioner, one Thomas Loosemore of Wayland Farm, was so troubled in his conscience that he forsook the church at Southcombe and was seen to worship here with us in Nympton Rogus for some ten years. During that time I did not spare to preach against the use of violence towards our betters, though in those unlawful times I was obliged to speak prudently about our martyred king. The man has now returned to his rightful parish church where 'tis said he lives soberly and is much respected.'*

His eyes lifted to Suzie's again. She stared back at him, new thoughts tumbling over each other.

'And when I walked into Southcombe church I thought that all the evidence of those times had been destroyed! So it *is* the same Thomas. We really are descended from him.'

'No doubt about it. Joshua was baptized in 1653,' he reminded her. 'So he couldn't be the result of Goring's cavalry raid.'

The others were listening, only half understanding.

Tom was trying to follow. 'I sort of see what you mean, Mum. Makes you feel kind of weird, knowing you're descended from a guy that killed someone. Sharing his name, even. And then the guy's so cut up he can't face seeing his mates every Sunday.' His gaze dropped to his hands, which were twisting his fork.

'Wayland Farm's right on the boundary with Nympton Rogus,' James told him. 'It was actually nearer for the Loosemores to go to that church than their own.'

'Why go at all?' put in Millie. 'I wouldn't.' A little smile flashed over her defiant face, aimed at James beside her. 'Not unless I fancied the vicar.'

'Nothing to do with the rector's rating in the charts,' James assured her gravely. 'It was the law. You got fined if you didn't show up on Sunday.'

'You're kidding!'

'But this guy came back,' Tom persisted. 'Ten years later. He faced up to what he'd done.'

'They made him churchwarden,' Suzie said. 'He'd have been the one counting them in every Sunday. His name's on a board in the church.'

'Big deal,' murmured Millie.

Tom stood up and walked to the edge of the green. He stood looking out over the valley of the Twisted Oak. After a moment, Suzie joined him and slipped her arm through his.

'I'm sorry. I didn't mean to wish all this on you again.'

'It's OK. It's Dave I was thinking about. Anyway.' He turned a brave smile on her. 'You're right. It's part of who I am, all this.'

'Only a tiny part of you. I gave you my name, but you look much more like your father than me. Anyone can see you've got more of the Fewings genes than the Loosemores.'

His smile broadened. 'Anybody researching Dad's family in Lancashire? We don't know what skeletons he's got in *his* cupboards.' He nudged her and whispered in her ear. 'Tell you what: which of us is going to break it to Millie that her rector's gay?'

She turned to him in utter astonishment. 'What do you . . .?'

The laughter faded in his face. 'Mum! You didn't . . .?'

'Oh, look!' cried Suzie. 'Here's the food.'

James swung round to include Suzie and Tom in his infectious smile. 'I was just telling Millie, the Church of England has provided me with a modern semi, but Madeleine lives in the Old Rectory. When we've eaten, I'll get her to show you the actual stairs.'

'Is there still a bloodstain on the floor?' asked Millie.

Suzie lifted the sheet of baptisms out of the way of the plates. The echoes of the woman's despairing cry sounded in her head. She stood looking down at the records.

'*Joshua, son of Thomas Loosemore*. That's all it says. So we're never going to know his mother's name.'

AUTHOR'S NOTE

The people, places and institutions in this book are fictitious. But I am indebted to many real life people and organizations who have done so much to help my own family history research in ways that have inspired this book, or have given me other advice. They include the following:

Devon Record Office: www.devon.gov.uk/record_office.htm

Westcountry Studies Library: www.devon.gov.uk/local studies/115498/1.html

Genuki genealogical website: www.genuki.org.uk

IGI International Genealogical Index: www.familysearch.org Access to Archives: www.nationalarchives.gov.uk/a2a

Moretonhampstead Historical Society: www.moreton-hampstead.org.uk

Devon Family History Society: www.devonfhs.org.uk

Kent Family History Society: www.kfhs.org.uk

Devon and Kent genealogical email groups: http://lists.rootsweb.com/index/intl/ENG

Online Census indexes: www.1901CensusOnline.com

Mr and Mrs Nigel Faulks of Yeo Barton, Mariansleigh

Mark Stoyle for *Loyalty and Locality* and *Devon and the Civil War*

John Wroughton, *An Unhappy Civil War*

John Walker, *Sufferings of the Clergy*

Devon and Cornwall Constabulary

While I have given free rein to my imagination here, many details owe their original inspiration to discoveries in my own family history research. You can find something similar to Suzie's experience in the following:

The painted tiles and ceiling in Southcombe church – Filleigh, Devon.

The churchwardens' board in Southcombe – Drewsteignton, Devon.

The parishioner who threw his rector downstairs – Chittlehampton, Devon, in *Walker's Suffering of the Clergy.*

The dishonest turnpike gatekeeper – James Avery alias Taverner. *Silvester Treleaven's Diary*, Moretonhampstead, Devon, in Moretonhampstead Historical Society's virtual archive.

Smugglers and Revenue Men – The Deal Boatmen, Kent.

Entries in churchwardens' accounts – Rose Ash and Cheldon, Devon.

St Juthwara's church – St Sidwell's, Exeter.

The carved initials at Wayland Farm – Yeo Barton, Mariansleigh, Devon.

Anne FitzRobert's Proof of Age – Anne Pauncefoot, Proof of Age, Inquisition 1502, IPMs in Westcountry Studies Library, Exeter; Chancery Series II. VII 15 (57).

Field names – Mariansleigh, Devon.

Goring's Crew – Mark Stoyle, *Devon and the Civil War.*

Revd Arthur Chambers' printed sermon – Epistle Dedicatory to *A Golden Topaze*, a sermon preached by Revd Francis Whiddon in Moretonhampstead, Devon, and printed in 1656, Westcountry Studies Library, Exeter. Whiddon, however, was on the Parliamentarian side in the Civil War.

Rector's comments in the parish register – Revd Lewis Southcombe, Rose Ash, Devon.

DUDLEY

DUDLEY